BEIGNETS AND BROOMSTICKS

A Selection of Titles by J.R. Ripley

The Maggie Miller Mysteries

BURIED IN BEIGNETS *
BEIGNETS, BRIDES AND BODIES *

The Tony Kozol Mysteries

STIFF IN THE FREEZER
SKULLS OF SEDONA
LOST IN AUSTIN
THE BODY FROM IPANEMA
BUM RAP IN BRANSON
GUNFIGHT IN GATLINBURG

The Gendarme Trenet Series

MURDER IN ST BARTS
DEATH OF A CHEAT

* *available from Severn House*

BEIGNETS AND BROOMSTICKS

J.R. Ripley

This first world edition published 2017
in Great Britain and the USA by
SEVERN HOUSE PUBLISHERS LTD of
Eardley House, 4 Uxbridge Street, London W8 7SY.
Trade paperback edition first published
in Great Britain and the USA 2018 by
SEVERN HOUSE PUBLISHERS LTD.

British Library Cataloguing in Publication Data
A CIP catalogue record for this title is available from the British Library.

ISBN-13: 978-0-7278-8761-0 (cased)
ISBN-13: 978-1-84751-877-4 (trade paper)
ISBN-13: 978-1-78010-939-8 (e-book)

All Severn House titles are printed on acid-free paper.

Severn House Publishers support the Forest Stewardship Council™ [FSC™],
the leading international forest certification organisation. All our titles that
are printed on FSC certified paper carry the FSC logo.

Typeset by Palimpsest Book Production Ltd.,
Falkirk, Stirlingshire, Scotland.
Printed and bound in Great Britain by
TJ International, Padstow, Cornwall.

ONE

'Let me get that for you.' The man coming out the entrance of Maggie's Beignet Café switched the bag of freshly fried beignets from his right hand to his left and held the door to the café open for me to pass.

'Thanks,' I replied, sliding awkwardly past him. 'Have a good day.' I had just come back from the thrift store and my arms were full.

I wobbled across the floor, steering awkwardly between dining tables. I was anxious to relieve myself of my bulky load. A shopkeeper's assistant had given me a ride back to my place. Not owning a car, my transportation options were limited and that limited my ability to travel, let alone transport, big, bulky items like this one.

Schwinns are nice but, even with a basket between the handlebars, they are no match for a minivan or station wagon at such times.

There were days I regretted selling my car but I'd needed the cash to open my café.

'What's that?' asked Kelly.

With a grunt, I hefted the unwieldy machine up onto the front counter and slid it back from the edge. I winced as I watched deep new gouges form in the green Formica countertop.

'An espresso machine,' I huffed, picking up a shiny loose bit that had fallen to the floor and slapping it down next to the polished copper and brass beast. 'It's vintage.'

'An espresso machine?' gaped Kelly. 'Looks more like a steampunk spaceship.' She took a step back. 'What did you bring it here for, Maggie?'

I frowned as I looked out the window and across the street toward my competitors, Karma Koffee. 'I thought it might help us drum up some more business.'

There was a line out the door at the Gregorys' shop. I had one paying customer at the moment, Belinda, from Salon de Belezza, the beauty shop next door. She ordered coffee and a plate of beignets, her usual mid-morning snack. It was going to take more than an espresso machine to compete with the Gregorys.

'Maybe.' Kelly fiddled with the loose bit then popped it over one of the spaceship's nozzles. Kelly Herman had been my second employee here at Maggie's Beignet Café. She's a quiet, twenty-three-year-old half Havasupai, half Jewish beauty with long black hair and soupy brown eyes.

She works part-time for me in the café and part-time for my sister, Donna, and her husband, Andy, at their business. They owned Mother Earth/Father Sun Grocers a couple blocks' away.

I had moved from Phoenix to Table Rock a few months back to open my fledgling business after divorcing my dead ex-husband, Brian. He wasn't really dead but a woman could dream, couldn't she?

My sister and her family, a husband and two boys, and my mother were already here, so I figured it was the place for me too.

Table Rock is a lovely little town located in the scenic northern Verde Valley of Arizona, halfway between Sedona and nowhere. People around Table Rock like to say it's where people move to who think Sedona is too mainstream. Anybody who's ever been to Sedona knows that the town, with its New Age and metaphysical culture, is about as far from mainstream as one can get, so that was really saying something.

It didn't hurt that prices in Table Rock were cheaper than in Sedona. New Age dreamers were more interested in all things spiritual and in developing their consciousness than they were in inflating their bank accounts.

Folks around town also like to say that aliens outnumber Table Rockers four to one. I wasn't sure yet about the aliens but I was certain that pickup trucks outnumbered people by at least that ratio.

'Thanks. I was wondering where that goes.' The machine had set me back three hundred bucks – a steal, according to the woman who had sold it to me, Laura Duval. It looked terribly complicated, although Laura had assured me I could manage it.

'No problem. Where did you get it?'

I blew out a puff of air and felt the tiny hairs on my forehead dance. 'Laura's Lightly Used.' Laura's Lightly Used was the thrift shop a couple blocks east of Maggie's Beignet Café. The sprawling store sold vintage clothes, items for the home, outdoor goods, sporting equipment and more, such as secondhand restaurant equipment.

I had purchased much of the equipment from Laura's store when

I was setting up my café. She had also sold me my Schwinn. At this point, I figured Laura had more of my money than I did.

Maggie's Beignet Café sold beignets, coffee and soft drinks. I was slowly adding additional sweet-flavored beignets and savory beignets to the menu in an effort to increase foot traffic. Well, mouth traffic, really.

As for my hair, it was finally starting to grow back. I studied my reflection in the shiny espresso maker's thirty-eight-ounce boiler. Definitely a sign of hair growth. My green eyes looked a little sallow and my face a little sickly. I blamed that on the brass. All in all, I didn't look bad for a fifty-year-old. Too bad I was only thirty-nine.

I guess I should have been grateful my hair was now long enough to reach my forehead. I shot a furtive glance at Belinda as she scarfed down her third powdered sugar-covered beignet. The woman's boss, Caitie Conklin, had recently shaved me bald and I wasn't in a forgiving mood yet. It had been done in the name of charity – with all of the hair being donated to cancer patients along with the money charged for the cuts – but still . . . A woman can only tolerate so much.

And though my red hair was beginning to grow out, the nickname Cueball had obstinately stuck around.

I hoisted the piano-hinged section of the countertop and scooted around behind the counter. The eight-table café sits on Laredo Street, at the edge of the Historic Old Town and just a few blocks from Table Rock Town Square. The café still contained remnants of the deli it had once been, like some signage and even some deli-branded paper napkins I'd found in storage and was determined to use up before having to order new ones.

I'd been told by a man named Cosmic Ray over at the Table Rock Visitor Center that my café had been a head shop in one of its previous incarnations. So far, I'd found no evidence of that. Not a bong in sight.

The front counter also contained the deep fryer and prep station. Customers could watch the beignets being fashioned and fried behind the protection of a glass divider.

The big mixer sat on the floor to the right of the accordion-style swinging doors that led to the storeroom. The back wall contained the coffee and drinks machines, a couple of small coolers and a sink.

Beignets, the state donut of Louisiana – though they look more like puffy golden pillows than donuts – are sweet, fried pieces of dough smothered in powdered sugar. I didn't expect to get rich selling them but I was hoping they would pay the rent.

'Give me a hand, Kelly.'

'Sure thing.'

With Kelly's help, I moved the espresso machine next to the French-press coffee makers. Kelly moved some napkins and cups out of the way to make room.

I tilted my head at the new machine. 'I don't suppose you know how to operate this baby?' I twisted the burnished wood grip of the lever.

'I'm afraid not.'

'Too bad.'

'Didn't it come with a manual or some instructions?'

'No. Laura told me how it worked.' I scratched my head. 'I can't exactly remember what she said.' I forced a smile. 'I'm sure it will come back to me.'

'Maybe we can look it up online.'

'That's a good idea,' I said brightly. I ran a finger along the open wings of the eagle at the machine's peak. 'Laura said it's a Belle Époque-inspired design built by La Floriano.'

The machine was fifteen inches wide and over two feet tall, not counting the majestic eagle. I admired the intricate details.

'What's this here?' Kelly stuck her hand in a cavity near the top of the boiler.

'That's for the espresso cups. Laura explained that the cups are kept warm there by the hot water in the boiler. According to the date on the bottom, this machine was built in the late nineteen thirties.'

'All we have is paper to-go cups and regular coffee cups.' Kelly bent until she was eye level with the opening. 'They won't fit.'

'I know. Laura didn't have any cups for it. I'll have to find someplace else to get them. If Laura didn't have them, I doubt I can find them locally. I may have to order them online.' It wasn't worth a hundred-plus mile trip down to Phoenix to shop for them.

'In the meantime, let's give it a good cleaning and reconditioning. I'm sure that between us we will have this baby figured out in no time.' I slapped it lovingly on its side.

'This isn't going to end up like the waffle maker, is it, Maggie?'

Kelly asked as she reached for the cleaning supplies under the front counter.

'What do you mean?'

Kelly set the green bottle of environmentally friendly cleaning fluid my sister insisted I use next to the espresso machine. 'I mean this.' She ran a finger along the authentic Liege-style Belgian waffle maker I had picked up for a song online. She held up her finger.

Dust.

'You bought this what? Six or seven weeks ago?' She wiped her finger with a damp rag.

'Has it been that long?' I picked up the waffle maker. The machine was capable of making genuine, chewy and delicious Liege waffles and came with eight additional waffle plates. 'Trust me, we can make everything from ice-cream cones, heart-shaped waffles, stuffed waffles, croque monsieurs and galettes with this baby.' At least, that was what the online advertisement for the machine promised.

I didn't know exactly what a croque monsieur or a galette was yet and was dying to taste each. Whatever they were, sounding French, the tourists would probably go for them – and pay big bucks for the privilege – and the waffle maker would pay for itself in no time. I had only paid about a hundred and thirty dollars for it, and that included shipping.

'Yeah,' Kelly said, the corner of her mouth turning down, 'but you haven't even made a regular waffle yet, let alone any of that other fancy stuff you mentioned.' She wiped my fingerprints from the side of the espresso's boiler. 'And we don't sell ice cream.'

'Fine. Front and center.' I picked up the waffle maker and moved it to the center of the counter. 'Since we are going to have to wait to get cups for the espresso maker, we can start making waffles now.'

While I intended to make my own waffle mix, eventually I had purchased a couple bags of imported Liege waffle mix and Belgian pearl sugar for a start. 'Do you remember where we put the mix?'

'You put it in the cupboard behind the powdered sugar.'

'Would you mind running in back and getting it?' I reached for my apron on the shelf under the counter. Like me, Kelly wore the standard Maggie's Beignet Café uniform: a periwinkle polo shirt, khaki slacks rather than shorts, this being October, and a visor.

The uniforms had been Aubrey's idea. Aubrey Ingridson had been my first hire. Not only had having uniforms been her idea, she had sketched out the logo and gotten a local embroidery firm to make up the patches that she'd then handsewn onto our shirts and visors.

Our aprons were pure white with the addition of the café's logo. With all the powdered sugar flying around over the course of a day, it was the only color that made sense.

'Of course not,' Kelly replied quickly with a smile on her face. 'That's what you pay me for.'

As she pushed through the swinging accordion doors to the storeroom, the tinkle of bells announced a customer. 'Good morning,' I called.

'Hello, Ms Miller.' It was Nancy Alverson, a bookish woman with curly brown hair and brown eyes framed by delicate silver glasses. 'What's all this?' Her eyes went from the waffle maker to the espresso machine.

'We're trying some new things.'

The young woman nodded appreciatively. 'I can see that. I guess a girl can't live on beignets alone.' She patted her stomach with her free hand. Her left hand clutched the strap of a colorful red, blue and brown-striped cloth bag that I knew from experience held her purse, a notebook, a laptop computer and who knew what else.

'Not that I haven't been trying,' Nancy added. The thirty-five-year-old Ms Alverson was single and wan, spending much of her time indoors, from what I could tell. When she did venture out, like now, she wore a floppy sapphire-blue sunhat with a brown leather cord, olive cargo pants, flannel shirt and a black fleece vest with over-the-ankle hiking boots. The flannel shirt *de jour* was a plaid tan and sangria-colored affair.

We shared a laugh.

Nancy had been coming into the café for several weeks now but she kept to herself. Once or twice, a brave soul of the male variety had tried to engage her in conversation. She had remained aloof.

Not unfriendly, from what I could see and hear. But not welcoming of uninvited attention.

I knew she was a writer and scant else. She spoke little and rarely smiled, not because she seemed to have a dour disposition, but rather because she seemed lost in herself and as if the act of smiling might break something, like one of her facial bones.

'The usual?'

Besides the traditional New Orleans-style beignet, Maggie's Beignet Café now offered chocolate, blueberry and lemon beignets.

For Halloween, I had also added pumpkin spice beignets to the menu. If they were popular, I'd keep them on the menu permanently. If not, using a chalkboard for a menu made it easy to erase them from our list of offerings.

'Yes, please.' She lifted her hat, letting it fall to the back of her neck.

I did know that she was renting a room across the street, up above Karma Koffee, a high-end beverage and bakery shop. That she preferred walking across to the café rather than frequenting Karma Koffee made me like her all the more.

Belinda dumped her trash in the receptacle and returned her tray to the counter.

'Thanks again!' I called as she went out the door. She raised her left hand in reply.

'How's the writing going?' I inquired as I prepared Nancy Alverson's habitual order of three blueberry beignets and a black coffee. We make our coffee the traditional way too, with chicory. I'd read that chicory was originally added to coffee during a time of shortage during the Napoleonic Wars as a way to extend the coffee supply. Donna told me chicory has all kinds of health benefits and can reduce stress, relieve constipation, fight osteoarthritis and more.

I grabbed the French press and measured out portions of coffee and chicory, using a mix of two parts coffee to one part chicory root.

'It's going,' she said just as enigmatically as she did every time I asked her.

She watched in silence as I sliced and rolled out the blueberry beignet dough and dropped a trio of three-inch wide, quarter-inch thick squares into the fryer. The 370-degree cottonseed oil hissed and bubbled.

In a minute, the beignets were golden brown and ready to serve. I scooped them out with the long-handled, stainless-steel skimmer ladle and set them on the draining tray for a minute before dusting them with powdered sugar. I'd learned that if you added the sugar too soon, it melted and disappeared.

I grabbed a plastic serving tray from the stack at the edge of the counter. I plated the beignets and placed the tray on the counter between us. I added a couple of napkins and her coffee. 'Here you go. Enjoy.'

'I will.' She paid in cash, dropping fifty cents into the tip jar beside the cash register. Then she quietly took her tray to the corner table against the window, angling herself in such a way as to get the best view of the busy street and keep the glare off the screen of her battleship-gray laptop.

'Here.' Kelly set a five-pound bag of waffle mix and a smaller bag of pearl sugar next to the waffle maker.

'Thanks.' I read over the instructions on the back of the bag and got busy. One way or another, for better or for worse, I was making waffles. 'Hand me a mixing bowl, would you?'

Kelly went to the back, returning with a mixing bowl and several sizes of spoons. Together we managed to quickly complete a batch of waffle mix.

'Now all we have to do is wait for the waffle iron to heat up.' I rubbed my hands in expectation.

After several minutes, the iron chimed. Kelly raised the lid and I dolloped some thick waffle batter onto the hot plate. 'OK.' I licked my thumb, which had somehow gotten into the bowl.

Kelly shut the lid slowly.

I moved to the sink and started rinsing the mixing bowl and two of the spoons under warm water. I turned, my Pavlovian response to the tinkle of the leather belt of brass bells on the front door that announced the coming and going of customers.

It wasn't a customer. It was my employee, Aubrey. 'Good morning!' I waved a soapy hand and dried myself quickly with the end of my apron.

A moment later, two men and a woman, all dressed for business, stepped inside and Kelly greeted them. She picked up a pencil and the order pad.

Aubrey stepped behind the counter. I followed her to the store-room, where she took off her light fleece jacket and hung it on the hook in the backroom next to mine. Though late October, and I'd heard there had been snow in Colorado, the temperatures in this part of Arizona were near perfect: highs in the seventies, lows in the forties.

'What's that chirping noise?' Aubrey is a strawberry blonde with jade-green eyes. She's a Table Rock native and still lives with her parents and brother in the house she was raised in. For a Table Rocker, she was relatively normal. Which, for a Table Rocker, was anything but normal.

'We're making real Belgian waffles,' I explained.

Aubrey grabbed a clean apron and we both returned to the front of the café.

As we rounded the corner, Aubrey's eyes grew wide. 'What's that doing here?' Her eyes were on my Belle Époque copper and brass espresso machine.

'You like it?' I said from over the young woman's shoulder.

Aubrey stepped back, jostling me. 'I don't like it at all!'

I frowned. 'Why not?'

'Because it's cursed!'

TWO

'I've got three orders of beignets, two regular, one lemon!' Kelly called, waving the ticket over her shoulder. 'Two coffees, one cola!'

The door opened and yet more customers filed in. I smiled at them, then turned and narrowed my eyes at Aubrey. 'What do you mean, cursed?' I demanded softly so as not to upset our customers.

'I mean cursed. You want to get the beignets and I'll get the drinks?'

I nodded and went to the fryer, grabbing both regular and lemon-flavored dough as I moved.

'Excuse me.' One of the dark-suited men leaned over the glass divider, a troubled expression on his face. Businessmen were always pressed for time.

'Your beignets will be up in a minute,' I promised.

'I think something's burning.'

I glanced at the deep fryer. Everything looked just perfect but the smell of something akin to burnt cake was unmistakable.

He pointed behind me.

The waffle iron was puffing out smoke like a steam locomotive climbing a steep Rocky Mountain pass.

'Maggie!' scolded Aubrey. She reached for the hot waffle iron and popped the lid. She grabbed a plastic fork and prodded the charred lump. Her eyebrows went up in a *this is what you get for buying a cursed espresso machine* manner.

By the time I turned back to the fryer, the beignets were over-cooked too. I sighed, fished them from the fryer and started over. The businessman, now joined by his two companions, looked meaningfully at his watch.

Once their orders were ready, the three of them took up a table against the wall near the counter. While I prepared a dozen beignets to go for the next customer, I saw one of the two businessmen at the table lean toward Nancy. 'Do I know you?'

Nancy glanced up from her computer, her hands hovering over the keyboard. 'No. I don't think so.' She turned her face back to the laptop, scooted her chair, angling herself further from the three, and resumed typing.

The two men whispered between themselves while the woman, hair in a bun, dressed in business attire, blue jacket, matching skirt and pale pink blouse, sipped her soda.

Several hushed words passed among them, and then the middle-aged man in the dark suit tapped Nancy on the arm. 'Excuse me, but I'm sure I know you.'

I bagged the dozen beignets, then sprinkled in a generous helping of powdered sugar. I rolled the top of the bag closed and gave it a good shake to make sure each beignet got a good coating of sugar.

'I'm afraid you are mistaken,' I heard Nancy say. She gently closed the lid of her laptop and stood. She grabbed her coffee and remaining beignet and tossed them in the trash.

'Leaving already?' I said.

'Things to do,' she replied vaguely, pulling her lips taut.

'OK. Don't forget to stop by tonight.'

'Tonight?' She propped the door open with her shoulder.

'Halloween,' I replied. 'We're going to be handing out special treats!'

'Of course. Halloween.'

I watched as she walked quickly across the street and disappeared through the street-level door leading to her third-floor apartment.

It was the first time I'd seen her not finish her food.

I couldn't help noticing the two men and the woman watching her the whole time.

Not more than a minute or two later, Nancy came down to the street once again with her bag slung over her shoulder. She glanced toward the café then climbed inside her ancient white Land Rover, which had been parallel parked on the street.

The man whose approach Nancy had brusquely brushed off rose quickly and strode with determined long steps out the café and directly to her vehicle as she attempted to maneuver out of the tight space she was trapped in. He rapped on the window and she rolled it partially down. He gesticulated with his arms.

I couldn't hear Nancy's reply, of course, but even from a distance I could see that she didn't look happy. The man jumped into the road as Nancy stepped on the gas and drove off.

The man, clearly agitated, returned to his companions. He was tall, with a shock of gray-black hair and sharp sideburns, a tanned complexion and a narrow nose and jaw, as if his face had been stretched too far. His dark eyes blazed. 'She's impossible,' I heard him say.

The three business people rose and left soon after, leaving their trash on the table. I couldn't complain too much because they'd also left a three-dollar cash tip, which I added to the tip jar for Aubrey and Kelly to split up later.

Detective Highsmith came in right before closing. The café generally closes at three in the afternoon, although once I had come up with some successful savory beignet additions to the menu, I hoped to bring in enough business to justify staying open into the early evening hours. Kelly was already gone for the day but promised to be back before six o'clock that night.

'Am I too late?' The six-foot-plus brawny cop glanced at me and Kelly. His brown suit and tie were dull and ordinary, but his M&M-brown eyes were as scrumptious-looking as the candy-coated chocolate morsels.

I glanced at the clock on the wall. A local artist had offered to transform the deli clock and sandwich menu board into a one-of-a-kind Maggie's Beignet Café sign. Since he was offering to do it for free in exchange for allowing him to hang a half-dozen of his pieces on the café's walls, I let him.

The sign now read Maggie's Beignet Café and pictured a highly stylized candy-red and teal-blue javelina's head. Javelinas run wild in Arizona. They have long snouts and large heads. A typical adult has a thick coat of dark gray, bristly hair and a band of white hair around its neck. They have a noticeable mane of long, stiff hairs running down their backs from head to rump. The average adult male is four to five feet long and up to two feet tall, and weighs forty to sixty pounds.

Javelinas travel in small herds of fifteen to twenty. They look scary but are relatively harmless. While they eat the occasional grub or insect, they, like my sister, are vegetarians.

Javelinas also look similar to a wild boar or pig, and the tourists often mistake them for such, but they are unrelated. I've also been told they are quite tasty, but have no interest in testing the veracity of that claim.

'Too late for what?' I asked. I made a mental note to text Jakob. Jakob Waltz was the local artist who'd reimagined the sign and whose six paintings now hung in the café. Make that five. I'd sold one of his pieces, a multicolored, postmodern interpretation of the Verde River Valley, a few days ago to a tourist.

Jakob had explained to me that he had sketched out the bones of the painting from the gondola of a hot-air balloon. It seemed the determined young man would do anything for his art.

I needed to let Jakob know to come down to the café and pick up his check. He had offered to let me keep a percentage of each sale but I had refused. The life of an artist was hard. He deserved every penny for himself.

'A couple dozen beignets,' Table Rock's lone detective explained. 'I promised the guys at the station that I'd bring the treats this afternoon.'

'What?' I teased. He and I have a special relationship. 'Are you expecting to confiscate less candy than usual from the little trick-or-treaters tonight?'

'Ha ha. Very funny, Cueball,' he teased.

I colored.

Highsmith plucked his wallet from the inside pocket of his sports coat. 'Two dozen to go, Aubrey.'

'Drinks with that?' she asked.

'Nah.' He slapped his credit card on the counter and Aubrey ran it through the scanner.

I took care of the order, happy to use up the rest of the regular beignet dough. I intended to switch over to pumpkin spice after that.

The plan was to close, as usual, at three, then reopen at six p.m. It was a tradition for downtown Table Rock business owners to offer candy and other treats to the children on Halloween night. Now that I was a fully-fledged business owner celebrating my first Halloween, I intended to do the same.

I'd hand out pumpkin spice beignets and gobs of candy from the big bags that Mom was generously providing. Donna and Andy would also be handing out sweets at Mother Earth/Father Sun, but I was convinced that trick-or-treating parents and children alike would prefer sugar-coated fried dough and sugar-filled candy to stuff made out of the tapioca syrup and rice starch in Donna's kitchen.

I dropped the filled beignet bags on the counter and turned to wash my hands. 'Thanks again,' I said, my back to him as I scrubbed the dough from beneath my fingernails. 'Say hello to the men in blue for me and tell them that they and their families are all invited to come back this evening – and you too, if you want a free treat.'

'Treat?' the detective asked.

I pushed the bulky espresso maker to the side to make some extra room on the counter.

Aubrey explained, 'We're opening for Halloween. Treats for the kiddies. Parents, too. Anybody really. We're going to wear costumes and everything. It's going to truly, truly be a blast.'

We had hung the Halloween decorations up a week ago – crepe paper pumpkins, spooks, goblins and witches. A black-and-orange Happy Halloween banner extended from one side of the café ceiling to the other. Cardboard tombstones with pithy inscriptions such as Paul Bearer, 1813–1842; Barry D. Alyve, 1794–1851 and Ricky D. Bones, Dates Unknown, sat in the front window.

'Sounds good,' Highsmith agreed. 'But we have plans.'

'We?' I turned around. 'You and VV?' VV stood for Veronica Vargas. Considering VV's looks, it could have stood for voluptuous vixen. From my personal experiences with the woman, I had the feeling it really stood for venomous viper.

Mark Highsmith and VV were a thing, although every now and again I felt Highsmith and I could have a thing of our own.

VV was everything I wasn't: beautiful, cool, aloof, toney, tailored and trendy. She was also successful, with her own law practice in addition to being Table Rock's prosecuting attorney. To rub more salt in the wound, her daddy was mayor of Table Rock.

I could say that I didn't see what Highsmith saw in her, but he saw what everyone else with one X and one Y chromosome saw: a woman to drool over.

'That's right,' Highsmith said with a smile. 'We're taking part in the Haunted Halloween Hop.'

I pulled my brows together. 'What's that?' I asked as Aubrey locked the front door and turned the *Open* sign to *Closed*.

Highsmith explained, 'It's Halloween for grownups.' The way he was looking at me as he said grownups, I was getting the feeling he thought that let me off. 'We go to seven different bars and brewpubs here in Table Rock, Cottonwood, then Jerome and over in Sedona, hear some ghost stories—'

'And drink too much beer?' I finished. I'd been to Jerome. The road to the town at the top of Cleopatra Hill was steep and twisty. Jerome was almost a mile high. If this Haunted Halloween Hop's revelers weren't extra careful, there might be some new ghosts born that night.

'That's right.' When he smiled big like that, his dimples blossomed and the big galoot looked adorable. Not that I cared. 'You should come. Bring a date. It's fifty dollars a person and all the proceeds go to charity.'

'Thanks.' I wrapped my hands around the sides of the espresso maker. 'But as you heard, I have plans of my own.' Not to mention, fifty dollars per person was too steep for me. Nor did I have a date, let alone one willing to spend fifty dollars on me.

'Will you be wearing costumes?' inquired Aubrey.

'Of course,' replied the detective. 'It's Halloween. That's the whole point.'

'What are you going as?' I asked.

'A Victorian London bobby.'

'Cute. Dare I ask what VV will be dressing up as?' The Wicked Witch of the West was the first and best option that came to my mind.

'A Victorian lady.'

'Like Lady Audley?' I quipped, in reference to a Victorian-era novel called *Lady Audley's Secret* written by Mary Elizabeth Braddon. I had read the sensationalistic story in my downtime between clients while working as a hair stylist over in Phoenix. The lurid novel had made an impression on me.

Thinking of VV in particular brought back memories of Lucy Graham, the bigamous 'heroine' who deserted her child, pushed her first husband down a well, considered poisoning husband number two, then set fire to the hotel where other male conquests were lodging.

Veronica Vargas could star in the movie if they made a modern film version.

'Huh?' He clearly had no idea what I was talking about. 'I guess. If you say so.'

I nodded. 'I can see that.' I hoisted the machine with a grunt and it tilted toward me, bumping me in the nose. 'Ouch!'

'Here . . .' Detective Highsmith leapt over the counter. Sheesh, the man had moves. 'Let me help you with that, Maggie!'

Still in shock from the alacrity of his actions, I stepped back and gladly released my grip on the heavy machine as he nudged into my side. 'Thanks.'

'Don't mention—' A string of cuss words followed while Highsmith grabbed his left foot with his right hand and did a dance across the narrow space behind the counter.

I had dropped the espresso machine on his foot. 'Are you OK?' I gasped, reaching for his arm to steady him.

'Don't touch me!' He sounded pained, and no doubt he was.

'Sit,' I begged him. 'I'll get some ice.' I pointed to Aubrey. 'Get Detective Highsmith some ice from the freezer!'

Aubrey hurried to the storeroom. As she did, I heard her whisper harshly in my direction. 'Cursed. I told you, Maggie.' Her eyes were on the fallen espresso maker. 'That thing is truly, truly cursed!'

THREE

I looked for the third time at my reflection in the tall mirror in the small employee bathroom located in the café's storage area. 'What am I supposed to be?'

'Don't you get it?' Aubrey brought her hands to her cheeks. 'You're Little Dead Riding Hood!'

I frowned. 'Little Dead Riding Hood? I thought you were going to make me a Little Bo Peep costume?' I said over my shoulder. With my black, knee-length hooded cape, shredded black knee-length skirt, tattered black nylon hose and white peasant blouse and white apron, both spattered with fake blood, I looked like Little Red Riding Hood going through her Goth phase.

'Oh, Maggie. That's so boring. Trust me.' She patted my shoulder. 'This is so much better.'

'Much more Halloween,' agreed Kelly, looking quite as lovely as Aubrey.

'Sure,' I said gloomily. 'That's easy for you to say.' I tugged at her sleeve. 'You get to wear all this chiffon and makeup.'

I stepped out of the cramped bathroom that had never been intended for three people and turned my attention to Aubrey. 'So how come Kelly looks like a Native American princess and you look like that girl from *The Little Mermaid*? Why aren't the two of you dressed like ghouls? I look like something some grave digger just dug up.'

'That's the whole point,' Aubrey said with a smile that I wasn't feeling myself. Sure, she looked sexy in her flowing, form-fitting green skirt that looked like real fish scales with a spaghetti-strap sparkly purple top. 'Contrast.' She probably thought I hadn't seen her wink at Kelly, but I had. Aubrey's luxuriant orange-red wig was a wistful reminder of my own once-long red hair.

'That's right.' Kelly's chin bobbed up and down. 'Contrast, Maggie.'

For Kelly, Aubrey had crafted a beautiful brown ultra-suede dress with short sleeves and a pointed hem with a darker brown fringe. The dress was trimmed in a three-inch-wide detailed tribal print of orange, yellow, purple and pale blue. Aubrey had even included matching arm and head bands with dangling feathers.

All that was missing was the bow and arrow with which Kelly could shoot me and put me out of my misery.

'Whatever.' I sighed. It was too late to change costumes now. Aubrey had offered to design and sew our costumes and this was Halloween night. I was stuck with it. 'We'd better get out front and unlock the door.' I put my hand on the swinging door.

'Don't forget your basket, Maggie!' Kelly giggled as she thrust a woven basket that she had spray-painted black into my hands. A nest of spider web lay at the bottom.

'Thanks,' I said with a frown. I stopped in the passageway and looked down at my feet. Two brown, fuzzy spiders stared up at me where my shoes should have been. Aubrey had really pulled out all the stops.

It was going to be a long night.

I wondered how Detective Mark Highsmith was getting along. He had left the café in a huff – and with a significant limp. While I had offered to take him to get his foot looked at, he had insisted on driving himself to the Mesa Verde Medical Center, and that was the last I had seen of him.

Hopefully, the small matter of a smashed right big toe wouldn't put a crimp in his beer drinking.

Kelly unlocked the door just as my mother pulled up at the curb. Mom's metallic-green VW Beetle sported long black eyelashes over the headlights, a pink lips decal on the front bumper and an Aliens Onboard bumper sticker on the rear. And the Bug wasn't dressed up in honor of it being Halloween. That was just Mom being Mom.

A two-inch-long milky crystal dangled from a silver chain lassoed around the rearview mirror. Mom said it was a good-luck charm. Funny how she'd added that right after getting the car back from the body shop after I had accidently driven it into a small boulder – well, not much more than a pebble really.

'Hi, Mom!' I wrapped my arms around her then stepped back. 'You look adorable. Meow.' I held up my right hand and clawed at a nonexistent scratch post. My mother had opted for one of her yoga outfits, a long-sleeved black leotard, to which she had added a pleated black skirt and black cat ears. A pair of black ballet flats protected her feet.

'Thank you, dear.' Mom tilted her head as she said, 'And you look . . .'

'Hideous?' I suggested. 'Gruesome?'

Mom chuckled. 'Let's say spooktacular.'

I groaned, although Kelly and Aubrey seemed to think my mother was a hoot because they laughed uproariously.

Mom handed me a grocery bag which was itself filled with several bulging sacks of assorted popular candies. 'Thanks, Mom. We'll be a hit.'

I turned the candy over to Kelly, who had come in from the back, but not before helping myself to a cherry Tootsie Pop and a KitKat. Aubrey turned on all the lights and I began cranking out the pumpkin spice beignets.

'Will Connor and Hunter be stopping by?' Mom asked. She adored her grandkids.

Mom also liked to comment that the boys were growing up too fast and how she only wished *somebody* else would provide her with fresh young replacements. Donna and Andy had insisted they were finished having children. That left little old me. Emphasis on the *old*.

According to my mom, if I didn't have kids soon, I could be my own grandmother.

'I mentioned we'd be having pumpkin-flavored beignets and treats and she said Andy would try to bring Hunter. I'm not sure about Connor. He's attending a school dance.'

Though both of my nephews were homeschooled – Donna had been a school teacher in her previous life – they occasionally attended public school events as a way of making friends and maintaining those relationships.

The night flew by. Aubrey helped fill orders, Mom worked the register and Kelly kept everything stocked and cleared tables.

When I wasn't busy frying beignets, I was busy scaring young children. It wasn't my intention – it was the costume. At least my gruesome appearance didn't appear to have put a dampener on anyone's appetite for sweets.

In fact, I was thrilled with the crowds we were getting. It looked like it would be a big night for the town and a big night for me. Of course, I was giving the beignets and the candies away for free. I hoped it would lead to some new customers, not to mention some good word of mouth.

I was charging for drinks, and we did pretty well in that department.

Too bad I hadn't had the espresso maker up and running. At least it hadn't been harmed in the fall. Highsmith's foot had softened the impact. Despite Aubrey's absurd claim about the machine, I expected it would turn us a sweet little profit as soon as it was operational.

My brother-in-law, Andy Singer, came in at around seven-thirty with my nephew, Hunter. The boy was twelve years old, two years younger than his brother, Connor.

Andy is six foot four and skinny with long, dirty blond hair, frequently tied up in a ponytail. For as long as I've known him, a hemp bracelet has been tied around his right wrist.

Andy was a UCLA graduate and, as he liked to say, a reformed corporate attorney. Now he eked out a living, along with my sister, as an organic farmer and grocer. They both seemed happy to have given up high-powered careers, the flashy cars and the house in one of the best neighborhoods in Scottsdale for the slower pace of life in Table Rock.

'Hi, Andy.' I waved and looked at Hunter with a grin on my face. 'What have we here?'

'Hi, Aunt Maggie.'

'Hunter, are you in there?' I was gazing at a five foot green and leafy . . . something. Fake green fronds covered my nephew from head to toe. A fuzzy purple pompom sprouted from his head and fuzzy purple mittens covered his hands. Those hands clutched an old-fashioned burlap sack that bulged with treats.

'What are you supposed to be?' I asked. I was afraid to guess. I might hurt his feelings.

Hunter tugged at his costume. 'I'm an artichoke.'

'I think you look wonderful, baby,' cooed my mother. She grabbed a generous helping of candies and chocolates and dumped them in his bag.

'Thanks, Grandma!'

'You're welcome, baby.' Mom turned to me. 'Doesn't he look darling, dear?'

'Just darling,' I replied, dutifully. 'Can I get you men some beignets?'

'We wouldn't say no, would we, Hunter?' Andy answered.

The artichoke shook noisily.

'I'll take that for a yes,' I said. I got busy on their orders. Mom took a break and joined Andy and Hunter at a table for a few minutes while they ate.

'Say hi to Connor for me!' I called later as they left to resume their trick-or-treating. 'And tell him to stop by! I'll save some treats for him!'

The artichoke waved.

I took that for a yes, too.

At one point in the action, I looked up to see a large group of adult revelers in costume strolling loudly past the café. Aubrey had mentioned that Hopping Mad, a local brew pub up the street from us, was one of the designated stops for the Haunted Halloween Hop. I expected that was where they were all headed.

Among the merrymakers, I spotted Mark Highsmith and Veronica Vargas strolling shoulder to shoulder. The detective, in his tall, silver-tipped black hat with the big, shiny silver badge on the front, stood out above the crowd like a beacon in a storm.

Jakob came in just before nine p.m. and waved to me from the back of the line of customers leading to the sales counter.

'Come for the pumpkin spice beignets?' I hollered above the din of the trick-or-treaters and grownups.

'No. I came for my check. But since I'm here . . .' He smiled. Jakob wasn't handsome in a traditional sense. His teeth were slightly off but he had a pleasant oval face, a frizzy mop of brown hair with long, tapered sideburns and sharp yet welcoming green eyes.

'Go for it,' I said, ladle in hand. Heat from the fryer blasted my face. 'Mom, can you hand Jakob his check when he gets up there? It's under the till.'

'Will do,' she promised.

Several minutes later, Jakob wormed his way through the line and I handed him a paper plate with three pumpkin spice beignets atop it.

'Thanks, Maggie.' Halloween seemed to have made no impression on him. Like every other time I had seen him, he wore loose-fitting jeans and a black V-neck T-shirt. The only thing different about his attire this time was that there were less paint stains in evidence than usual.

'My pleasure.' I ran the back of my arm across my forehead.

'Nice costume.'

I couldn't help frowning every time somebody said that, and I couldn't help it this time either.

'What? You don't like it?' he asked with a smile.

'Let's just say that next year I'm in charge of making the costumes.' I shot a meaningful look at Aubrey, who was filling a glass with lemonade, into which she plopped one blue and one red gummy eyeball. She pretended not to hear.

Jakob leaned over the glass divider. Despite the cloud of pumpkin spice in the air, I caught a hint of something musky. 'I don't suppose you've seen Nancy?'

I shook powdered sugar over what I hoped was my last order for the day. My feet were screaming, my knees buckling and my arms felt like my bones had been replaced with lead rods. 'Nancy Alverson?'

He nodded.

'No. I haven't seen her.' I set down the aluminum powdered sugar shaker and moved the plate to the waiting customers, a thirtysome-thing pair in normal attire accompanied by a sallow-skinned zombie with big yellow teeth and a bug-eyed green alien with black nostrils the size of vacuum hoses and a solitary antenna poking up from the center of his skull; their boys, or so I hoped.

'Should I have?'

'No. I knocked on her door and rang the buzzer. There was no answer. I was just wondering . . .' He turned his head and looked out the window toward the building across the street. 'Nancy mentioned that she comes in here sometimes.'

'Come to think of it, when I told her we were having Halloween treats tonight, she said she'd come by.' I wiped my hands against my apron, mixing sugar with faux blood stains. 'Then again, we've been so busy, I might never have noticed if she'd come and gone.'

I turned to my mother. 'Mom, do you remember seeing Nancy tonight?'

Mom slammed the register shut with her hip. 'Who, dear?'

'Never mind.' Clearly, she didn't know the young woman. I turned back to Jakob. 'Sorry.'

'No problem.' He held up his plate. 'Thanks for these.' He patted his shirt pocket. 'And for the check.'

'Happy to be able to do both. Don't forget to bring something new to fill that hole in the wall.' I pointed to the space that the two-by-three-foot painting had occupied.

'Soon,' Jakob promised. He exited the café, balancing the plate of beignets in the palm of his left hand.

'Time to lock up!'

Kelly was dancing between the tables with a damp cloth and a gray plastic bus tub, clearing and wiping. 'Hallelujah.' The Native American princess for the night set the tub on the table nearest the door and thumbed the lock. She turned the sign to *Closed*.

I thanked Mom for her help and sent her on her way. 'Thanks for pitching in, Mom. We'll get this.' Mom worked in the café part-time, too. Her idea, not mine. Since she was a startup investor and had helped me out in more ways than I could ever count or hope to pay her back for over the course of my life, letting her work in the business was small payback.

'Are you sure? I don't mind staying and help you clean up.'

I grabbed my mother's coat and helped her into it. I pushed her toward the door. 'You've done more than your share already, Mom.' I handed her a half-filled bowl of candy. 'Here. Why don't you take the rest of this home?'

Mom eyed the candy – millions of calories and billions of grams of sugar in each scrummy bite. 'I don't think I'd better.' She pulled back her hands. 'I won't be able to help myself.'

'Me either. Do you think Connor and Hunter would want the rest of this?'

'Are you joking? I think they'd love it!' Mom shook the bowl. 'But can you imagine what Donna and Andy would say?'

My sister would say I was poisoning my poor, defenseless nephews. She would probably then dump the whole bowl of candy in the trash – the stuff probably wasn't even good enough for her composter.

I couldn't let all this lovely candy go to waste. 'I'll set a few pieces aside for Connor like I promised.' I fished out several candy bars and a box of Cracker Jack.

How could Donna or Andy object to that? Corn and peanuts. Two vegetables. It was like a nutritious meal in a box.

I lifted the bowl in the air. 'Anybody else want this?'

Kelly and Aubrey declined.

Mom took the bowl from my hands. 'I'll leave it in the community room.' Mom poured the candy into a bag and dropped it in her purse. She lived in a sprawling condo complex. No doubt it wouldn't take long for the candy to disappear.

We cleaned up as best we could. Kelly and Aubrey left together. Kelly had been dropped off by her brother and Aubrey was her ride home, although they mentioned they would be going to a friend's party first.

As for me, Little Dead Riding Hood, I was dead tired. I had my Schwinn and would be pedaling home. However, there were a dozen beignets left, keeping hot under the infrared lights of the freestanding stainless-steel warmer next to the deep fryer.

During busy times like that night, we tried to stay ahead of the orders by having some beignets fried up in advance of the demand in an effort to cut down on the customer wait time, although beignets are delicate and it's a fine line between precooked and rubber.

I'd had my fill and hated to throw the remaining beignets in the trash. There was a dim glow of light coming from Nancy Alverson's apartment, visible from my window. I bagged up the remaining beignets, sprinkled them with sugar and sealed the bag. I'd deliver them to Nancy – my last treat of the day before going home to treat myself to a nice hot bath and a nice cold drink.

Margaritas and bubble baths. Two of life's little pleasures, especially when enjoyed together.

Speaking of pleasures, I realized – as I wrapped my hideous black cloak around myself after double-checking that all the equipment had been properly shut down and the cash was in the floor safe – that this had been the best Halloween I had had in years. When my cheating, dead ex-husband Brian left me, I thought for a while there that my life was over. Little had I known that it was only beginning.

I crossed the street quickly. Traffic was lighter now. There were a few trick-or-treaters wandering around, high-schoolers by the looks of them, and they had barely bothered with costumes, opting for such simple gestures as high-school football jerseys and sexy cheer-leader outfits, all bearing the Table Rock H.S. mascot, the roadrunner, with a football tucked under its wing.

A couple of lights were still on at Karma Koffee but the lavender neon sign above the storefront was dark and the sign on the door had been turned to *Closed* as well. I didn't see anybody inside the shop.

Squeezing between two tightly packed parallel parked cars at the curb, I crossed the sidewalk to the small door in the side of the speckled brown brick-fronted building.

A narrow, unmarked red door tucked in a small alcove in the brick wall protected the entrance from the elements.

I yawned, rolled up my sleeve and glanced at my watch. It was nearly ten p.m. Most days I was in bed by now. Hawking beignets and coffee for a living meant early rising – something I wasn't cut out for. In my old life, I was rarely up before seven.

There was no chance of getting away with that now, what with employees and customers waiting. Not to mention a certain cat that lived with me and who would probably gnaw my toes off one by one if I didn't drop some kibble in her dish at five a.m.

As I pressed the brass buzzer, I heard a rumble and felt a slight tremor. The door was windowless and there were no sidelights. I pressed my ear to the wood. 'Nancy? It's me, Mag—'

The door flew open without warning and a dark blue blur shot past me as if being chased by the Devil.

FOUR

Speak of the Devil.

I quickly recognized that blue blur. It was Veronica Vargas herself.

I jumped out of her way, bouncing off the rough brick alcove. 'Veronica? What's going on? What are you doing here?'

VV spun on her Victorian black, lace-up boots, her billowy blue satin skirt rustling as she lifted it with both hands. 'You!' she cried. 'Get out of here before you ruin everything, Ms Miller!'

'What do you mean?' I hoisted the sack of beignets. 'I'm only delivering these.' I was taken aback. I didn't know which was more frightening, VV standing there on the sidewalk screaming at me or the fact that she recognized me despite the dark shadows engulfing us and the Little Dead Riding Hood outfit I was wearing.

I narrowed my eyes at her. VV was costumed in a long-sleeved blue velvet top with a plunging princess neckline with a bustled peplum. The matching royal-blue skirt drifted to her ankles. A matching blue velvet hat was fixed on her head. Her elegant auburn locks hung in perfect curls. The hat was accented with a small bouquet of pink and white carnations.

Who did she think she was – Eliza Doolittle? With all that cleavage hanging out, she looked more like a Victorian vixen. It wasn't fair. No woman should be that voluptuous and that thin all at once.

Especially not while I was dressed as the Crypt Keeper's wife.

VV's eyes danced madly up and down the street. Those eyes were the color of hazelnuts, though her shell was twice as hard.

She pointed her finger at me. 'Do not go upstairs.' The Latino accent she routinely kept at bay was poking through. 'Go home, Miller. I've got to find Mark!'

With that, she spun away and ran up the street, her feet clopping like horse's hooves and echoing off the brick walls and stone pavers.

I stood transfixed for a minute, clutching my bag of pumpkin spice beignets. 'What the devil has gotten into her?' I'd always thought the woman a bit mad. Had she made that fancy hat herself? Had she been sniffing too much glue?

More likely she was drunk. Hours of Haunted Halloween Hopping could do that to a person.

I looked at the bag of beignets growing cold in my fingers. Whatever was bothering VV was no concern of mine. She was a grown woman and could take care of herself.

I trudged prudently up the steep, unlit wooden steps to the third floor. The stairwell was unlit. Wasn't that some sort of safety violation?

The door to the apartment stood partially open.

I had never been inside. Nancy and I were not exactly friends. What would she say about me barging in on her this late at night?

I probably should have turned around and gone home, but VV ordering me to stay out had only had the opposite effect. Now, more than ever, I was determined to deliver the pumpkin spice beignets to Nancy. Whether she liked it or not. If Nancy didn't like my stopping by unannounced, she could ask me to leave, beignets and all.

I rapped my knuckles lightly against the gaping door. 'Nancy? It's me, Maggie Miller. From the café.' I held my breath for a moment, listening. 'I brought you some extra beignets.' I peeked through the crack. 'Can I come in? Nancy?'

Nancy had to be home. VV had just come from the apartment. Why wasn't she answering?

I squeezed through the door and found myself in a tidy little apartment. The living room, no more than a fifteen-by-twelve-foot space, contained old yet serviceable upholstered furniture in unremarkable shades of green and brown. A small, walnut-stained coffee table with turned legs held an assortment of books, magazines and regional tourist information.

To my left, the orange glow of a nightlight revealed a compact bathroom with subway tiled flooring. Straight ahead, a small galley kitchen with white cabinets stood empty, although the unmistakable smell of cumin hung in the air. I knew the bedroom was to my right on the street side. Light spilled out from there onto the worn gold carpet.

'Nancy?' I moved through the living room and into the bedroom.

The twin bed cut the front left corner. A six-drawer bureau was on the wall opposite the window. Nancy Alverson sat at her desk against the wall to the right of the window, her left arm dangling limp, her right arm stretched out.

Her unmoving hand rested on the keyboard of her dark-screened laptop.

I stepped closer. Her head slumped. Her eyes were half-lidded. There was a bluish tinge to her complexion.

The young woman was clearly dead.

The bag of beignets dropped from my hand to the carpet and I struggled for my cellphone, which was deep in the bowels of my purse.

My eyes on Nancy, I dialed 9-1-1. I reported where I was and what I'd found.

'Don't worry, Ms Miller. The authorities are already on their way,' assured the voice on the line.

I slipped my phone back in my purse. Nancy was dressed as she had been earlier in the day at the café, minus the hat and with the addition of a creamy white cashmere scarf that was tied tightly around her neck.

Too tightly was my guess.

I reached out a tentative hand to feel her flesh and check for a pulse – just in case. Maybe I could give her CPR until the professionals arrived. I knew *I* had a pulse because mine was going a million miles per minute.

Leaning closer to Nancy, I caught a whiff of Joy Parfum. I had a feeling such a perfume, at hundreds of dollars per ounce, was far beyond Nancy Alverson's budget.

It was, however, VV's signature scent. I held my nose an inch from the cashmere scarf around Nancy's neck. The smell of jasmine and roses was strongest there.

Had Veronica Vargas signed her confession to murder by employing the scent-laden scarf to kill Nancy Alverson?

Was VV on the run now and halfway to the Mexican border? What would the Mexican authorities say when Lady Victorian Vixen showed up seeking asylum?

The desk held assorted brochures, pamphlets, books, papers, pens and pencils. A nearly empty Karma Koffee cup sat in the left-hand corner nearest the wall. I smelled chamomile.

'Don't touch anything!'

I nearly jumped out of my skin. 'Detective! I – I didn't hear you!'

Detective Highsmith stood at the entrance to the bedroom in full London bobby glory: navy-blue trousers and a high-necked, navy-blue tunic-style jacket fastened with big silver buttons along each side. A wide brown leather belt with a big silver buckle attested to the trimness of his waist. A foot-long wooden nightstick hung from the belt. There was an officer number pinned to the collar of the jacket and a silver police badge over his heart.

Highsmith was breathing heavily. He bounded into the room and grabbed me gently but firmly by the shoulders. I noticed he was favoring his right foot. 'Step back, Ms Miller.'

I nodded and let myself be pushed away. A team of EMTs followed, squeezing past me, their arms laden with medical equipment, as I exited the bedroom. Highsmith sat me on the sofa and pointed his truncheon at me. 'Don't move.'

I nodded once again and folded my hands in my lap. It looked like it was going to be a long night for Little Dead Riding Hood.

As time passed, more police entered but there was no sign of VV. Pictures were taken, voices conferred and eventually Nancy Alverson was taken from the premises.

Detective Highsmith came forward, rubbing his hands over his face. I noticed he had removed his hat, probably in an effort to look less farcical.

'Can I go now?'

The detective laid a gentle hand on my shoulder. 'Are you up to answering a few questions?'

'I guess so.'

He smiled. 'OK. Give me a minute to wrap up. Then we can talk.'

Highsmith returned to Nancy's bedroom with a couple of uniformed officers, Officer Ellen Collins and Officer Ravi Singh. I knew them both, sort of. I'd had the misfortune to be around a dead body or two in Table Rock already. The two officers had had the misfortune of having been around them with me.

A third officer, Chip Kurkov, a pleasant young fellow relatively new to the force, offered me coffee. 'Here you go, Ms Miller. I hope you like it black.' He carried a cardboard tray holding half-a-dozen lidded paper cups.

Chip was a frequent customer at Maggie's Beignet Café, despite having been one of the first responders on the scene the time I'd discovered a dead body there. A lesser man might have found it off-putting.

'Black is fine. Thanks.' I took a sip. It was blazing hot. I wrapped my hands around it. I had a chill, more from fright and sadness than the cold, I was sure. The heat coursing through my hands was soothing. Nancy Alverson had seemed like such a lovely young woman. She hadn't deserved to have her life cut short and in so hideous a fashion.

'Of course,' I said, looking at the logo, 'I'd like it better if it wasn't in a Karma Koffee cup.' They had definitely been closed for the day when I crossed the street. 'How did you get this?'

Officer Kurkov seemed embarrassed as he explained. He knew

how I felt about my competition. 'The Gregorys opened up when they heard about the incident.'

'They heard about it already?'

'Kurkov!' shouted Highsmith. 'Get in here!'

'Be right there, sir,' he said over his shoulder. Turning to me, he explained, 'The Gregorys were the woman's landlords. They own this apartment.'

I sighed. I should have known. The Gregorys were my landlords too, not of my café, but of my apartment. The fact that they owned the apartment Nancy Alverson had been renting directly above their business wasn't surprising at all.

I took another sip. The coffee was delicious, not that I'd ever admit it to a living soul. Why did everything they brewed or baked have to be so perfect? I was a particular fan of their Heaven's Building Block muffin, a pumpkin flour-based, maple-glazed miracle containing raisins, walnuts, cinnamon and something I hadn't been able to identify – probably crushed angels' wings.

To kill time, I picked up a supple, leather-bound book the color of burnt umber. It was titled *The Sacred Church of Witchkraft: Our History and Mission.*

I idly flipped through its thick pages, which were accompanied by frequent full-page, four-color illustrations. Someone had spent a pretty penny publishing the arcane tome.

Come to think of it, much of the reading material in the apartment, at the table and at her desk revolved around the topics of witchcraft and New Age religions.

I had a hard time reconciling the quiet, studious young woman I had known with such quirky interests. Then again, I hadn't really known Nancy Alverson.

Detective Highsmith appeared several minutes later. He opened a small spiral notebook and took a seat at the other end of the sofa. 'Thanks for sticking around.'

He pulled a pen from his pocket and jotted down a few lines. 'So,' Highsmith began, 'let's start at the beginning. What were you doing here, Ms Miller? Were you friends with Ms Alverson?'

'You can call me Maggie, you know. You have before.'

He dug the fingers of his left hand into his thigh. 'Let's keep this professional for now and save the first names for social occasions, shall we?'

I shrugged. 'If you say so.' Better to be called Ms Miller than

Cueball. 'Nancy, Ms Alverson, had been coming into the café regularly, mostly in the mornings. We weren't friends by any stretch. In fact, I feel like I hardly knew her.'

Glancing at the coffee table, I said, 'I certainly had no idea of her interest in witches and witchcraft.'

Highsmith frowned. 'It wasn't witchcraft that killed her.'

'She was strangled, wasn't she?'

'The coroner will give us something conclusive, but yeah, it seems pretty definite.' He tapped his pen against the pad. 'What were you doing here?'

'Bringing her a bag of beignets.'

'The bag on the floor in the bedroom.'

'That's right.'

'You deliver now?'

'No.' I explained how I'd had some leftover when we closed up for the night. 'Nancy had never stopped by for some. From the café, I saw the light on up here and thought I'd bring them by.'

'She didn't call the café and order them?'

'No.'

'You used the stairs off the street?'

'Yes, of course.'

Highsmith must have noticed my confusion because he explained, 'There's a second door over there.' He waved his thumb over his shoulder.

'I had no idea.' I leaned past him for a look. There was a door on the far wall. I had assumed it was a closet. 'Where does it go?'

'Down.'

'And?'

'Up,' he said rather drily.

'Fine. Be that way.' I'd find out from somebody else where that second staircase led. 'Yes, Detective, I crossed the street and knocked on the door at the street.'

Highsmith nodded as if following my steps. 'Go on. Did you see or hear anything unusual when you arrived?'

I hesitated, drinking coffee while I considered my next words. In the end, I had no choice but to say, 'I saw VV.'

A pained expression crossed Highsmith's face before he got his emotions under control. 'Yeah.'

I gulped and continued. 'I knocked on the downstairs door and said something.' I scratched my scalp. 'My name, I think. Then I heard sounds, like running.' I swiveled and faced the detective. 'Then the door flew open and . . .' I shrugged helplessly. 'There was Veronica.'

'She told me she ran into you.'

'Literally,' I added with a chuckle. 'How is she, by the way?'

'Holding up. She's at home.'

That explained why she wasn't hovering around the crime scene making everyone nervous. 'Do you think she . . .'

The corner of Highsmith's mouth turned down. 'Murdered Nancy Alverson?'

I nodded.

'No.' Highsmith came to his feet, towering over me. 'Why would she?'

That was what I wanted to know. I stood and lifted my black cloak over my head. 'Is it OK to leave?'

'Sure.' He walked me to the door. 'Would you like one of the officers to give you a ride?'

'No, thanks. I've got my bike.' It was a good thing it was late. What were passers-by going to think as they saw Little Dead Riding Hood pedaling through the dark streets on Halloween night? Hopefully, I wouldn't get mistaken for a witch and tossed in a deep well or burnt at a stake somewhere in the desert.

'OK. One more thing.'

'What's that?'

'What are you supposed to be, anyway?'

'Huh?'

He tugged at the black cloak. 'The costume.'

'Aubrey made it. According to her, I'm Little Dead Riding Hood.'

That brought a smile to Detective Highsmith's lips.

'Smirk all you want,' I said, pulling myself together. 'Let me know when you catch Moriarty, Copper.'

'Excuse me?'

'Moriarty, from Sherlock Holmes.' I gave him a quick up and down with my eyes. 'In that getup, you do look like you ought to be rubbing shoulders with the great detective and Inspector Lestrade.'

Highsmith rubbed his solid jaw. 'Not a bad idea. Next year I just might dress as Sherlock Holmes.'

'Great, although I can't picture VV dressed like Doctor Watson.'

'True,' Highsmith said with a wink, 'but I think *you* could pull it off.'

I was pretty sure there was an insult or a compliment in there someplace but I was too tired to figure out which he had intended.

'Goodnight, Detective.' I headed down the stairs and back to the café to collect my bicycle, feeling more like the Grim Reaper than Little Dead Riding Hood.

FIVE

Because Aubrey and Kelly had worked extra hours for Halloween and planned to attend the Halloween costume party afterward, I had promised them the morning off. That left Mom and me to open the café. The young ladies were due in at noon.

As a business owner, I had one assigned parking space behind the store between two garbage bins. Because I didn't own a car, Mom had parked there. At the sound of her honk of arrival, I went to the storeroom and let her in the back door.

'Good morning, dear.'

'Hi, Mom,' I said, returning her hug, the tone of my voice unable to match my mother's own cheerfulness.

Mom peeled off her black-and-gray-checked coat and hung it on a hook. 'Everything OK, dear?'

'Sort of,' I said. 'Let's get some coffee and I'll tell you about it.'

Mom tied on her apron. 'That sounds ominous.'

'Don't worry. It's nothing you should be alarmed about.' I followed my mother out front and poured us each a cup of coffee. I'd already had one strong cup at home, along with a cinnamon and sugar toasted pastry. It may not have been the breakfast of champions, but it had been all I could stomach.

'I've got some frozen bagels in back,' I said, adding sugar and milk to my cup. 'Would you like one?'

'No, thank you.'

'OK.' I lifted the hinged countertop. 'Let's sit.'

Mom preceded me and went to the table and the exact seat that Nancy Alverson had favored.

'Not there.'

Mom froze, her butt hovering over the chair but not landing.

I plopped down at the middle table with my coffee. 'Let's sit here.'

My mother gave me a look signifying that she recognized funny behavior when she saw it but joined me nonetheless without saying a word. She sipped quietly, her gaze following the activity on the street, which wasn't much at this hour. There was a Table Rock police car sitting across the street in front of Karma Koffee. Nancy's Land Rover rested two spaces away.

Finally, I spoke. 'Remember when I asked you about Nancy last night? Jakob was looking for her.'

'Yes. He's a nice young man. A good artist, too. I don't think I know her, though.'

'I'm sure you've seen her.' I described her briefly.

'Yes, I remember now.' Mom turned and looked behind. 'Always sits at that table with that laptop of hers.'

'She won't be sitting there today.'

'Oh?'

'She was murdered last night.'

'Murdered!' Mom's hand shook and she set her cup down.

'Yes.'

'Not here?'

'No.' I clamped my hands over my mom's. Anyone knowing the history of Maggie's Beignet Café would know that her question wasn't all that unusual. 'Across the street. In her apartment.'

Mom played with her wedding band. 'I didn't see anything in the newspaper about it.'

'It happened late last night. There will probably be something in it tomorrow.'

'How did you find out? Is that what the police car is doing there?'

We both looked at the empty squad car.

'Yes. I mean, I guess. I found her last night.'

'You did?' Mom's eyes grew wide. 'Oh, Maggie!'

'Sort of.' I explained how after locking up I had gone across the street to give her the leftover pumpkin spice beignets. 'Veronica Vargas came running down the stairs. I went up.'

I paused, picturing the scene in my mind. Nancy slumped at her desk. 'That's when I saw her.'

'Do the police have any idea who the killer is?'

I pressed my hands against the table and leaned back in my chair. 'Besides VV, you mean?'

'Maggie, you don't think—'

There was a sharp rap on the glass. We both turned our heads.

It was Veronica 'VV' Vargas, suspect *numero uno*. And, unlike her usual svelte self, she looked a wreck.

She banged again, her rings hitting the glass with a jarring metallic clang. 'Let me in, Miller!'

My mother and I shared a look. 'You had better let her in before she breaks the glass.'

'OK.' I pushed back my chair. 'But if she murders us, I'm blaming you for it.'

Mom's hand on my arm held me back. 'How was Nancy murdered?'

'Strangled,' I said, wincing each time VV's ring struck the window. 'With a scarf that I think belonged to you-know-who.' I raised my left palm to cover the jab I was making in VV's direction with my right index finger.

Mom's brow rose. 'I see.'

'Still want me to let her in?' I was half-joking. I went to the door and thumbed the lock. 'Good morning,' I said. 'We aren't quite open yet.' A subtle sniff on my part revealed no hint of the perfume I had smelled the night before.

VV stepped inside. She looked at my mother, who waved hello. VV looked more frumpy than fashionable in baggy gray sweats and white sneakers. A large hat hid half her head; the oversized pair of dark sunglasses hid the rest. A silver-toned leather bag with studded trim hung from her shoulder.

Mom rose and returned behind the counter. 'I'll get started on the beignet dough.'

'Thanks, Mom.' I turned the *Closed* sign to *Open*. No point turning away customers now that I'd let VV in.

VV sat at the table in the corner, facing away from the street. It was the table Nancy had favored but I wasn't up to asking her to move. I joined her reluctantly.

'Care for some coffee?' Mom called from behind the counter.

I raised my brow in question. Veronica nodded. 'Yes, please, Mom.'

Mom hustled over with two coffees and a handful of creamer packs, sugar and sugar substitutes, including some packs of something called Stevia that my sister, Donna, insisted I carry. I'd tried it once.

Trust me, there is no substitute for sugar.

VV dumped two creams and two sugars in her coffee and sipped tentatively.

'So,' I said, leaning both elbows on the table, 'what can I do for you, Veronica?' Seeing that Veronica Vargas had thus far remained mum and I had better things to be doing that morning, such as running my business, it seemed I was going to have to be the one to get this conversation going despite the fact that she had come knocking on my front door.

'You and I need to talk.' She pulled off her sunglasses and set them on the table between us.

'If you've come to confess, you've come to the wrong place. It's the police you ought to be talking to.' It was probably a low blow but I'd been unable to resist.

'Maggie!' Mom scolded.

VV sneered. 'That's exactly what I'm talking about.' She flitted an empty creamer across the table with her nail.

'What?'

'That smart mouth of yours.'

I bit my cheek to hold back a smart reply.

VV locked eyes with me. 'There was a murder last night, Miller.'

'Yes. I was there, remember?'

'It isn't what you think.'

'I think – no, I'm sure I saw you running from the victim's apartment.'

If looks could kill, VV's look just then would have sent me to my grave. 'You saw me running to get help.'

'Why didn't you use your phone?' I brought my cup to my lips, keeping my eyes on my companion.

'Because I was in costume. I didn't have my cellphone. I didn't even have my purse.'

I drummed my fingers on the table. I had to admit, that made sense. I didn't have to admit it to VV, though.

'Mark told me you went to the apartment to deliver Ms Alverson some of your beignets?'

'That's right.'

'Did you see anybody else? Did you hear anything unusual?'

'Just you,' I said with a smile.

VV glared some more. 'When was the last time you saw Ms Alverson?'

'You mean alive?' VV's pained expression told me not to expect

a reply. 'Around ten yesterday morning. She came in, ate and left.'
Two pairs of customers strode in the door and I started to get up.

'Don't worry, Maggie,' Mom called. 'I've got this. Good morning,
folks.'

'What were *you* doing there?' I asked VV.

It was a solid minute before VV answered. As she did, we watched
a blue uniformed officer step out from Karma Koffee and enter the
squad car at the curb. It was Chip Kurkov. The poor guy must have
been up all night.

'Not that it's any of your business, but . . .' VV paused and
studied her blue polished fingernails. The color matched the costume
she'd been wearing the night before.

'But?'

'I thought Mark might be there.'

I stiffened. 'Highsmith?'

'That's right.' Her fingers wrapped around the cup on the table.

I pinched my brow together. 'I thought he was with you?'

'He was.' VV blew out a breath. 'We were at Hopping Mad up
the street. Mark got called away. He said there was a report of some
vandalism at the middle school. With the department being shorthanded last night and the middle school being just around the corner,
he said he would check it out.'

A.B. Honicker Middle School, named after our town founder,
was just around the corner. Parents often came into the café after
dropping off their kids and I frequently got parents and kids stopping in after school for a treat.

I leaned back in my chair, aware now of the others in the room
who had taken up seats around us in the tiny café. I lowered my
voice. 'That doesn't explain what you were doing at Ms Alverson's
apartment.'

VV answered without looking at me. 'I thought maybe he had
gone to see her instead.'

'Nancy?' I squeaked.

VV nodded once, her fingers tightening.

'Why would Mark be going to see Nancy? What does she have
to do with the middle school?'

'Nothing, Miller,' VV hissed. 'That's my point. I thought maybe
Mark was lying and was going to see Nancy instead.'

The implication of VV's words had been slow to sink in but when
it did it hit me hard. 'You don't think that Mark was . . . what?

Having an affair with Nancy?' It sounded too preposterous to even consider, let alone say out loud.

VV shrugged a shoulder. 'I wanted to check on him. See for myself. I was jealous.'

'You? Jealous?' I couldn't believe what I was hearing.

Frankly, I was in shock. And I didn't know what shocked me more: the idea that Veronica Vargas had murdered Nancy Alverson or the idea that Veronica Vargas might be jealous of Nancy. Of anyone, for that matter!

VV lowered her eyes and nodded once. I didn't know what to say. She worried her fingers. 'I'd heard he had been to her apartment before.'

'From whom?'

'It's a small town. People talk.'

'Did you ask Mark about it?'

'Yes. He said Ms Alverson had wanted to consult with him on some legal issues.'

'Legal issues?' This was getting interesting. 'Like what?'

'Oh, town regulations, ordinances. That sort of thing. I really couldn't say more.'

'I'm sure that's all it was, then.' Pretty sure, at least.

'I know.' VV pushed a finger behind her ear. 'I'd had a lot to drink last night. I think I simply got a little crazy.'

'Been there, done that,' I muttered. 'And then you went to Nancy's apartment and found her there?'

'Yes. Nobody answered the buzzer and the door was unlocked. I went up.' Her eyes darkened. 'The door to the apartment was unlocked too. I knocked. She didn't answer. There was nobody in the living room.' Her voice drifted off.

'And you wondered if she and Mark were doing the horizontal hula in her bedroom?'

VV winced. 'Something like that.'

I didn't ask what she'd found. We both knew the answer to that. Unless . . .

Unless VV had discovered Nancy Alverson alone and wrung her neck.

'I didn't kill her,' VV spat, as if reading my mind.

More and more customers were flooding in. My Halloween promotion seemed to have done its job. 'I have to get to work, VV. What do you want from me? Why are you here exactly?' The only time she ever came into the café was on the arm of Detective Highsmith. Was this some sort of rapprochement?

'I just thought you should know what really happened.' She pushed back her chair and stood. 'Before you go blabbing all over town. I, my family, has a reputation in this town. I do not want anything or *anybody* ruining that reputation.'

I frowned. So much for our detente. 'One more thing,' I said as she threw some money on the table for the coffee I hadn't asked her to pay for. 'Last night, why did you tell me not to go upstairs to Nancy's apartment?'

VV looked at me like I was an idiot. 'Because it was a crime scene, Ms Miller. I didn't want you messing it up.'

OK, I was an idiot and that made sense. Once again, no point telling her that.

She rolled her hard eyes as she settled her purse over her shoulder. 'I ran back to Hopping Mad to call it in. Imagine my surprise when Mark told me he'd found you standing over the body.'

There was a mad glint in her eye. 'A case could even be made that maybe you killed her. It is mere steps from your little café to Ms Alverson's apartment.'

VV looked out the big picture window and up at the building across the street. She slid her dark sunglasses over her eyes. 'You've got an excellent view from here.' She pointed. 'That window there. That would be Ms Alverson's apartment, wouldn't it?'

I bristled and blushed. Every customer in the place was looking at me.

VV sashayed to the door. 'What is it they say, Ms Miller? The killer always returns to the scene of the crime?'

The door opened and VV stepped through, ignoring the two dapper men coming in.

VV turning her back on me was like a spell being broken.

'Good morning, Mag—' Clive began.

'One sec—' I pushed past Clive and ran into the street. VV was sliding behind the wheel of her metallic-blue Mercedes. I grabbed the window of the open door and held on.

'What is it, Ms Miller?'

'Your scarf,' I panted.

'What about it?'

'What was your scarf doing wrapped around Nancy Alverson's neck?'

VV tossed her purse on the passenger seat. 'What makes you think it was my scarf?'

'Oh, please. Everybody from here to Tucson can smell you when the wind is right. And there aren't too many women around Table Rock who could even afford to buy a bottle of Joy Parfum, let alone use it as liberally as you do.'

VV appeared at a loss. She whipped off her hat and fluffed her hair with her fingers. 'I must have left it there earlier in the day.' She pulled at the door handle.

I held on, preventing it closing. 'Wait a minute. Earlier in the day? What were you doing at Nancy Alverson's apartment earlier in the day? I thought you only went there last night because you thought Mark was there?'

She tugged at the door once more but I was ready for her and held the window with both hands.

'Did you think he was there earlier in the day too?'

'What I was doing at the apartment is really none of your business, Ms Miller. The same way that Nancy Alverson's murder is none of your business.' She pushed a button and the luxury car sprang to life with a roar as her foot hit the accelerator. 'I suggest you stick to frying donuts in your little café and leave the police work to the experts.'

VV shoved the gearshift lever into drive and I was forced to release my grip on the window. She yanked the door closed and sped down Laredo.

If she was on her way to Mexico, she was heading in the wrong direction. Nonetheless, I hoped she had packed her passport. I would have hated to see her get turned away at the border.

Life in Table Rock wouldn't be the same without VV, but it wouldn't be any the worse.

SIX

'What did *she* want?' demanded Clive Rothschild as I re-entered the café. Clive and his partner, Johnny Wolfe, had some history with VV.

'Don't tell me you two are still holding a grudge against Veronica?'

'Not long ago, that woman locked us up and wanted to throw away the key!' Clive replied. 'She accused us of murder!'

'You did sort of confess.' Clive, Johnny and I had been involved in a recent murder investigation and, as prosecuting attorney, VV had seemed rather keen on seeing that Clive and/or Johnny fried for the crime.

Clive stuck his nose in the air and crossed his arms. 'I took it back.'

It wasn't much of a legal defense but it was sincere. 'She wanted to talk to me about Nancy Alverson's murder.'

Clive's brow shot up. 'That woman who was killed across the street?' Clive has red hair and green eyes like me. He also has a few freckles, which I did not. He was a dapper dresser. At the moment, he wore designer jeans, a bronze sports coat over a black shirt and a black-and-white polka-dot bowtie. He stood a hair over six foot but only weighed about one-fifty.

'You know her?' Clive and Johnny ran The Hitching Post next door. Though this was the Old West, they didn't sell stirrups, saddle soap and lassos. They sold tiaras, sashes, garters – all things of a bridal rather than bridle nature. This was the New Age Old West, after all.

Plus, they carried the West's most beautiful designer wedding gowns, many of which were created and sewn by Johnny Wolfe himself. The former Olympic-class figure skater – a bronze-medal winner – was an accomplished fashion designer.

If I ever got married again, which no way, never, no, not me and I mean never, uh-uh, ain't gonna happen in this lifetime, I'd be pleased to have Johnny design me a wedding dress, providing he did the job at cost. The Hitching Post's prices were way out of my league.

'Asha told us about it this morning,' Johnny said from the counter where he stood giving Mom his order. 'I'll take the pumpkin spice to go.' He turned to me and Clive nearer the door. 'You want anything Clive?'

'The same, please,' Clive said.

'Double that,' I heard Johnny tell my mother. Johnny and Clive have been married for over three years. Johnny is a half-foot or so shorter with white flesh, skinny hips and shoulders. There's a feminine quality to voice. He is overly fussy about his wavy, glossy black hair. His eyes are charcoal blue. He's a bit of a coxcomb but I was fond of him, not that I'd ever tell him that to his face.

'Who is Asha?'

'Asha Anand,' explained Clive. 'She's one of our seamstresses. She works freelance out of her home.'

'Was she a friend of Nancy Alverson's?'

'She never said so.' Clive was handling one of my cardboard tombstones. The Hitching Post had refrained from decorating their display window for Halloween, preferring to advertise wedding gowns to wedding ghouls.

Johnny placed a dollar in the tip jar and joined us with his bag of beignets. 'Asha takes a yoga class with Rob Gregory. She was there yesterday evening.'

'How did she learn about the murder?' I asked.

'She was in Karma Koffee this morning. Rob and Trish mentioned it.'

Clive was nodding. 'She told me and Johnny all about it when she dropped off her work this morning.'

I looked over at Karma Koffee. Seeing Nancy's unwashed white Land Rover out front was a sad reminder of her death. That and the fact that she wouldn't be in for her usual blueberry beignets and coffee anymore.

I tilted my head. 'Huh.'

'What?' asked Clive.

'I'm not sure.' I scratched my head.

'I think Maggie's having another of her brain seizures,' quipped Johnny. 'Let's get out of here, Clive. She could be contagious.'

I stuck my tongue out at him as he grabbed Clive's elbow and headed for The Hitching Post. I moved closer to the window, my breath clouding the glass. Was it my imagination or had Nancy Alverson's Land Rover *not* been parked there on the street last night?

'I'll be right back, Mom!'

'Yes, dear.' Mom was scooping beignets from the fryer and placing them under the warmer. Business was more brisk than usual, so maybe our Halloween giveaway really was showing dividends already.

I pulled my collar tight around my neck and marched across the street to Nancy Alverson's Land Rover. I placed my hand on the hood. It was cold.

Snoopiness won out over pride and I found myself opening the door to Karma Koffee, where my senses were instantly bombarded.

My eyes were dazzled by the upscale eatery's designer interior and to-die-for original tin ceiling, my nostrils overwhelmed by the smell of Heaven's Building Blocks and all the other lovely muffins and pastries that they baked each day.

My stomach, traitor that it was, grumbled loudly.

Every seat in the place was taken.

A bookshelf displayed several books, all written by Rob and his wife, Trish. Topics included fortune telling, baking, coffee brewing and a slender tome that promised to help the reader to find their spiritual identity. Judging by the relative thinness of the latter, it was easier to find your spiritual identity than it was to brew a good cup of java.

Rob Gregory folded his arms across his chest, as if preparing for battle, as I approached the sales counter. Two uniformed employees worked efficiently behind him. Another was refilling the napkins in the dispensers along the counter at the far wall. 'Are you here to pay your rent, Ms Miller?'

'Excuse me?' I stopped in front of the counter, inhaling the smell of heaven in muffin form.

'It's the first of the month.' He held out his open palm. 'I assume you'd like to give me a check for your rent.'

'It's in the mail.' The Gregorys owned the fourplex where I rented my one-bedroom apartment. Truth be told, I hadn't mailed it yet but vowed to myself that I'd do it the minute I got home. Well, after I fed the cat and did some laundry. Maybe buried my Little Dead Riding Hood costume out on the front lawn in an unmarked grave.

The property I was renting had originally been shown to me by a real estate agent. If I had known Rob and Trish Gregory owned it, I would have pitched a tent in the hills first rather than give them any of my hard-earned money. 'Was Nancy Alverson's Land Rover parked outside last night?'

'What business is that of yours?' Rob replied.

'It may not be any of my business but I'm sure the police would like to know.'

'Know what?'

I spun around to face the mountain that was Detective Mark Highsmith. 'Hi, Detective. Am I glad to see you. I was just asking Rob if he remembers seeing Nancy Alverson's SUV parked outside last night.' I pointed out the window. 'That's it there, the Land Rover.'

'I know that, Ms Miller.'

'But do you know whether or not it was parked at the curb here last night?' I asked. 'Because, personally, I don't remember.'

Mark opened his mouth to reply, then apparently thought better of it. 'Can I speak with you for a minute outside, Ms Miller?'

I frowned. 'I suppose.'

He pulled open the door and I followed him as he limped out to the sidewalk. Instead of stopping beside him, I marched over to Nancy Alverson's vehicle, cupped my hands around my eyes and peeked in the windows.

'What are you doing, Maggie?'

'Looking for clues.'

'She was killed in her apartment, remember?' The detective sounded tired, and I was sure he was.

I peered some more into the vehicle. There was camping gear, empty water bottles, wrappers from local food joints, a couple of maps and lots of touristy brochures, bits of clothing like balled-up socks and jackets, a camera and a pair of binoculars. I turned to face him. 'I don't think the Land Rover was here when I came to see her last night, Detective.'

Highsmith stroked his chin. 'I'll look into it. Anything else?' His rumpled brown suit looked as worn out as he sounded.

I started to say something then shut my mouth. I wanted to ask him about his purported relationship with Nancy Alverson but so far it was only purported, and by Veronica Vargas at that. It was probably nonsense.

This was not the time to make him angry. I wanted information.

'No. Do you have any suspects yet? Do you know who killed her?'

Highsmith shook his head. 'Nope. But don't worry, we'll find him.'

'Or her?'

Highsmith locked me in his sight. 'Or her.' He glanced briefly in the rear window of the Land Rover. 'Do me a favor: be nice to Veronica. She's having a tough time.'

'I'll bet. The reporters are going to be all over her.'

'Not if they don't know that it was her scarf wrapped around the victim's neck.'

'You haven't told them?'

'We're keeping it quiet for now. I'm asking you to do the same thing. If not for the sake of our investigation, then for Veronica's sake.'

I snorted. 'You have got to be kidding? The woman treats me like dirt.'

'Nonsense. You're being too sensitive, Maggie. You aren't giving her a chance. Veronica is really very sweet.'

I was pretty sure my eye-roll could have been seen from the dark side of the moon. The man was clearly gaga for VV. I, on the other hand, had no such delusions clouding my judgment. 'Are we talking about the same person?'

'She's not as tough as you think she is, Maggie. She only acts that way. She's a lawyer and a prosecuting attorney. She has to act tough. It's part of her job.'

I shook my head side to side. VV was suckering Highsmith and he was suckering me.

'You owe me, Maggie.' Highsmith thrust his left hand into the pocket of his trousers.

'How do you figure?'

He looked down and raised his right foot.

Rats. I did, sort of. But really, it was that cursed Belle Époque espresso machine's fault, not mine.

'Fine. I won't tell a soul.' My hand flew to my mouth. 'Oh . . .'

The detective narrowed his eyes at me. 'What?'

'I might have mentioned VV's scarf being the murder weapon to my mom.'

Highsmith groaned audibly.

'Don't worry,' I added quickly. 'I'll tell her that mum's the word. Promise.' I held up my hand.

'Fine. Now, if you don't mind, I've got a job to do. I believe you do, too.' He pointed to the small crowd of customers entering Maggie's Beignet Café.

'Right, thanks.' I slid past him and pulled open the Karma Koffee door.

'Miller!' The detective growled and took a step toward me.

'What? I'm just going in for a muffin. I'll be out in a jiff.' I crossed my heart. 'Promise.'

I heard a mighty sigh that could have sent a galleon skipping across the Mediterranean from Tunis to Constantinople as the detective turned and headed for the door in the alcove that led up to Nancy Alverson's apartment.

The line was three deep when I got back inside Karma Koffee, and I was forced to wait my turn.

The counter, like each table, was thick with customers, many with open laptops taking advantage of the free Wi-Fi. With Maggie's Beignet Café being in close proximity to Karma Koffee, I did the same. I suspected Nancy Alverson had also done the same. I hadn't hooked up Wi-Fi of my own yet, though Aubrey and Kelly had been pestering me to. Such things were a drag on the café's bottom line.

The thought of Nancy sitting dead at her desk brought another pang to my heart. Suddenly, I felt like crying. I grabbed a napkin and dabbed the corners of my eyes.

'You OK?'

I looked up. It was Lee, a Karma Koffee employee. 'I'll be OK.' I dabbed some more. 'It's all this Arizona dust.'

Lee was a quiet, sixtyish churchgoer with fuzzy, short gray hair, a long face, full brows and wide-set eyes. He was something of a loner but a whiz at making coffee drinks. Aubrey knew him well. She used to work at Karma Koffee too but had quit without notice to come work for me – her idea, not mine.

I couldn't say which bothered the Gregorys more: the fact that she left Karma Koffee or the fact that she came to work for me. A little of both, I hoped.

Lee slid a big tray of blueberry scones onto a shelf in the glass-fronted display case. 'When I'm feeling . . . dusty . . . I find there's nothing like chocolate.' He handed me a bite-sized biscotti then returned to the kitchen.

'Thanks.' I sniffled, dropped it on my tongue and chewed. It was fresh-baked and rich with the combined flavors of chocolate and almond.

Trish handed a customer a cruller and a scone. She passed his cute female companion two large coffees. She wished them a good day, then turned to me. 'Now what, Ms Miller? Can't you see we're busy here?'

They were indeed. Busier than I was, no doubt. 'Where did Rob go?'

Trish planted her hands on her hips. 'That's not an answer, that's another question.'

'I wanted to tell you how sorry I am about Nancy.'

'Thank you,' Trish said rather sharply. 'Now, if you don't mind, I'm trying to run a business here.'

'Did you know her long? Do you know if she has any family in the area?'

'Ms Miller, really. This is not the time or the place.' Trish looked past me to a fellow in a flannel coat who had cleared his throat quite pointedly behind me. 'Can I help you, sir?'

I twirled and smiled at the stranger. 'One second?'

The man looked up from his cellphone. He didn't look happy. 'Please?'

Nor did he reply. He simply returned his attention to whatever was so important on his phone screen.

'Thank you.' I spun back to Trish, knocking over a small chalkboard announcing the day's special blend. 'Sorry,' I muttered, setting it back on its easel as best I could.

The Gregorys were a handsome couple in their mid-thirties, both tan and fit. Rob has short, wavy brown hair with sun-bleached streaks at the temples of his rectangular face. His eyes are dark gray.

At the moment, however, Trish was looking rather ugly. 'Ms Miller, please, order something or leave.'

'Actually,' I cleared my throat, 'I was wondering . . .'

'Yes?' she said, her patience clearly strained.

'Do you have room for one more student?' Rob taught yoga part-time at his studio up on the second floor directly above Karma Koffee. Nancy Alverson's apartment was on the floor above the yoga studio.

Trish's long lashes batted at me. Her hair is two shades darker than Rob's and shoulder length. I've never seen her wear earrings, but she does sport a delicate silver navel ring, which shows frequently as she is a fan of small halter tops and billowy skirts when not wearing the Karma Koffee uniform: fern-green polo shirts, matching visors and khakis.

Both were into yoga and all things New Age. Today, I saw that Trish's fingernails were painted white and intricately decorated with black spirals.

'You'll have to ask Rob. I don't handle the classes – he does.'

'OK. Would you ask him for me, please?'

She wiped her hands on a damp towel behind the counter. 'Fine. I'll have him call you. Anything else?'

I drew in a deep breath. I knew I was pressing my luck and Trish's patience but I asked anyway. 'Do *you* remember seeing Nancy Alverson's Land Rover parked on the street here last night?

For a second there, I really thought there was honest-to-goodness steam coming out Trish Gregory's ears, but it was only an employee frothing milk at an intricate espresso station six times the size of my own recently acquired machine.

Trish Gregory pressed her knuckles into the quartz counter and got in my face. 'Ms Miller,' she said, her voice as tight as a balloon at the end of its tether.

'Yes?' I gulped.

'If I give you a muffin, will you go away?'

I took the muffin but the joke was on Trish, because I was going to leave anyway.

SEVEN

I spent the rest of the day doing normal stuff, like trying to earn a living. Aubrey and Kelly were as busted up as I was about Nancy Alverson's murder. Neither had known her any better than I had but it was still difficult to accept.

It was hard enough accepting any death, let alone the murder of a frequent customer who lived across the street. That third-floor apartment window would forever be a reminder of what had happened.

Toward closing, my nephew, Connor, rolled up on his bike. Connor, like his younger brother, Hunter, takes after his dad, Andy. Fourteen years old, Connor already was nearly six foot tall. He had the same fine blond hair as his father, although he kept his a more normal length with bangs that spilled over his forehead. His eyes, like Hunter's when he wasn't disguised as an artichoke and you could see them, were blue-gray.

'Hi, Connor.' I lifted the hinged countertop and met him just inside the door. He tolerated my hug about as well as any fourteen-year-old would. 'Lemonade and beignets?'

'Yes, please.'

'OK. Make yourself at home. I'll be right back.'

Connor set his olive-green backpack on the nearest table, pulled out a chair and sat. 'Dad mentioned you had some leftover candy, too?'

I smiled. 'It's right here behind the counter.' I scooped up half-a-dozen pumpkin spice beignets and placed them on a tray. I added two large lemonades and set the candy bars and Cracker Jack box beside the rest.

I carried everything over to the table, where I was met by a big grin. 'Thanks!' Connor grabbed a beignet and bit it in two. 'These are great, Aunt Maggie!'

'Glad you like them.' I picked up a warm beignet, rolled it around in some extra powdered sugar on the plate and took a bite. 'I never get tired of beignets,' I said, licking my fingers afterwards.

'Me, too.' Connor polished off a couple more. He picked up the candy bars one by one, added them to a small, zippered pocket of the backpack and set the Cracker Jack box in an exterior mesh pocket. 'Is this all the leftovers?' he asked greedily.

I laughed and leaned forward conspiratorially. 'Just between us, your grandmother has the rest. She's going to leave it in the community room. I'll bet if you get there quickly enough, you may be able to add to your stash.'

Connor smiled. 'Thanks. I might.' His eyes clung to his lemonade. 'Aunt Maggie, can I ask you something?'

'Sure, you can ask me anything. What else are aunts for?' We each plucked another beignet from the pile.

'I was wondering if you could talk to Mom for me.'

My brow went up. 'OK, about what?'

'You see, I'm in ninth grade now. At least, I would be if I was in regular school.'

'Yeah.' I nodded. 'I guess you would.'

'And I'm not a kid anymore.'

'No.' I tried not to grin. 'No, you're not.' I had no idea where this was leading.

'Well, there's this girl . . .'

Bingo!

I knew exactly where this was leading. I put my hand over Connor's. 'And you would like to ask this girl out on a date?'

Connor blushed and looked at his plate. 'We met last night at the school social. Her name is Madison and I was hoping to take her to the movies.'

'That sounds wonderful.' I frowned. 'What's the problem?'

'Mom thinks I should have her over for dinner first.'

Yikes! Forcing a fourteen-year-old girl to eat Donna's home-cooked vegetarian cooking? That could be considered a cruel and unusual punishment.

I had to tread carefully. I was only the aunt. 'What does your father think?'

Connor toyed with his fingers. 'I think he sort of agrees with me. But I don't think he wants to say that to Mom.'

Smart man. I couldn't say that out loud either. I patted my nephew's hand. 'I'll have a talk with her, how's that?'

The smile returned to his face. 'That would be awesome, Aunt Maggie. Thanks.'

I tilted my head, narrowing my eyes at him. Although he'd said thanks, he still didn't look happy. 'Is there more? Something you are not telling me?'

Connor gulped as he nodded. 'I was thinking . . .'

'Yes?'

'Maybe,' his eyes darted to mine then returned to some unknown point in the distance. 'Maybe you could talk to Mom about letting me go to public school?' He glanced quickly into my eyes.

I took a deep breath.

'Public school, huh?' My fingertips tapped the table nervously. This was a whole lot bigger than her son's first date. This was her son wanting to cut the strings.

How would Andy and my sister react to that little bombshell? Why, oh why, must I be the one to open the bay doors and drop the bomb?

'Have you tried talking to your mother and father about this yet?'

'No. It's kind of hard.'

'I can imagine.' Donna loved homeschooling her boys. I let out a breath. 'I'll talk to her. That's all I can promise.'

Connor leapt to his feet with a squeal of chair and floor that sent a shiver up my spine. 'Thanks again, Aunt Maggie!' He grabbed his backpack and started for the door.

'What about the beignets and the rest of your lemonade?'

Connor blushed, hurried back to the table, stuffed two pumpkin spice beignets in his mouth like the world's hungriest squirrel and snatched the paper cup of lemonade. 'Fthankphew fewee mumph!'

And he was gone.

The remainder of the day was relatively eventless. We were all happy and relieved to put an end to it and close up shop.

I pedaled home, pondering how I was going to approach talking to my kid sister about her oldest boy wanting to go on his first date – one not involving parents and sketchy meals – and attend public school.

I arrived home with no clear plan. While I would have liked to put the conversation off for as long as possible, I knew that doing so would not be fair to Connor.

I'd have to talk to Donna and Andy soon.

I parked my pink Schwinn on the patio. I walked around to the front, turned the key in the lock and was immediately attacked by Little Dead Riding Hood. I screamed and lunged sideways, knocking into the small wooden table beside the door and sending a small potted cactus to the floor.

Little Dead Riding Hood mrowled at me and a fuzzy orange, white-and-black-striped tail wagged quickly back and forth from the folds of the hideous cloak.

I laughed and bent down to lift the cloak from Carole Two. I wasn't quite sure how old Carole Two, my calico cat was but, according to the vet, she was middle-aged, like me.

I'd sort of inherited the cat and the name. According to the cat's previous owner, Carole was the name of his deceased wife. Whether he had named the calico Carole Two in her honor or as a slight was open to interpretation.

I kicked off my shoes at the door and scooped up the cactus mess as best I could, vowing to run the floor sweeper over the dirt later. C2 followed me to the kitchen, where I pulled the big bag of kibble down from atop the refrigerator. Her primary food was some organic stuff that Donna and Andy insisted I buy from them. The dry bits were full of rice, corn, soybeans, kelp, chia seeds and a hundred other natural vegetable ingredients, all of which sounded totally unnatural to me.

For the cat's sake and mine, I kept a mixed case of tuna, salmon and chicken canned food hidden where my sister was unlikely to discover them behind the pots and pans inside one of the lower cabinets.

I refreshed the cat's water bowl and gave her a scoop of dry and a can of wet. It was probably too much food, but neither of us had a boyfriend so we weren't worried if we put on a few pounds.

I grabbed some nacho chips from the pantry and a frozen burrito from the freezer. With the burrito nuking for a couple of minutes, I grabbed a relatively clean glass – cat hair sticks to everything –

and poured a generous serving of chilled strawberry and mango sangria.

I ate at the kitchen table with Carole Two sitting on the chair beside me, watching my every move. It was a little unnerving having her silvery-blue cat's eyes on me the whole time, but cat company was better than no company at all.

Running back over the events of the last couple of days, from Nancy Alverson's appearance at the café, to her death, to VV, and to my run-in with the Gregorys, I remembered that it was indeed time to pay the rent.

I went to my bedroom, dug my checkbook out from the bottom of my underwear drawer and wrote out a painful amount. I had some envelopes and postage stamps in a drawer in the kitchen so I went there and prepared the mail, writing out the name TR Properties, LLC in big, bold letters.

I slipped into my flip-flops and walked down to the bank of four mailboxes that sat side by side on a horizontal wooden post nailed atop a rustic wagon wheel buried several inches into the hard ground. It was too late for today because the mail generally came early on my street, but at least my telling Rob Gregory that the rent check was in the mail would now be true – and my conscience clear.

I pulled open the mailbox. Sure enough, the mail had come. There were several pieces, all bills except for an ad for a new Chinese takeout place. There was also a small padded envelope.

I set my rent check in the mailbox and raised the red flag, then returned to the apartment. I put the bills in the drawer with the rest of the mail I would rather ignore, like something from the IRS about quarterly business taxes, and sat down on the green sofa. I laid the padded envelope on my lap. C2 hopped up beside me. The couch was old and lumpy, like I would probably be one day. It had come with the apartment, already in such bad shape then that the last tenant hadn't even wanted it.

I didn't want the couch either but I couldn't afford to replace it, so it stayed. Everything in the apartment was secondhand, found or donated by my family and friends. The one bedroom, one bathroom apartment is only six hundred square feet, so it didn't take much furniture to fill it. The front door opened onto the living area with the dining and kitchen area to the left and a walled-in courtyard patio beyond that. The bedroom was straight back.

Humble but home.

I studied the manila envelope. There was no return address, only the handwritten address to me in the center. I ripped off the top of the envelope and peered inside. There was something hard and dark at the bottom, along with a small square of off-white paper. 'You want to see, too?'

Carole Two mrowled and poked her nose in. After that, she lost interest and settled down on the window ledge looking out across the front yard, a barren desert landscape of rock, gravel and dirt. The occasional lizard or bird kept it interesting for her, although there were times I thought C2 might be sitting there in telepathic communication with her home planet or, perhaps, her mothership orbiting our planet.

I dumped the contents of the envelope onto the end table. It was a flash drive, black with a plastic blue cap. The piece of paper stuck to the inside of the envelope. I could see cursive writing, small and tightly compressed. I pulled it out and read: *Ms Miller, I suppose you will think I am paranoid. But, just in case, humor me. I do not know anyone else I can leave this with and I feel I can trust you. Please hold this for me until I ask you for it. And, please, do not tell anyone about it.*

Thank you.

Nancy Alverson

I looked at the note through tears and realized that not only was I crying, I was shivering. I set the note atop the envelope beside me on the sofa and picked up the flash drive. What was on it? Why had she sent this to me? Why hadn't she given it to me in person? Was she afraid I would ask questions that she was either unprepared or embarrassed or couldn't be bothered to answer?

I looked at the postmark. The envelope had been mailed yesterday. The day she was killed. Did she, I wondered with a frisson, have a premonition of her pending death?

I went to the kitchen table, picked up my glass and poured myself a second dose of sangria. I carried it to the green sofa and leaned back, pushing my head into the too-soft cushion. I drained my glass and picked up the flash drive, holding it out at arm's length while I eyeballed it.

Whatever was on the small drive could have been what got Nancy Alverson killed. It might also reveal her killer.

I knew I should take the flash drive to the police now that Nancy

Alverson was dead. On the other hand, she had sent it to me. She had not said anything about not looking at the contents of the drive.

I considered my options. My only computer was a laptop and I kept that at the café most days. My need for sleep was greater than my need to know what was on the drive. I told myself that I would take it to the café in the morning and look at it there. Afterward, if I found anything worth reporting, I would hand it over to the authorities.

For all I knew, it could have been nothing more than a copy of her grandmother's favorite recipes. Though I had a feeling it wasn't . . .

I heard a thump. Carole Two had jumped from the window ledge to the floor and was scurrying toward the bedroom, bushy tail waving goodbye. Then again, that tail could have been a cleverly disguised alien radio antenna.

A moment later, there was a tentative knock at the front door. I glanced toward the window. It was well after six p.m. and growing dark. I approached the door in my stockings, moving quietly across the carpet. 'Yes?' I called through the door.

'Ms Miller?'

'Who is it?' I rested my hand on the doorknob.

'It's me, Jakob Waltz.'

I pursed my lips even as I opened the door. 'Jakob? What are you doing here?'

The young artist stood at my door in loose-fitting blue jeans, scruffy cowboy boots and a faded denim jacket that had seen better days. The collar of a red turtleneck shirt protruded from under it. In his hands was a three-foot-square object wrapped in heavy brown paper. 'I went by the café but you were closed.' He extended his arms. 'I brought you this.'

I tilted my head, felt the tickle of cold air wrap around my ankles. 'Come on in.' I stepped away and motioned for him to follow.

He wiped his feet at the door. 'It's another painting for your wall. Like you asked.'

'Thanks. Set it by the door. I'll take it to the café tomorrow.' I moved to the kitchen. 'Can I get you anything?'

'If it's no trouble.' He leaned the covered painting against the table by the door and shuffled from foot to foot.

'No trouble at all.' I yanked open the fridge. 'Beer OK?'

'A beer would be great.'

I popped open a cold can of Miller for each of us – sadly, no relation – and returned to the sofa. I handed him his can. 'Have a seat.' I returned to my spot at the sofa.

Jakob sank into the mismatching used-to-be-a-recliner. The mechanism allowing it to move back and forth had long since broken. 'Thanks, Ms Miller.'

'You really didn't have to come all the way out here after hours to bring me the painting.' I glanced toward the object in question. 'It could have waited until morning.' It could have waited until anytime, really.

'No problem. I was in the area.'

I noticed his eyes move from the envelope to the flash drive on the end table beside me. 'How did you find me, anyway?' I casually picked up the flash drive and the accompanying note and dropped them both back inside the padded envelope.

I slid the envelope between the seat cushion and the side of the sofa.

'One of the other girls, Aubrey or Kelly, I don't remember which, mentioned where you lived.' Jakob slowly unbuttoned his jacket.

'Oh, of course.' I was suspicious but I didn't know why. There was no reason on earth that one of them couldn't or shouldn't have mentioned where I was living. It wasn't like my address was a state secret or anything. Nancy Alverson had had no trouble getting my address, so why should Jakob?

Then again, why the urgent desire to bring me a painting?

I took a healthy swig and realized the beer didn't mix well with the two glasses of sangria. I set the can down on a cork coaster I'd got from a local bar.

Jakob leaned forward in the unsteady, overstuffed recliner. If Table Rock ever held an ugly recliner contest, I'd win hands down. He pressed his arms between his knees, clutching the beer can in his hands. 'You heard about Nancy?' His voice was soft, tentative.

'Yes.' Remembering my promise to Detective Highsmith, I paid particular attention to my words. I wasn't so much worried about besmudging VV's reputation, such as it was, as I was about mucking up the ongoing police investigation into Nancy Alverson's murder. I wanted her killer found and brought to justice. 'I was shocked. I can't imagine anyone wanting to harm her.'

'Me, too.' Jakob nodded solemnly.

'Of course,' I said, tentatively, 'I barely knew her. She came into the café regularly but I never really got to know her. I guess you knew her, though?'

He acted surprised.

'You did come in last night asking about her.'

Jakob leaned back with a sigh. 'Yeah, I knew Nancy. We were kind of seeing each other.'

'Kind of?'

The young man shrugged. 'We went out a few times.' He cast a disarming smile my way. 'I really liked her, you know?' I nodded and he continued. 'I don't know if she felt quite the same way about me as I did about her, but she liked me.'

It sounded like someone had been smitten. My heart went out to him. 'You might have been the one person in town closest to Nancy. Do you have any idea who might have wanted to harm her, Jakob?'

'No,' gasped Jakob. 'That's just it. I have no idea at all. Nancy kept mostly to herself except for her work, I mean. She did ask a lot of questions.'

'Questions?'

'Yeah, research.' Jakob fell back into the blue-and-yellow houndstooth recliner.

'Do you know what she had been working on?'

Jakob shook his head adamantly. 'Not a clue. She didn't like to talk about stuff like that. I don't suppose she mentioned anything to you?'

'Not a thing.'

The corner of Jakob's mouth twitched. 'Too bad.'

'What sort of a writer was she? Do you know?'

'How do you mean?'

'Did she write fiction?'

'No.' Jakob sounded sure of that much. 'She was into historical stuff, exposés.'

'Exposés?' I couldn't imagine anything in Table Rock that needed or was worthy of exposing. The town had a long and colorful history but there were no deep, dark secrets that I was aware of.

'Yeah, she said she liked to do books that had some sort of investigative angle. She showed me a copy of one she wrote a few years ago. It was a book about the solar industry but focused on some company that was running a scam down near Tucson. They were claiming they were running this big solar farm but it was a sham.'

I sighed. There was nothing like that in Table Rock. My sister and brother-in-law had a number of solar panels, as did a lot of Table Rockers, but nothing on a large scale. Nothing worth getting killed for. 'Do you know if she had any family?'

'Oh, sure. Her parents are here in Arizona someplace. Winslow, I think she said. And she has a brother. I'm not sure where he is.'

Winslow was no more than a hundred miles east of Table Rock and was near Meteor Crater. I thought carefully about how to phrase my next question before saying, 'Did you ever find Nancy last night?'

Jakob was quick to shake his head no. 'I wish I had,' he said morosely. 'Maybe if I had, she wouldn't have been murdered. Do you think it was a robbery?'

'I really don't know.' I had seen no signs of a break-in or a robbery in the apartment. 'You would have to ask the police about that. In fact, have you talked to the police?'

'No.'

'You should. You said yourself, you were one of the few people in town who knew her well. Nancy was new in town. I'm sure the police would like to pick your brain. She might have said something that meant nothing to you at the time or you might have seen or heard something yourself. Something that might help the police find her killer.'

'I can't imagine what.'

'I can't either but it's worth a try, right?'

'I suppose.'

'When did you last see Nancy?'

Jakob worried at his lower lip a moment. 'The day before yesterday. We had dinner.'

'How did she seem?'

'What do you mean?'

'Did she seem worried? Distracted?'

'Nope. She acted the same as she always did.'

Thinking back, I had seen no signs of a break-in at the apartment and Detective Highsmith hadn't mentioned any such thing. Had Nancy known her killer? There was a good chance that she had. That was a very scary thought. 'Did you have plans with Nancy last night?'

'No, I just thought she might want to hang out. I called first but she didn't answer. She got that way sometimes when she was working – single-minded, she called it. I thought I would surprise her.'

'Jakob, do you remember if Nancy's Land Rover was parked outside the apartment last night?'

'I couldn't say for sure but it must have been.'

'Why do you say that?'

'She was there, wasn't she?'

'Yes, but maybe—'

'I never had lunch today,' interrupted Jakob, hoisting his beer can. 'I don't suppose you've got anything to go with this?'

'Can I fix you something to eat? I have a whole bag of frozen burritos.'

'No, thanks. I'm having dinner with friends later. Maybe some pretzels?'

'I'll check.' I went to the kitchen, opened a cupboard or two and came up empty in the pretzel department. I grabbed a near substitute.

When I returned to the living room, Jakob was pacing near the sofa. 'Will nachos do?' I held out the open bag of blue corn chips.

Jakob grinned. 'Yeah, thanks.' He stuck his hand in the bag and grabbed a handful, which he quickly devoured. 'I guess I'd better get going.'

I walked him to the door.

He paused. 'You know, it's ironic.'

'What is?'

'Nancy was leaving at the end of the month.'

'Do you mean leaving Table Rock?'

'That's right.'

'How can you be sure?'

'She was renting month to month. She told me she gave the Gregorys notice yesterday that November would be her last month.'

Instead, yesterday had been Nancy's last day.

I chewed my lip, standing in the open doorway, watching Jakob walk slowly back to his pickup truck at the curb. Jakob was wrong. It wasn't ironic, it was sad.

I closed and locked the door, then picked up Jakob's beer can to carry it to the recycle bin in the kitchen. He hadn't taken a single sip. I poured the beer down the drain and cleaned up.

Finally, I pulled the drapes and went to bed.

I switched on the small television set under the window. The local station was running nothing but horror movies featuring slashers and hackers.

Fortunately, one of the big cable stations was running *Abbott and Costello Meet Frankenstein*. Dad and I used to watch it every Halloween. Dracula, Wolf Man and Frankenstein's monster were old friends and didn't scare me in the least.

Although why anybody, including a monster, would want Chick's feeble brain, I never understood.

I fell asleep during the movie with Carole Two on my stomach and woke beaded in sweat with the top sheet twisted around my legs. I'd dreamt that a mad doctor was about to put a scalpel to my brain.

I heard a rustle outside the window and took a sharp breath.

It took me a moment to summon my courage, but once I did, I rose from the bed and tiptoed to the curtain. I pulled back an edge and looked outside.

There was nothing to see. Relieved, I crawled back into bed.

As my head hit the pillow, I realized there were no trees directly outside my bedroom window. So what had caused the rustle?

Had the sound been nothing more than my imagination run wild?

Was it Nancy's killer, come to retrieve the flash drive?

I heard the soft pitter-patter of Carole Two padding into the bedroom and called her to me. She leapt onto the bed and I rubbed her head.

This was not a night to be alone.

EIGHT

I pedaled to the café at five a.m., anxious to discover what was on the flash drive that Nancy Alverson had mailed to my house. I tucked the Schwinn in a corner of the storeroom and sat at the small makeshift desk, an old reclaimed barn door atop two wooden trestles. My brother-in-law, Andy, had built the desk for me and I was glad to have it.

Plus, it looked rather funky.

I sat at the short wooden stool, turned on my laptop and stuck the flash drive in an empty USB slot. There were numerous files in half-a-dozen folders. I pointed the cursor to a folder called Master and clicked on it. The folder contained a single file titled: MMGSST.

I clicked on the file and her word-processing program sprang to life, opening the file on the fourteen-inch screen of my laptop. The title of the document was *Money and Magick – Greed and Sin in a Small Town*.

I understood the file's name now. MMGSST was shorthand. It stood for the first letters of the main words of the document's title.

A glance at the bottom of the word-processing program's screen indicated that the document was nearly three hundred pages long and over ninety thousand words.

Nancy had been busy. No wonder she had had time for little else.

I scrolled down, reading quickly through the table of contents and the draft introduction. Jakob appeared to be right about one thing: Nancy had been working on an investigative book-length work of nonfiction and it appeared to be centered on this Sacred Church of Witchkraft.

Her four-page introduction hinted that this would be a tale of murky business practices, greed, deceptions, bogus rites, fraud and malfeasance.

I leaned back and thought. The *Sacred Church of Witchkraft*. They were one of many peculiar religions headquartered in and around Northern Arizona. I had seen some of their notices for events and classes. I was pretty sure they were located west of town near the mountains.

Nancy had had a lot of books about Wicca, witchcraft, magic, religion and other similar topics lying around her apartment. It all fit.

I went out front, turned on the deep fryer to heat up the oil for the day, then made a pot of coffee in the French press. Aubrey let herself in with her key. Kelly showed up not a minute later.

Aubrey followed me to the storeroom. Kelly was getting everything ready for opening in front. There's a long table in the center of the backroom with a sink and prep area. Aubrey grabbed a four-quart stainless-steel bowl from a shelf beneath the counter. 'OK to start making Belgian waffles in earnest now, Maggie?'

'Sure,' I replied, carrying a cup of coffee to my work desk. 'Go for it.' I set the coffee down carefully and tapped a key of the laptop, bringing it out of its stupor.

'What are you reading? More beignet recipes?' inquired Aubrey, dumping waffle mix into the bowl.

'No. It's—' Once again, I realized my dilemma concerning how much or how little I should say. 'Just catching up on my reading.'

Aubrey shot me a funny look as she carried her bowl of waffle mix to the front. 'If you say so.'

Alone once again, I dove into the manuscript. Nancy was a good writer and her subject was compelling. My forgotten coffee turned cold.

'Hi, Maggie.'

My eyes jumped from the laptop's screen to the swinging door to the storeroom where Brad Smith stood smiling. 'Brad? What are you doing here?'

Brad grinned. 'Good to see you, too.' He glanced at the computer. 'What are you up to?'

'I was researching some new recipes.' I looked past him as I lowered the screen.

'In case you are wondering, the ladies said it was OK for me to come on back.'

'No problem.' I pushed a hand through my hair as I rose. My muscles were stiff from leaning over. I'd been reading for over an hour.

'Don't let me keep you.' Brad unzipped his lightweight tan jacket to reveal a button-up navy-blue shirt tucked into a pair of nicely fitting blue jeans.

Brad was a reporter for the *Table Rock Reader*, a local newspaper. Being tall and of slender-waist with electric-blue eyes and wavy brown hair, he was also trouble. The fact that he looked a bit like my not-really-dead ex-husband Brian was something I tried but didn't always succeed in not holding against him.

There's the cutest little gap between his two front teeth that's revealed every time he smiles. Like he was doing at that moment.

'That's OK.' I rubbed my knuckles into the small of my back. 'I was about to take a break anyway.'

'Stiff? Let me get that.' Brad swept behind and began digging his fingers deep into the flesh of my lower lumbar region.

I was in heaven. I closed my eyes. It was all I could do to keep from groaning out loud. As the pleasure grew, so did my discomfort.

I twisted around. 'Thanks.' I felt my face heat up. 'I'm good now.'

His eyes danced. 'Are you sure? We don't have to stop.' He wriggled his fingers seductively.

'Yes,' I said, straightening the bottom hem of my long-sleeved polo shirt. 'We do.' I moved to the other side of the island, putting some distance and a nice solid object between us. I was pretty certain I could trust Brad.

It was me I wasn't too sure about.

'Are you here for any particular reason?'

With Brad Smith, reporter, there practically always was a reason. Brad and I had some history too. There was even a point, the tiniest speck really, where I'd thought, and I'm sure he had too, that there might be something developing between us – something more than the two of us trying to find the same murderer.

But that moment had passed several weeks ago and we had seen little of each other since. The reason for our rift stemmed from what had happened over Labor Day weekend. We had made plans to meet up at an outdoor fair, the annual Labor of Love, on the town square. Brad showed up with a beautiful woman on his arm. Hurt, I took my revenge by spending the afternoon with Dr Daniel Vargas, a fortyish, six-foot Latin looker. He was VV's older brother, but I did not hold that against him because the two siblings were as different as could be.

Speaking of siblings, the beautiful young woman on Brad's arm turned out to be his kid sister, Sophie.

Oops.

Things had been uncomfortable between us ever since, which was why I had avoided him. Maybe I was a little embarrassed, too. Brad had apparently been avoiding me as well because this was the first time that he had come into the café since our little misunderstanding.

'I was chasing down leads on the Nancy Alverson case,' explained Brad. 'I heard you were on the scene.'

'You did?'

'Yeah. Am I wrong?'

I hesitated. 'Where did you get your information?'

Brad shrugged and strolled over to my laptop. 'Chip Kurkov told me you were at Ms Alverson's apartment.' He turned and pulled a small notebook from his inside jacket pocket and clicked open his pen. 'Tell me what you saw.'

'There's nothing to tell. When I got there, she was dead.'

'Come on, Maggie. Help me out here. I've got a story to write.'

'You've already spoken with the police. I'm sure they can tell you much more than I can.'

Brad's face said it all. 'They've told me practically nothing.'

Kelly stuck her head through the opening and looked from Brad to me. 'Maggie, we're getting a little backed up out here.'

'I'll be right there, Kelly.' I looked at Brad. 'Sorry, I've got a business to run.' I grabbed my apron.

'I've got a job to do too, Maggie. Haven't I helped you out before?'

I suppressed a sigh. That he had. He had even suffered speeding tickets and broken bones. 'What do you know about the Blessed Witchkraft Church?'

'You mean the Sacred Church of Witchkraft?'

'Right, that.'

'The place at the edge of town with all the kooks?' Brad scrunched up his brow. 'What's that got to do with anything?'

'I don't know, but buy me lunch and maybe between the two of us we can figure it out.'

'Sounds weird. But OK, Maggie Miller, woman of mystery.' Brad closed his notebook and stuck it and his pen in his outside pocket. He zipped up his jacket. 'I'll meet you. Shall we say Señor Sapo's at noon?'

Señor Sapo's was the Mexican restaurant a few doors down.

'Fine. No, wait. Make it Hopping Mad at one-thirty and it's a date. Well, not a date,' I stammered, seeing the smug look take over Brad's face and remembering the time I had taken him by surprise and kissed him full on the lips on my front porch. 'A meeting. A lunch meeting.' My face was burning.

Brad smirked. 'One-thirty, Hopping Mad it is. My treat.' He let himself out the back way.

I waited for my cheeks to drain and my blood pressure return to normal before going out front to pitch in. I couldn't wait to get back to the laptop and read some more, and found myself praying that business would slow down.

Eating lunch at Hopping Mad would give me a chance to interrogate the staff. Not that I was investigating anything, but I felt I owed it to Nancy to find out what was going on and who was responsible for her death.

Business remained brisk. Mom showed up at noon to lend a hand.

We were working side by side, me cranking out beignets, Mom now on the register, and Kelly and Aubrey handling the rest, when the café phone rang.

I grabbed the receiver off the wall and answered. 'Maggie's Beignet Café. How can I help you?' It was Rob Gregory wanting to confirm that I was intent on signing up for his yoga class. 'Yes,' I turned my back to the others, 'that's right.'

'Are you interested in the yearly plan or the monthly?' Rob inquired.

'Um, I hadn't really thought about it.'

'Maggie! We're getting backed up over here!' Kelly stood at the counter with a handful of drinks waiting for beignets.

I clamped my hand over the receiver. 'Aubrey, can you handle the fryer for a minute? I need to take this.'

Aubrey nodded and scooted over to the deep fryer.

I removed my hand from the receiver. 'I'm not really sure. Do you have some sort of free trial membership?' Free being the key word.

'No, but I do accept walk-ins.'

'Great. I'll go with that.'

'Are you sure? I can save you a bundle if you go for the yearly plan. Even the monthly option is a far better rate. Think about it, Miller.'

I promised I would. 'What time is the next class?'

'I've got a beginners' group that meets tomorrow at seven.'

'In the evening?'

'That's right. Don't be late. It's disrespectful.' He hung up on me. Sure, no disrespect there.

I replaced the handset on the wall and returned to the fryer station. 'I'll take over, Audrey. Thanks.'

Audrey moved back to handing out orders.

'Do you know a place where I can get a yoga outfit cheap, Mom?'

I had seen the way some of those women going into Rob's studio dressed. Some of the men, too. I had a really good feeling that Rob Gregory wouldn't be pleased to have me show up at his fancy yoga studio in my Walmart sweatsuit.

Mom closed the cash register and handed her customer a receipt. 'Yoga clothes?'

'Yeah.' I ran a towel across my forehead. Working the fryer for hours left me hot and wet. 'You know, yoga pants, maybe a tank top.'

Mom looked pensive. 'There's a shop at the spa, of course.' Mom taught yoga part-time herself at a local green-certified spa retreat called Sol Serena.

'Right. Maybe I'll try there.' Although I knew their prices would be outrageous. 'Thanks.'

'Why?' Mom asked. 'What do you want yoga clothes for?' She refilled the napkin dispenser beside the register.

'I'm taking a yoga class tomorrow night.' I busied myself at the fryer, avoiding eye contact.

'You are? Where? With who?'

I tucked my chin into my neck. 'Rob Gregory.'

Mom looked incredulous. 'Rob Gregory? Yoga By Rob?' That was the name of his yoga studio. 'You're taking a class at Yoga By Rob?'

'Yes,' I said softly. I felt not only my mother's but Kelly's and Aubrey's eyes boring into me. It was like being drilled by six hungry yellow sapsuckers all at the same time.

'Maggie Miller, I have been trying to get you to do yoga with me ever since you came to Table Rock.' She planted her hands on her hips in indignation and hurt. 'You know I teach a class twice a week at Sol Serena. Why would you go to Rob instead? You don't even like the man!'

I grabbed my mother's hand and dragged her through the swinging doors to the storeroom. We had provided enough entertainment for the customers and the employees. Besides, I didn't want word spreading about what I was up to.

As the saying goes, loose lips sink ships. And I've never seen a ship in Table Rock. Tells you something, doesn't it?

'It's not what you think, Mom. It's not the yoga that I'm interested in.'

She eyed me suspiciously. 'It isn't?'

'No.'

'What is it then?'

'It's the fact that Yoga By Rob is directly above Karma Koffee.'

'And?'

'And Nancy Alverson's apartment is directly above Yoga By Rob.' I pointed my finger upward and raised my brow suggestively.

Mom's eyelids fluttered in confusion for a moment, and then she smiled. 'Oh. Oh, yes. I see. You want to do a little snooping.'

I put my finger to my lips. 'Our secret, OK?'

'Don't worry. Your secret is safe with me.'

'Thanks, Mom.'

'Promise me one thing, Maggie, dear.'

'Yes?'

'That I won't have to come and post your bail.'

'I'll do my best.' There was no point in making promises I might not be able to keep.

Mom returned to the front and I went to the laptop on my desk to continue reading Nancy Alverson's book.

I flipped open the lid and hit the space bar. The screen was empty. I clicked the directory to open the file but there was no file.

There was no directory.

My hand flew to the side of the laptop.

The flash drive was gone!

NINE

B rad was seated at a black vinyl upholstered booth near the middle of the brick wall to the right of the bar inside Hopping Mad. The Hopi-Irish pub was owned and operated by Johnny Honanie, a colorful and gregarious local. He insisted that everybody called him Joho.

Brad's jacket was hanging off the end of the booth. I had left my sweater in the café. It was warm enough outdoors this time of day to walk around in shirtsleeves.

A bottle of orange cream soda stood waiting for me. There was another in Brad's hand and he had ordered a basket of pepper-and-lemon-seasoned buffalo wings. He was nibbling on one as I slid into the seat across from him.

'Glad you made it.' Brad dabbed at his greasy fingers with a paper napkin.

'Was there any doubt? Thanks for this.' He knew what I liked. I grabbed the neck of my orange soda and took a quick sip. I helped myself to a couple of wings, dropping them onto the small plate beside me.

'With you, there's always doubt.'

It was true that I might have stood him up once or twice – and it might have been on purpose – but it was time to let bygones be bygones.

We spent a few minutes nibbling buffalo wings and catching up, now and then drifting into awkward silence.

We had hit one of them. I snatched up my laminated menu and studied the offerings, not that I didn't know them by heart. 'What looks good?'

'I'm having the cheeseburger and fries,' Brad said, reaching for the last buffalo wing. 'You want this?'

'You can have it.' I loved the wings but I loved the hand-cut French fries more. I threw down my menu. 'When in doubt, go with the classics.'

Brad laughed and folded his hands atop the table. 'I did some digging back at the office before coming here.'

'Oh?'

He nodded. 'I found out quite a lot about the Sacred Church of Witchkraft.'

'Anything suspicious?'

'No.' Brad straightened as a college-aged waitress stopped at our booth and asked if we were ready to order.

'Hi, guys. I'm Chloe and I'll be your server today.' Chloe's hair was short and dark and curled forward along her jawline. A blue Kokopelli tattoo danced on the back of her left hand. On the back of her right hand was a tattoo of a feather.

Representations of Kokopelli were as common as cacti in Arizona. Kokopelli was supposed to represent fertility, both human and agricultural. I wasn't familiar enough with Native American culture to know what the feather represented.

Maybe it meant she was ticklish.

Chloe held up a small electronic tablet. 'Are we ready to order?'

'A cheeseburger and fries. Hold the tomato for me, please.'

'Same here,' I said. 'Except you can give me his tomato.'

'You got it. Done with these?' the waitress asked, reaching across the table for the now-empty tray of wings, her chest passing so near Brad's face it could have been considered foreplay.

'Nah.' Brad was smiling. Sure, of course he was. 'We're good. Right, Maggie?'

'Right.' I bit my lip to keep from saying more.

She disappeared, taking the empty tray, our orders and a little piece of my dignity with her.

Brad laughed. 'Now, what were we talking about?'

'You were telling me what you found out about this church.'

Brad shrugged and took a pull on his soda. 'Lots of stuff. They have an extensive website. Plus, there was the usual ranting from disgruntled ex-members who've posted their own stories on the internet. Nothing that I wouldn't have expected.'

He played with his bottle, making a series of damp rings on the paper placemat that bore pictures of numerous area tourist sites.

'Your turn.' He made come-hither motions with his fingers. 'Why the interest in the Sacred Church of Witchkraft and what does it have to do with Nancy Alverson's murder?'

'First, you have to promise that this is just between us.'

'What do you mean just between us? Come on, Maggie. We're talking about a murder here. My readers want to know what happened.'

This being Table Rock, not Los Angeles or even Phoenix, I wasn't sure just how many readers that was but I understood his point.

'I want to know what happened too. I knew Nancy, sort of. She was a regular at the café.'

'Sorry.' Brad patted the back of my hand.

'Thanks. Had you ever met her?'

'Never. I didn't know she existed until the murder. If there's anything you can tell me, it would help with the personal angle for the story.' He pulled his little notepad and pen from his jacket and set them on the table beside his plate.

'Nancy Alverson was a person, Brad. Not an angle.'

'You know I didn't mean it like that.' He looked genuinely offended.

'Sorry. How about this? We work together, share information.'

'Sounds good,' Brad replied eagerly.

'But.' I held up my index finger.

Brad pulled a face. 'But what?'

'But you don't write your story until we are absolutely sure we've found the killer. Or that the police haven't found him or her first.'

'No deal.' Brad shook his head. 'If the police do solve the case first then I've got nothing.'

'Nothing?' I arched my brow. 'Or maybe a chance to tell the story that Nancy Alverson intended to tell?'

Brad held his breath as Chloe brought our burgers. She set a red lacquered tray holding bottles of catsup, mayo and mustard – all made in-house – between us.

'Anything else, guys?' inquired our waitress. We both shook our heads no and she moved on to her next table.

I dug into my burger as I waited for Brad to speak.

'What story?' He finally broke the silence.

'A story of greed, deception, fraud.' I tried to remember the words in Nancy's introductory text. Brad's eyes lit up with each word.

I swallowed and washed the bite down with orange soda. 'Do we have a deal?'

Brad snatched a fry and crammed it in his mouth. 'Fine.'

I grabbed my cheeseburger with both hands and brought it to my lips.

Brad clamped his fingers firmly around my wrists and lowered my arms. 'Come on, Maggie. You're killing me here. What have you got?'

I pushed back, freeing myself from his grip, and took a big bite, feeling the grease and the mayo ooze down my chin. I slowly picked up my napkin and wiped my face and neck.

'What I've got is an appetite and I think and talk better on a full stomach.' I balled up my napkin, dropped it on the table and snatched a fresh one. 'Eat,' I said. 'Your burger is getting cold.'

Brad sighed in defeat and dug into his food. Halfway through the meal, I took pity on him and relented. Besides, I was tired of hearing him talk sports.

I pressed my hands against the edge of the tabletop and blew out a breath. I still had half a basket of fries but was as stuffed as a Thanksgiving bird. 'Nancy Alverson sent me a flash drive in the mail.'

Brad looked at me, a long French fry dangling between his fingers with a dollop of catsup on its tip. 'She did?'

I nodded. 'Along with a note asking me to hold on to it until she asked for it back.'

'Why you? When?'

'I don't know. Because she didn't know anybody else? Maybe I've just got one of those trusting faces.' I pressed my hands into my cheeks and smiled.

'Maybe.' Brad sounded dubious. 'You know, you look like a chipmunk when you do that.'

Color rose to my cheeks. 'Anyway, in answer to your second question.' I cleared my throat. 'I received the flash drive in the mail yesterday. It was waiting in my mailbox when I got home from work.'

'The day *after* she was murdered.'

'Yes, and it was postmarked *the day* she was killed.' I leaned back and let the weight of my words sink in.

Brad leaned closer and I could smell his musky aftershave. 'What was on it?'

'What makes you think I looked on it?'

The expression on his face said enough. Too much, really. 'Fine. I looked. Nancy was working on an exposé that included the Sacred Church of Witchkraft. She called it *Money and Magick – Greed and Sin in a Small Town.*'

Brad whistled. 'That's some heavy stuff. Those folks have some money. They've got branches – churches, I guess I should say – all over the world.'

'I didn't know that.'

'Trust me, I wouldn't mess with them unless I was certain of my facts. I'm sure they've got lawyers who'd sue the butt off the newspaper if given the chance.' He shook his head. 'Solomon would just love that. And you say she was writing an entire book about them?'

Solomon Winchell was the publisher of the *Table Rock Reader*. I'd never met the man but I had seen his photo and his name inside the newspaper.

'Not just them, but mostly, yes. I didn't get a chance to read the entire manuscript.' Now, with it missing, I probably never would know the extent of Nancy Alverson's investigation.

'So what are we waiting for?' Brad slid out of the booth and grabbed his jacket. 'Show me. I want to get a look at this manuscript.'

'No can do.'

Brad froze, one arm in his jacket. 'What?'

'You can't read it.'

'Come on, Maggie.' Brad's voice was laden with frustration. 'We had a deal. I thought we were going to share information.'

'Sit back down, Brad.'

He hesitated.

'Please.'

Brad extricated himself from his jacket, slid back into the corner of the booth and placed the jacket beside him. 'Why do I get the feeling that there's more to this story than you're telling me, Maggie?'

'Remember when you came by the café this morning?'

'Of course I do.'

'Remember when you left?'

'Maggie, really. Will you get to the point?'

'Fine.' I slid my plate to the end of the table. 'The flash drive is missing.'

'Missing?' Brad practically hit the ceiling.

'Shh. Keep your voice down. For a reporter, you have a real lack of decorum.'

Brad glared at me. 'Explain what you mean by missing, Maggie,' he demanded through gritted teeth.

I explained what happened at the café. 'After you left, I went out front to help. When I returned a couple hours later to continue reading, I discovered that the flash drive was gone.'

Brad rubbed his jaw. 'Maybe one of the employees pulled it out of your laptop for some reason?'

'I asked them. Neither Kelly nor Aubrey used the laptop.'

'Then your mother—'

'She swears she was nowhere near it.'

'Damn.'

'Yeah. Now we may never know what was on that drive. I can't figure out who knew that I even had it.'

'Maybe Nancy told someone else.'

'Maybe. But what would be the point of that? I mean, I got the impression she was trying to keep what she was working on and the flash drive secret. Otherwise, why mail it to me in the first place?'

'Good point.' Brad squeezed his empty soda bottle until I thought it would burst. 'What I don't get is how somebody managed to get past the four of you and sneak into your storeroom.'

'It was your fault really.'

'My fault?'

'You went out the backdoor.'

'So?'

'You left it unlocked.'

'In other words, you forgot to lock it behind me.'

We glared at each other.

I had been a little flustered at the time. But that had been Brad's fault too.

'Now what?' I asked finally.

'Have you got any plans?'

'Not really.'

Brad looked at the check, counted out some money then wrapped his fingers around his jacket. 'Let's go.'

'Where are we going?'

'To get religion.'

TEN

I excused myself to go to the ladies' room first. Joho, dressed in a tan leather vest with fringe, long-sleeve white shirt and relaxed fit jeans, was tending bar and entertaining his customers as was his custom.

'Hi, Joho. How are you today?' I asked.

'Hello, Maggie.' He held a beer mug in his hand and was wiping it dry with a white cloth. 'Enjoy your lunch?'

'It was perfect, as always.' I leaned against the bar. 'How did the haunt go the other night?'

'Swell. We had a full house. Too bad you couldn't make it.'

'We were open until nine that night handing out treats. Then things got kind of crazy.'

Joho's face turned serious. He returned the mug to a rack and rested his elbow on the bartop. 'I heard about that. Tough. A young kid like that.' The pub owner was nearer sixty from what I could tell, although with his dark, unwrinkled skin and rich black hair, he could have passed for forty.

'Did you know her?'

'She stopped in now and then for a meal.'

'Alone?'

'What?'

'Was she alone each time she came?'

Joho stepped back and scratched behind his ear. 'Most times. There was this young fella that was with her sometimes.'

I described Jakob Waltz.

'Yeah, I suppose that could've been him. Hard to say. Your description sounds like a lot of people. And I see a lot of people,' he said with an accompanying wink to the man seated on the barstool to my right.

'Mark Highsmith and Veronica Vargas were here for the Haunted Halloween Hop?'

'Sure,' he drawled. 'They were part of the group doing the haunt.'

'But Mark left early and then Veronica left a little after that?'

'I don't know, Maggie. We were jammed that night. I really couldn't say who came and went when.' He leaned closer. 'The police asked me the same question.'

'They did?' I whispered back.

'Yeah, yeah. They wanted to know who was here that night, how they acted and if I noticed anything suspicious. I told them they were crazy. Everybody was acting just like you would expect. They were having a good time, drinking, swapping ghost stories.' Joho shook his head. 'If one of them was the killer, you could've fooled me.'

Maybe they had.

'Thanks, Joho.' I turned to leave.

'You know, now that you mention it . . .'

'Yes?'

'I do remember seeing Veronica Vargas in here for lunch earlier that same day.'

'Oh.' That was hardly an item of interest. Hopping Mad wasn't that far a walk from the town hall or VV's private office. 'I suppose she was with Mark Highsmith?' I pictured the two of them all snuggly and googly-eyed in a corner booth.

'No, she was with that dead girl.'

'Nancy Alverson?'

Joho nodded. 'The two of them were sitting right over there.' He pointed to the same bank of booths along the wall where Brad and I had had our lunch. I noticed Brad eying me and Joho curiously.

'The reason I remember is because it all started off normal enough, and then . . .' Joho shrugged.

'Then what?'

'The two of them started arguing. It got so I thought I was going to have to go over and have a word with them.'

'But you didn't?'

'No. There was no need.'

'They quieted down?'

'Nope. They left together but they were still going at it.'

I fell back on my heels.

'That's the last I saw of either of them – well, the dead woman, that is. Like you said, Veronica Vargas was here that night.'

I thanked Joho for his time and rejoined Brad after a quick stop in the ladies' room.

'What was that all about?' Brad asked as we walked to his car in the public lot around the corner.

'What?'

'You were asking Joho a lot of questions. Anything interesting?'

'That depends. We were sharing recipes.' I stood beside the car. 'He suggested beer-flavored beignets. What do you think?'

'I think you're a poor liar.' Brad unlocked the car and settled in behind the wheel. 'Do the police know about this flash drive?'

'I haven't told them yet.' And I didn't relish doing so now that I'd lost it or, rather, had it stolen from me. 'Have the police told you if they have any suspects?'

'No. Like I said before, they keep speaking in generalities. Your friend, Highsmith, seems to be stonewalling me.'

'I'm not so sure I'd call us friends. And for your information, he stonewalls me all the time too.'

'If you say so.' He sounded a bit put out.

'What? Are you jealous of Mark?' Brad had once seen Detective Highsmith kiss me, innocently, on the forehead after a minor fender bender.

'Not the least. Besides, he's still going out with Ms Vargas, right?'

'Right.' I turned on the radio, hoping to avoid further conversation that neither of us was enjoying. My choices were country music and New Age instrumentals. Where was Duran Duran when you needed them? I yearned for an *ordinary world*.

Brad was the first to break the silence. 'I tried a couple of times to speak with Ms Vargas but she turned me down flat.'

'What did she say exactly?' Joho's recounting of Nancy Alverson and VV's heated discussion had me wondering more about VV's involvement in the young woman's death.

'Nothing. I couldn't even get past her assistant. I tried her office at the town hall. She's keeping out of sight.'

His hands squeezed the wheel. 'My sight, anyway.' We had left downtown Table Rock, such as it was, behind us, and were now moving quickly down a state road through majestic red rock country.

'You know where you're going?' I asked as Brad left the main road and took the dark blue Honda sedan down a smaller paved road.

'Yep. I was out here about a month ago.'

'You were?'

'Yeah. Not at the church. But close by.'

'Are we even in Table Rock anymore?'

'An early settler deeded all the land out this way to the town – well, except for a few other privately held parcels like the church. Besides, we are not as far from town as you might think. These roads circle around and double back quite a bit due to the topography.'

'I suppose so.' While beautiful, the Arizona setting wasn't built to accommodate the automobile. I couldn't begin to imagine what it must have been like back in the covered wagon days. 'What were you doing out here?'

Looking at the bleak landscape, I saw nothing worthy of a story.

'I was doing a piece on a treasure hunter.' Brad abandoned the narrow paved road and turned onto a gravel and dirt track. Two tall pillars, constructed with piled river stones, hugged the road on either side. Shiny metallic gold plaques mounted on each pillar read: Sacred Church of Witchkraft. A tall, carved soapstone pentacle sat atop each column.

This was the place. The road was uneven and I felt every filling in my mouth shaking loose. 'If they have as much money as you claim, you'd think they could at least pave this in asphalt, if not gold,' I complained. 'Can't you avoid the bumps?'

'And drive through the cacti and rocks instead?'

I ignored the question because I had no good answer.

We didn't see a single car but one man, in baggy tan trousers, dusty boots and a loose-fitting green-and-black flannel shirt suddenly appeared as we took a sharp turn past a massive boulder.

Brad jammed on the brakes and I flew into the dash. 'Sorry,' he said. 'You OK?'

'Yeah.' I shook my arms. 'Fine.' I peered out the windshield. 'Who is that guy?' A dusty Indiana Jones-style hat protected his head from the harsh Arizona sun. His scraggly hair was long and his beard longer and scragglier. His hands, neck and face were deeply tanned.

The man walked awkwardly toward us. A small blue pack hung off his shoulders.

'That's him.'

'Him who?'

'My treasure hunter.' Brad rolled down his window. 'How are you, Herman?'

Up close, I realized that the hundred-year-old-looking prospector couldn't have been more than forty, maybe younger. A lack of hygiene and too much time out-of-doors had done more to age him than a team of Hollywood makeup artists could have dreamed of accomplishing on their best day.

'Good, Brad. Real good.' He smiled at me, revealing yellow but otherwise healthy-looking teeth. 'And who might this be?'

'Maggie Miller, meet Herman the Swede.'

Herman put his fingers to the brim of his hat. 'Pleasure meeting you, Maggie.' An earthy odor emanated from him, not terrible, but nothing I'd want to dab on my wrists or behind my ears before a date.

'How goes the hunt? Find your City of Gold yet?'

'Well, now.' Herman the Swede licked his dried and cracked lips. 'If I told you that, I'd have to slit your throats and bury the two of you right here in the desert where even the vultures couldn't find you,' he replied rather unnervingly.

I gasped. A long knife with a stag grip hung in a sheath attached to his leather belt.

Brad chuckled and swung his head around to face me. 'He's kidding, Maggie.'

'Sure, Maggie. I'd never take the time to bury you. Ground's too hard.' Herman the Swede stamped his heel against the ground to prove his point, then leaned back and hooted. He resembled a crazed coyote howling at the sun rather than the moon.

Brad joined in.

I tugged at Brad's sleeve. 'Shouldn't we get going?'

'Of course,' Brad replied.

'You two are off to the church, I suppose?'

'Yeah, we thought we'd take a look around.'

Herman removed his hat, wiped his forehead with a red cloth then placed the hat back on his head. 'You two be careful.'

'How do you mean?' Brad asked.

Herman the Swede shrugged vaguely. 'They're a strange bunch. Plus,' he said, tugging his right ear, 'I hear things.'

Brad wished Herman the Swede well and rolled up his window as we drove on.

'Talk about a strange bunch,' I quipped. 'That Herman is one odd bird. It doesn't surprise me at all that he hears things. Probably aliens.'

Brad cracked a grin. 'Herman's not so bad.'

'How exactly do you know him?'

'Like I said, I did a story on him a while back. Don't you ever read my byline? Herman is a treasure seeker.'

'Looking for the City of Gold?'

'That's his dream.'

'Fairy tale is more like it.'

Arizona had been and probably always would be home to those seeking mythical long-lost treasures. If it wasn't for having to live without running water and air conditioning, I might have been willing to put in a few days looking for one myself.

'What exactly is this City of Gold?'

'Herman told me a bit about it. I read up on it a little afterward too. It's actually based on the old tale of the Seven Cities of Gold.'

'I've heard that story. Wasn't that supposed to be down near the Mexican border?'

'Herman thinks the remains of one of the lost cities lies hidden up here near Table Rock.'

'What makes him believe that? Does he have proof?'

'If he had proof, do you really think he'd share it with me?' Brad asked with a grin.

'Not without having to slit your throat afterwards.'

'Exactly.'

The road split in two and Brad followed the branch to the right.

'Look.' I spotted a big rock that the elements had carved to resemble a cactus and another that looked like a coffeepot, and said so.

'Yeah, I can see that,' Brad replied.

'You were telling me about the City of Gold.' I wanted to hear more.

Brad resumed. 'According to legend, in 1539, the Viceroy of New Spain sent an expedition, led by the Conquistador Francisco Vásquez de Coronado, to investigate the claims of a Friar Marcos de Niza, who reported seeing, albeit from a distance, one of the purported Seven Cities of Gold. The expedition spent years looking.'

'And they failed.' The good friar had probably been suffering sunstroke.

'That doesn't keep the legend from living on,' replied Brad.

And it never would. The lure of lost cities and vast hidden treasures kept many a dreamer forever searching. Like Herman the Swede. 'Where did you meet this Herman guy?' I couldn't picture Brad hiking around the upper desert in search of a story.

'I literally bumped into him in town one day. He was at Mother Earth/Father Son picking up supplies.'

'My sister's grocery?' She had never mentioned a Herman the Swede, a memorable character if ever there was one. Then again, Donna was a bit on the quirky side herself and probably never noticed Herman's out-of-the-normal behavior and appearance.

'We got to talking, hit it off and he told me his story for the paper.' Brad turned off the radio. We were getting nothing but static out here. 'He agreed to show me around his camp as long as I agreed that I would take no pictures there or tell anybody where his camp was.'

'He sounds a bit paranoid.'

'Aren't all treasure seekers?'

I supposed that was true. 'What's his real name?'

'I don't know. When I interviewed him for the article, all he would tell me was that his name was Herman. When I pressed him, he said to call him Herman the Swede. He didn't even want his picture in the paper.'

'Maybe he fancies himself a modern-day Dutchman,' I said, making reference to the well-known tale of the Lost Dutchman's Gold Mine.

'Could be. I guess he might seem a bit of a nut at first, but when I interviewed him for my article he seemed pretty normal.' Brad grinned. 'Except for the whole turning your back on society to go treasure seeking thing, of course.'

'I think he may have been out in the sun too long, if you ask me. But, in a way, I can appreciate what he's doing. Not that I'm about to join the expedition.'

'Me neither.' Brad pointed through the windshield. 'His camp is over near those hills. That's all I can tell you. Because,' he said with a lopsided grin, 'if I told you more . . .' He ran his finger along his neck like a knife.

'Very funny. You and Herman should take your act on the road.'

'This road?' Brad twisted the steering wheel.

'Ouch!' I complained as we bounced in and out of another deep rut. 'You did that on purpose!'

'Nonsense,' Brad was quick to reply, though there was no hiding the big, stupid grin on his face. 'Almost there,' he promised.

It was about time. I didn't think my butt could take much further abuse.

We bounced along for another half mile or so until we came upon a complex of buildings that left me gasping for breath.

ELEVEN

'I had no idea this place was even here.'

'Not everybody does. There's a lot of empty space in these parts. And, as you saw, access isn't easy. You could hide a whole city out here.'

'They practically are.' I looked around. The Sacred Church of Witchkraft complex consisted of perhaps a dozen brown adobe buildings. It was impossible to tell exactly how many from our perspective on the ground.

The buildings were of similar design but varying sizes with the largest, central edifice capped with a bright gold spire rising thirty or more feet above the roof of the structure.

Figures clad in white cloaks roamed the grounds, mingling with others like us dressed in civilian clothing.

The wide parking area had been graded as smooth as a runway and was covered in a fine layer of light brown and white pebbles. Brad parked in an empty space near a large tour bus.

An air-conditioned adobe-walled booth stood at the edge of the parking lot. The white-robed figure inside welcomed us. 'Good afternoon. Are you members of the Sacred Church?'

'No, visitors,' Brad replied.

'That will be five dollars per vehicle for parking. It is ten dollars per person for entry and twenty dollars each extra if you would like the behind-the-scenes tour.'

Brad pulled out his wallet. 'I think we'll stick with the self-guided tour.'

'No problem. Twenty-five dollars, please, sir.'

Brad slid a credit card through the slot in the window. 'Sorry, sir.' He tapped a sign on the corner of the glass. 'Cash only.' A silver pentacle medallion the size of a silver dollar hung round his neck.

Brad handed over the cash.

The man took his money and placed it in a cloth satchel. 'Sign here, please.' He tapped a lined page of a clipboard chained to the counter. We filled in our names and the time we had arrived.

Afterward, the attendant handed us Sacred Church of Witchkraft visitor stickers, green background with purple cursive lettering, to wear on our shirts to show we'd paid, a trifold brochure and a one-page map for the self-guided tour. 'The grounds and gift shop close at five. Seating in the restaurant is until four o'clock.'

'Thanks.' Brad pulled his cellphone from his pants and tapped the screen. He scrolled to a picture of Nancy and turned it toward the attendant. 'Have you ever seen this woman?'

The man blinked. 'Sorry, sir.' He motioned to the couple behind us. 'Next, please.'

Brad and I were forced to move on.

'Where did you get the picture of Nancy?'

'It was on her publisher's website.'

'What about her publisher? Have you spoken to anyone there? Surely her editor would know what she was working on.'

'The publisher was a dead end. It's a small press out of Brainerd, Massachusetts. A one-man operation. He basically published whatever Nancy sent him. He had no idea what she was working on beyond the fact that she was in Table Rock and promised him a book by the end of the year.'

Flipping through the brochure, I discovered that the Sacred Church of Witchkraft contained a herb and vegetable garden, dormitories for students, classrooms, three altars and a restaurant called Cocina Magia. According to the pamphlet, the church was self-sustaining.

The largest building was named the Church of the Sacred Vortices. I wanted to see it first so I led Brad straight for it. I tried one of the doors. It was unlocked. 'Come on, let's check this out.'

'Sure,' agreed Brad.

A red-cloaked man, his bearded face half-hidden by a draping cowl, appeared from an alcove in the entrance and told us it was closed for a private service. We could hear chanting coming from behind four highly-polished wood inner doors.

Stymied, we wandered deeper into the grounds. Following a path to a covered pavilion named the Altar of Many Times, we came to a purple-robed man with a flowing white beard, deep-set dark eyes and a purple conical hat covered in cryptic emblems. He sat cross-legged at the head of a low stone altar.

He spoke in a low, singsong fashion and neither of us understood a word he was saying. He could have been speaking in tongues for all we knew. A group of a dozen or so students or acolytes sat in a semicircle around him.

As Brad and I stood watching, a deep, soft voice behind us whispered, 'That is Wizard Ethereal.'

We turned to face a tall man with a triangular face and high cheekbones. Like Wizard Ethereal, he wore a heavy purple robe and a cowl of satin. An outfit like that had to be murder in summer. The gnarly fingers of his left hand were wrapped around a bent cedar walking stick. Atop the stick rested an entwined milky white globe.

'I am Wizard Silvermane.' He bowed ever so slightly. A silver pentacle hung from his neck. Everybody seemed to be wearing them.

'I'm Brad Smith. I'm with the *Table Rock Reader*. This is Maggie Miller.'

The old man's fingers swept lovingly around the orb on his walking stick. 'I understand you ask about a young woman.'

Brad and I exchanged a look.

'That's right,' I said. 'Nancy Alverson.' I nudged Brad. 'Show him the picture.'

The man placed his hand on Brad's arm. 'That will not be necessary. Accompany me, please.'

We followed Wizard Silvermane down the dirt path to a small building set off from the rest of the compound. It too was built of adobe. A covered porch with an intricately carved wooden railing ran the length of the low structure. Amulets and talismans hung everywhere along the top rail and tinkled with the slightest gust of wind.

The wizard knocked once on the stone porch with his staff then pulled open a heavy plank door and motioned us inside.

The smoky interior consisted of one large room with a smaller doorway to the right toward the rear. There were two desks side by side, spaced equidistant from each other in the middle of the room.

An exquisitely carved metal chalice, a foot in diameter and half as tall, sat on a stone plinth between the desks. The chalice's sides depicted a waxing and waning moon on each side of a large full moon with a pentacle in its center.

A deep purple-robed man sat at the desk to the right. A forest-green-robed woman sat opposite him. Her hair was as long and hoary as his own. Where his nose was squat and bulbous, hers was narrow and long.

Both the man and woman looked up from their massive dark-stained desks with piercing eyes.

The entire room seemed deadened and far removed from the outside world. There were no windows. No external sounds penetrated.

The sparse furnishings were heavy. A small wooden altar and lectern sat in the far left corner. There was a three-foot square black-and-gold rug at the foot of the altar with a large silver pentacle, matching the pentacle worn around the neck of each church member.

The floor was covered with candles – the source of all the gray smoke – of all shapes, sizes and colors. All of them were lit, their short wicks dancing like ensnared fairies. Rows of roughly cut wooden shelves ran up the walls, held by heavy iron brackets. The shelves were bursting with books, chalices and dusty, intricately carved small chests of various woods and metals.

There were several oil paintings on the walls, each depicting either a church building or something of the grounds. I couldn't help wondering if these Sacred Church people were cutting out human hearts and filling the chests with them.

I took a step closer to Brad. He was a man. His heart was bigger. Let him go first.

I heard a click and turned. Wizard Silvermane had performed a disappearing act.

'Sit.' The venerable man was small but his large voice filled the room.

'Thanks.' I chose the high-backed chair to the left with its fancy dragon-footed legs. Twin dragon heads were carved into the top and the entire wood frame was made to look like dragon scales. The seat was green velvet with a gold-studded border.

Brad was forced to sit in a chair that looked like it was intended to seat the Devil or burn an infidel to a crisp. The chair's frame had been carved to resemble flames and its velvet cushion was blood red and orange.

'I am Suryavayu, Head Master and High Priest of the Sacred Church of Witchkraft.' His face was gray with deep wrinkles. 'Meet Aditi Usha, Green Witch and Most High Priestess of the Sacred Church of Witchkraft.'

The green-clad Green Witch's only reply was a small wave of a hand clutching a short black stone wand that tapered to a dull point.

'I'm Brad—'

The headmaster high priest guy cut Brad off with a chop of his hand. 'You are Brad Smith and you are a reporter with the *Table Rock Reader*.' He turned his penetrating gaze on me. 'And you are Maggie Miller.' He grinned, revealing rows of uneven yellow teeth. 'Maggie's Beignet Café. Delicious.'

He knew our names and our occupations. This guy was really good at parlor tricks. I turned to Brad but his eyes were on our host.

The high priest nodded toward the high priestess. She rose with an accompanying rustle of fabric and disappeared wordlessly through the black-draped opening.

'You are here about Nancy Alverson.'

'That's right,' Brad answered. 'You know her?'

'Of course. Nancy was a friend of the church.'

'A friend?' I shot forward in my chair. That couldn't be right from what I'd managed to read of Nancy's latest masterpiece.

The high priestess rolled out a brass trolley atop which sat a black ceramic tea set. The oddly curved teapot and cups – they appeared half-melted – were decorated with white pentacles. The word *Blessed* was written along each thick handle. She stopped the tray between our chairs, poured us each a full cup and handed them carefully to us. She then returned to her seat.

'Thanks.' I took a sniff. It smelled like peppermint and cloves. I took a sip. It didn't taste bad but they could have used sugar.

I noticed Brad wasn't drinking.

'Yes, a friend. In fact, Nancy was writing some marketing material for us.'

Having read Nancy's book draft, I knew the man was either crazy or seriously deluded.

'Are you sure about that?' asked Brad.

'Certainly. She was a gifted writer. We considered our investment in her a wise one.'

'You were *paying* her to write about you?'

'Yes. Does that surprise you? We believe that truth benefits us all. It is part of what we teach here. I have the cancelled checks here in my desk.'

Even if that truth dug up dirt that might tarnish the church's image?

He opened a drawer to his left and removed a leather-bound ledger. He turned the pages slowly, then stopped. 'Ah, here it is.'

He turned the ledger toward us so we could read. Sure enough, there were several checks written out to Nancy Alverson. The total amounted to six thousand dollars.

'What exactly do you do here?' I said. 'If you don't mind my asking.'

Suryavayu repeated much of what I'd read in the brochure. The church provided teaching, guidance and holistic medicine. 'We offer degreed programs in a wide range of subjects, including cosmology, healing, divination and psychic arts.'

'All at a price, I'll bet,' Brad ventured.

The headmaster seemed unperturbed by the barb. 'How much is too much to pay for universal enlightenment?'

I decided to try a direct frontal attack to see if I could break his calm veneer. 'I heard Nancy Alverson was writing an exposé about you.'

His eyes flickered briefly. 'Nonsense. I am afraid you heard wrong, Mrs Miller.'

'It's Ms,' I replied. 'My husband is dead.' To me.

That got the old priest guy's interest. 'Is he now?' he said, leaning toward me with a twinkle in his eye. 'Perhaps you would like one of our priests to try and contact him for you? We have a special rapport with the spirit world.'

He probably did. And it was eighty-proof. 'Thanks, but that isn't necessary. If I want to contact him, I can reach him on his cellphone down in Phoenix.'

The high priest and high priestess exchanged a look.

I got a look from Brad myself. It said: *Shut up.*

I did.

Brad whipped out his notebook and pen. 'So if I wanted to write a story about you . . .?'

'The church would welcome you with open arms,' Suryavayu said.

'Great.' Brad flipped to a blank sheet of paper. 'Tell me, sir, where did you get the money for all this? What does it cost to attend one of your classes?'

The high priest shook his head. 'I'm afraid now is not a good time.' He rose.

The high priestess stood as well, clutching her black obsidian wand. I wondered if we were about to be turned into toads.

The high priest said, 'We are in the midst of a Summoning ceremony in the Earth's Portal and—'

'Yes,' interrupted Brad, 'but if one wants to get a degree in say, psychic arts, what are the fees—'

The door flew open. Wizard Silvermane was waiting for us. 'If you would, please?' He extended his hand.

We had no choice but to comply.

'You didn't try the tea,' I muttered to Brad as we followed Wizard Silvermane back toward the entrance to the church grounds.

'I was afraid it might be poisoned. Or drugged.'

I stopped dead in my tracks. OK, so that was a poor choice of words. 'You could have said something!'

Brad paused to take a photo of a small group of robed figures seated in the shade of a Western soapberry tree, talking into cellphones.

I caught up to Brad as he resumed walking. 'How did that priest know who we were?'

'We signed the register, remember?'

'Yes, but that didn't include our occupations.'

'Good point.'

'Hey, those are the guys I saw having beignets at the café.' I tugged at Brad's sleeve and he paused once more. Wizard Silvermane had not yet noticed we were no longer following him.

'So?' Brad eyed the two men and the woman. They were dressed much as I had seen before, business all the way. The taller of the two men I remembered chasing after Nancy. An aluminum attaché case hung from his left hand. A red-robed member of the church with a dense black beard was leading them. Where?

'They were in the café the day Nancy was murdered. In fact, that man on the left,' I said, 'tried to talk to her. She blew him off at first. I thought he was trying to hit on her. Nancy probably thought so too.'

'And?'

'And he tried again. Nancy got angry and left. A minute later, he ran out in the street and they had words.'

Brad stroked his chin. 'Any idea who those three are?'

'No.' Our escort was a good thirty yards ahead and about to disappear around a green hedge, still apparently unaware that we were not following in his wizardly wake. 'But let's shadow them and see where they go.' I hurried up the path to my right without waiting for a reply.

I heard the sound of Brad's footsteps as he followed me.

Dodging behind the occasional bush or cactus and the odd stone pilings we came across, we were able to stay low and out of sight. It didn't take long to figure out where the foursome was heading.

Stooped behind a low shed from which the sound of a running engine emanated, Brad and I watched as the red-robed figure knocked on the door of the same adobe cabin from which we had been asked rather unceremoniously to exit. This time, Suryavayu himself answered. All four disappeared inside.

Brad turned to me, his shoulder pressed against mine. 'What do you suppose that's all about?'

'I don't know, but I don't think they're here to enroll in a bachelor of mystic arts program.'

Strong hands clamped down on my upper arm. I twisted around. It was Wizard Silvermane and he had brought company. Two goons in orange robes, at least goons was what I took them for. The way they were filling out those robes and the dull, lifeless expressions on their faces seemed to confirm my diagnosis.

Wizard Silvermane tugged on my arm. He was surprisingly strong for an old wizard.

'Hey!' I complained.

'Yeah, watch it!' Brad moved in to help me but the two orange goons grabbed him, an elbow apiece, and lifted him easily off the ground.

Brad struggled some more, kicking, thrashing and cursing, but it was no use and I said so. 'Forget it, Brad. Let's go.' At least, I was hoping they would let us go.

'Very wise of you, Ms Miller.' Wizard Silvermane turned to his goons. 'Please see that our guests do not get lost once again on their way out.'

The two men, so far silent, released their grip on Brad and his feet hit the ground.

Two minutes later, we were in the car and on our way back to town.

TWELVE

'That went well,' I quipped. I was still feeling shaken. Shaken and confused. And not a little scared. 'What's next?'

Brad hit the highway and picked up speed. Normally, I had to goad Mr Leadfoot to step on the gas. That was no problem now. He seemed as anxious to put some distance between us and the Sacred Church of Witchkraft as I was.

'What's the hurry?' I teased.

'No hurry. I just thought I'd try to lose them. For kicks.'

'Huh?'

'Don't look now but we are being followed.' Brad's hands were in a death grip on the steering wheel.

I lowered the visor in front of me. I peeked in the mirror, making a show of checking my hair and makeup. I blanched. A white van sat about thirty yards back, matching our speed. 'What do you suppose they want?'

'Hopefully, to make sure we go back to Table Rock and stay there,' was Brad's reply.

I tilted the visor back into place. 'And not so hopefully?'

'Run us off the road? Maybe kill us out here in the middle of nowhere and away from the church to deflect any hint of suspicion on them?'

I frowned, wishing I'd never asked the question. Brad painted a vivid, if scary, picture. 'Go a little faster,' I urged.

The van locked pace with us for several miles, slowing when we slowed and speeding up when we attempted to break away.

'We're in luck.' Brad pointed out the windshield. Two vehicles sat along the side of the road. One was a Table Rock police cruiser, the other a navy-blue SUV. A uniformed officer was writing out a ticket to the driver of the SUV.

Brad tapped on the brakes, turned on his right blinker and slowed to a stop several yards in front of the two vehicles. 'If the cop asks, we thought the rear tire sounded funny.'

'Good idea.'

As Brad opened the driver's side door, the white van shot past. 'Did you get a look at the driver?' he asked.

'No. They were going too fast.' I climbed out and stretched my legs while Brad moved to the rear of his car and bent to inspect the tire.

I kicked the tire on my side. The blue SUV merged back on the road and the officer, whom I now recognized to be Officer Ravi Singh, wearing a police cap and a pair of green-tinted sunglasses, shambled over. He came to a stop beside Brad, who was standing near the trunk.

'Trouble, sir?' Singh asked.

'Hi, Officer. I thought maybe we had a flat.' Brad scratched the top of his head. 'Something sounded funny, you know?' Brad looked across the trunk at me. 'Right, Maggie?'

Officer Singh looked at me for a moment. 'Ms Miller. How are you?'

'Great, Officer. False alarm, I guess. Right, Brad?'

'Right.' Brad rapped the trunk with his knuckles. 'I guess we'll be off.'

We both looked up and down the road. There was no sign of the van. It hadn't doubled back. Was it and its driver waiting for us up ahead?

'I sure hope there's nothing wrong with these tires,' I said, doing my best to sound helpless as I lifted my leg and rubbed the back of my calf. 'I'd hate to get stuck out here in the desert.' I looked at the sky. 'It will be dark soon, too.' Well, sort of.

Officer Singh took the hint. 'You are heading into town?'

'That's right, Officer,' answered Brad.

'Why don't I follow the two of you? I'm going that way myself.'

'Would you?' I said with a flutter of eyelashes. 'You are a peach.'

Officer Singh blushed. 'It is my pleasure.'

'Haven't I always said how wonderful the police in Table Rock are, Brad?'

'Huh?'

I made a face that only he could see.

'Oh, yeah. You're always saying that. I mean, how wonderful your police are.'

'Super crime solvers, too,' I said, unable to stop myself. 'Speaking of which, have you found Nancy Alverson's killer yet?'

Officer Singh shook his head. 'Sadly, no. There are many, many suspects but no perfect match. Not yet.'

'You were on the scene, weren't you, Officer Singh?' asked Brad.

'Yes, that is correct. I was one of the first to arrive at the victim's apartment.'

'I never did hear, Officer. According to the police report, Nancy Alverson was strangled but the report didn't say how. Did the killer use their bare hands?'

'No, no. She was strangled with—' I snapped my mouth shut. I had almost spilled the beans and, if I did that, Mark Highsmith just might spill some of my blood.

'I am afraid that is confidential at this time.' Singh took a step back and motioned toward Brad's car. 'Shall we?'

Back inside the car, Brad said, 'Did you have to do that?'

'Do what?'

'Get all, I don't know, seductive and disarming?'

I grinned ear to ear. 'Is that what you thought, Brad? That I was seductive and disarming?'

Brad's face turned brilliant red and he didn't say another word to me until we reached the curb outside Maggie's Beignet Café.

'I've got to go interview the folks at Big Blue Outfitters. One of their hot-air balloons was stolen and the editor wants the story.'

I furrowed my brow. 'Who steals a hot-air balloon?'

'Beats me. It's hardly front-page news but BBO is a regular advertiser so off I go.'

'OK.' I started to open my door but his hand on my arm stopped me.

'Before you do.'

'Yes?'

'Back there at the side of the road when we were talking to Officer Singh—'

'You are not going to start that again.'

'It's not that, Maggie. When I asked Singh how Nancy Alverson was strangled, you,' he said, pointing the finger of guilt at me, 'started to say something. What was it?'

'I don't remember.' I climbed out and slammed the door before he could ask me anything further. 'Call me tomorrow!'

As Brad negotiated a U-turn, I looked up and down Laredo. There was no sign of the white van.

Maggie's Beignet Café was closed for the day. I opened the door and went to the storeroom to grab my bicycle. I knew it was hopeless but once again I looked on my desk and around the floor for the missing flash drive. There was no sign of it.

I closed the laptop and rolled up the power cord. I placed it all in the handlebar basket of my bike.

I rolled the Schwinn to the rear entrance of the storeroom and examined the lock for the umpteenth time. It wasn't broken and there was no sign of a break-in.

I slipped into my coat, secured the door and pedaled toward the town square.

I couldn't put off telling Detective Highsmith about Nancy Alverson's note and the now-missing flash drive any longer.

Table Rock Town Hall is located on the town square. The mayor's office, the town council and most town services were located within the rambling structure. Over the years, the town's offices had been expanded and remodeled innumerable times, often taking over spaces in the adjacent buildings, especially their upper floors. There was a two-bay fire station around the corner.

The town was undergoing one such change now. Table Rock Police Headquarters, which had originally been housed on the street, had been moved in the late seventies to its location just outside of the town proper. Police HQ was now being moved back to its original space, the thinking being that it would save the town money and improve communications between town services and the townspeople.

It certainly improved my ability to communicate. I no longer had to worry about taking public transportation, bumming a ride or borrowing a car whenever I wanted to drop in.

Which, for some reason, was more often than you might think.

A developer had purchased the old police station and was turning it into an outlet mall. Tempers still flared and the town was still divided into three camps regarding that plan. Some loved it, some hated it and a few just plain didn't care.

I slid my bike onto the bike rack and plucked my laptop from the basket. One of these days, I'd get a lock for it but, so far, I had been lucky. No one had had the nerve to steal my bright pink Schwinn.

I wasn't taking any such chances with the laptop.

I climbed the steps of the town hall and entered the regal old lobby. A neatly coiffed man, middle-aged, in a white shirt sat behind a large desk that contained a lamp, a radio and a guestbook.

'Hi, I'm here to see Detective Highsmith.'

The man nodded. 'Have you been here before?'

'Yes, but I see things have changed.' The building permits and inspections office was still to the immediate left. However, where the staff offices and human resources department had once been was now the entrance to the police department.

Along the back there were offices for dog licenses, public works, the public information office and a notary public service.

'You'll find the detective through there.' He glanced at his watch. 'I don't believe he's gone for the day yet.'

'Thanks.' I scribbled my signature in the guestbook.

'Is that a computer?'

'Yes.' I hefted the bag on my shoulder.

He stood and ran a metal wand up and down my body.

'You want me to open it?'

'Nah. You're good.'

'Tell me, is the mayor's office still on the second floor?'

'That's right, and I expect it's going to stay there.'

I wasn't surprised. The mayor, VV's daddy, had a posh office overlooking the square. I wouldn't have wanted to part with it either. 'And the prosecuting attorney?'

'Same, too. Third floor.' That would be VV's office, a smaller but equally posh space.

I thanked him once more and walked into the new police station. A polished wood counter extended from the wall. A glass partition rose from about six inches above the counter to the ceiling. Bulletproof, I suspected. Small speakers were built into the glass. There was a sturdy-looking gray metal door to the left of the counter.

A blue-uniformed officer stood behind the counter wiping his spectacles. He placed them on his narrow nose as I approached. 'Yes, ma'am?'

'My name is Maggie Miller. I'm here to see Detective Mark Highsmith.'

'Is he expecting you?' The officer glanced over his shoulder. I could see the detective hovering near a watercooler talking to a man in a black coat and tie.

'No, but it's about the Nancy Alverson case. I think he will want to see me.'

'One minute.'

The officer strode along between the rows of desks, some occupied, some empty. He tapped Detective Highsmith on the shoulder. Words were exchanged. Both men glanced toward me at the counter.

Was it my imagination, or did Detective Highsmith's shoulders sag ever so slightly when he saw it was me?

The officer, whose nametag identified him as E. Hunt, returned. 'You can go on back.' He pressed a button under the counter and the door buzzed.

The gentleman Detective Highsmith had been speaking with left as I approached. 'Come on into my office,' Highsmith said.

His office was a cubicle in the corner. He pulled an empty swivel chair from the cubicle beside his and rolled it my way. 'Have a seat, Ms Miller.'

'Thanks.' I settled in and placed my laptop and purse on the blue-gray industrial carpet floor. I rubbed my eyes and blinked. The flooring was new and some chemical in it was making my eyes itchy.

'Now what's this about the Nancy Alverson case?' He leaned back in his chair, resting his elbow on the cluttered built-in desk. A large, flat computer monitor behind him displayed a list of names with a photograph of a face beside each one.

'Suspects?' I asked.

'Huh?'

'On your computer.'

'New recruits.' He turned and hit a button on the side of the computer. The screen went blank.

I wasn't sure I believed him but it didn't seem important enough to pursue. 'Have you found any new leads?'

Highsmith grinned. 'That sounds almost exactly like the question you asked Officer Singh not an hour ago. You really, really have to stop interfering.'

I colored. 'For your information, I was not interfering. I merely ran into Officer Singh and I was simply making conversation.'

'Next time you want to make conversation, try talking about the weather.'

'I'll do that.' I jumped up, ready to leave. The man could make me so angry.

'Aren't you forgetting something?'

'What?' I grabbed my purse and laptop case.

'The Nancy Alverson case?' He motioned for me to sit. 'You told Hunt you had some information?'

I glared at him for a moment, then returned to my chair. 'I'm only trying to help.'

'I know,' he said, patiently. 'Can I get you something? Coffee, tea?'

'No, thanks. But speaking of tea, I noticed a paper cup of tea from Karma Koffee on Nancy's desk the night she was murdered. Any idea how it got there?'

'Not so far.'

'Were there any fingerprints on it?'

'Just hers, and before you ask, yes, she had ingested most of it before she was strangled.'

'So Nancy *was* murdered due to strangulation?' I asked. 'She wasn't poisoned first with the tea, perhaps?' It had been an idea bouncing around in the back of my mind.

Detective Highsmith leaned forward, planting his elbows over his knees. 'Why do you say that?'

'Well . . .' I shifted in my seat. 'If Nancy Alverson had been poisoned first, that might mean that the killer strangled her with a certain scarf afterward—'

'VV's scarf.'

I nodded. 'To pin the murder on her.'

Highsmith settled back in his chair and swiveled toward his desk. 'I don't know if I should be telling you this but the tea . . .'

'Yes?' I said eagerly.

He turned on his computer again and clicked on a file. 'Ms Alverson's tea wasn't poisoned exactly, but it was tampered with.'

'Tampered with how?'

'This is just between us, Miller.'

'Of course, Detective.'

'Fine. I'm only telling you because this whole murder thing has really got VV upset. People in the department are starting to wonder if she really could be involved somehow.' He stood and paced the small space between us.

'It's ridiculous. I have got to get to the bottom of this,' Highsmith growled, 'before things get out of hand.'

'The tea?' I interrupted. 'You said something about the tea.'

'It was spiked with approximately two hundred milligrams of diphenhydramine.'

'Diphenhydramine? What is that?'

'An over-the-counter allergy medication and sleep aid.'

'Did she have any allergies?'

'Not according to her family and physician.'

'Nancy had been drugged?'

Highsmith ran his hand over his face. 'It would seem so. It's unlikely that she would have taken such a strong dose herself. Besides, even if she wanted to take a sleeping pill or two, she would take them with her tea, not in her tea.'

'Unless she didn't like to swallow pills,' I noted.

'Good point.'

'Did you find a bottle of sleeping pills in Nancy's apartment, Detective?'

'Yes. And before you ask, the bottle was discovered in a kitchen cabinet. It had been open and a number of pills were missing – twenty-seven, to be exact.'

'Did you check the bottle for fingerprints?'

Highsmith looked insulted. 'The bottle was clean.'

'That's odd.'

'Tell me about it.'

I thought a moment. 'Could the drugging and the murder be unrelated? A coincidence?'

'Maybe,' he admitted. 'But when it comes to murder, I hate coincidences.'

'Would two hundred milligrams have been enough to kill her?'

'Not according to the coroner.'

'So the killer drugged her tea and then strangled her? Why? So she would be more docile and put up less of a struggle?'

'That's the assumption we are going on.'

Highsmith sat back down. 'Your turn. What brought you here, Ms Miller? If there is anything you know that can shed some light on this case, now is the time to share.'

I cleared my throat and pressed my knees together. 'I received a package in the mail from Nancy.'

The detective's brow shot up. 'When?'

'Yesterday.'

'And you're only getting around to telling me this now? Ms Miller, this is an active homicide investigation!'

'I know, Detective. Do you want to badger me or do you want to hear what she sent me?'

'What did she send you?'

I started to speak but he raised his hand.

'One sec.' He snatched a small notepad from the corner of his desk, dug around for a pen and found none. He grumbled as he grabbed one from the cubicle next door then took his seat once more.

'OK, go ahead.' He held the pen at the ready over the pad. 'Start at the beginning.'

'When I got home from work yesterday, I wrote out a check for the rent on my apartment and stuck it in an envelope. I knew it was probably too late to go out that day because the mail carrier usually comes earlier in the day. I decided to place the rent check in my mailbox, anyway, because I told Rob Gregory I already had. That way, I wouldn't have to think about it—'

'Ms Miller.' The detective looked about ready to burst. 'Unless your rent is somehow connected to this case—'

'I am trying to tell you, if you'd just let me finish.' I went on quickly despite the look he was giving me that said I was wasting his ever-so-valuable time. 'When I put my envelope in the mailbox, I saw that the mail had come as I expected. There was the usual junk plus an envelope from Nancy.'

Detective Highsmith visibly perked up. 'What sort of an envelope?'

'Padded. About so big.' I demonstrated with my hands. 'Inside was a note and a flash drive.'

Highsmith thumped the notepad against the palm of his hand. 'Did you touch it?'

'The flash drive? Of course! I touched the note, too. Why wouldn't I? Nancy sent them to me, didn't she?'

Highsmith was frowning. 'I suppose,' he admitted with some reluctance. 'Do you have this note? What did it say?'

'It's back at my apartment, Detective. She said something about . . .' I closed my eyes and tilted my head back, trying to remember. 'Something about how I should hold onto the flash drive for her until she asked for it back.'

'Why you? Were you friends? I got the impression you barely knew her.'

'I did hardly know her. In the note, Nancy said it was because she didn't know who else to trust with it.'

'It being the flash drive?'

I shrugged. 'Obviously.' An incessantly ringing phone in the background was finally answered and I sighed with relief.

'So you read the note. Did you look at this flash drive she sent you, too?'

'Yes. I mean, sort of. I had no way of looking at it last night. My computer was in the store and I didn't feel like going back. I didn't think it was anything urgent. I opened it on my laptop at the café this morning.'

Highsmith's eyes lit up with interest. 'What was on it?'

'Some files related to a book she was writing. I didn't get a chance to read the entire document. Then I got busy. I do have a business to run and . . . and some other things came up.'

'That's great.' He leaned forward. 'You know, whatever was on Nancy Alverson's computer is gone. That flash drive might be a big help in our investigation.'

'Gone?'

'Her computer has been wiped clean. We've sent it to a specialist to see if they can get anything off the hard drive but it's probably a lost cause. I'm assuming the killer wiped the drive, so you can see how important the flash drive might be.'

I found myself tensing up, knowing that I was going to have to get to the not-so-pleasant point very soon.

'I did want to bring the flash drive to your attention as soon as possible. That's why I am here.'

'Of course. You did the right thing bringing it here to me now. Is that it there?' he gestured. 'Inside that computer case?'

I squirmed. The seat of my chair suddenly felt like a bed of sharp nails.

'I'd like to examine it right away. Like I said, it may hold a vital clue as to who murdered Nancy, or at least tell us why.'

'Well . . .' I cleared my throat and tugged at my collar. 'Here's the thing . . .'

'Yes?'

'I don't have it.'

Highsmith rose to his feet and grabbed his jacket. 'OK, why don't we head over to your apartment now and get it. Do you need a ride?'

My jaw tightened and my face colored. 'Again, here's the thing . . .'

I looked around for help. This was a police station – couldn't somebody help me? I took a deep breath and blew out a stream of air, then said, 'I don't have it. It's gone.'

THIRTEEN

'You lost—' Highsmith turned his back on me and began swearing vehemently under his breath. His hands were clenched at his sides.

After a minute of this, the detective turned. His face was mottled and I could see that he was struggling with self-control issues. 'Ms Miller—'

I rolled my chair a foot or two back. 'I didn't lose it, Detective. And I don't appreciate you jumping to conclusions,' I snapped. 'It was stolen from me.'

Detective Highsmith slumped into his chair once more, tossing his notepad and pen on the desk in frustration. 'Stolen?'

'That's right.'

'Somebody broke into your apartment? Why didn't you report it to the police?'

I shook my head side to side. 'No. Nobody broke into my apartment.'

'The thief broke into the café?'

'No. If you would let me talk.'

The detective gestured for me to continue.

'Thank you. Like I told you, I took the flash drive to the café this morning to see what was on it and that's what I did. I was reading it in the storeroom – that's where I keep my laptop when I'm at the café. I went out front to assist for a couple of hours. When I returned to my desk to read some more, the flash drive was missing.'

'Just the flash drive or your laptop, too?'

'Just the flash drive. My laptop was right where I had left it. It hadn't been touched.' At least, I didn't think it had. 'I asked everybody – my mother, Kelly and Aubrey. None of them had taken the flash drive or even noticed it.'

'And you didn't see anybody else? You didn't let a worker or somebody else back there while you were working?'

'No. However . . .'

'Yes?'

'The door to the storeroom was inadvertently left unlocked.'

His sigh about bowled me over. 'So anybody could have gone into the back while you were all out front.'

'Yes, I'm afraid so. We are in and out of the backroom getting supplies, but yes, it would be easy enough for a thief to sneak in, take the drive and be gone without any of us knowing.'

'You really should keep that door locked during business hours.'

'Normally, I do. It was an accident.'

'I'll want the laptop.'

'What for? I told you, I didn't copy the file.'

'We'll want to check your computer for fingerprints. Whoever took the flash drive may have touched the laptop in doing so.'

'Oh.' That made sense.

'Who did you tell about the flash drive?'

'Nobody! Not before it was stolen, at least. I did mention it to Brad this afternoon. And . . .'

'And what?'

'And he was at the café earlier,' I admitted. 'He was there when the flash drive was in my laptop.'

'Would he have seen this?'

'Yes. He was in the storeroom with me. But he left out the back and the flash drive was still in the laptop.'

'Are you sure?'

'Definitely.'

'That doesn't mean he couldn't have come back after you'd gone out front and taken it.'

'But why would he?'

'Because he's a reporter and smelled a story maybe?'

'I suppose. But how could he have known I had the flash drive or what was on it? I only told him about it later at lunch.'

'Don't you think that Nancy mailing the drive to you meant that she wanted it kept private?'

'Nancy is dead, Detective. Telling Brad what was on the drive wouldn't change that.'

Highsmith merely shrugged. 'Did you tell anybody else?'

'No. I mean, my mother, Kelly and Aubrey knew that I was looking for a flash drive. They didn't ask what was on it and I didn't tell them. Although . . .'

'Yes?'

'Jakob Waltz came by the apartment yesterday evening.'

Highsmith held up a hand to stop me. 'Jakob Waltz.' He flipped through a file on his desk. 'A friend of the deceased. We interviewed him. He wasn't much help.'

'Yes. He brought me a painting for the café.'

'Why would he do that?'

'It is not unusual. I have half-a-dozen of his paintings in the café. You must have seen them.'

'If you say so.'

'We sold one recently and he brought me another to take its place.'

'But you didn't tell him about the flash drive?'

'No.' I shook my head firmly. 'He might have seen it, though. The flash drive and envelope were there in plain sight in the living room.' I rubbed my fingers. 'I got the sense that he was curious about it. I could be wrong.'

'Are you sure he didn't leave with it?'

'Definitely not. Like I said, I had it last night and I had it this morning.'

'But Jakob knew you had that envelope and flash drive?'

'Yes, but I don't see how he could have known that the envelope was from Nancy or what was on the flash drive.'

'Maybe he recognized her handwriting on the envelope,' Highsmith speculated.

That made sense too. Still, I couldn't believe Jakob Waltz could have had anything to do with Nancy Alverson's murder. What possible motive could he have? They were friends.

'What about the note? Did whoever took the flash drive get that too?'

'No. That's definitely in my apartment. The envelope too.'

'Good. Good.'

'I can bring them both to you tomorrow, if you'd like.'

'Let's not take any chances. How about if I stop by and collect them later on my way home?'

'I suppose that would be all right.' Though I hadn't cleaned in ages.

Highsmith, appearing to have recovered his calm, leaned back in his seat and laced his fingers. 'Tell me about the document.'

'Nancy was writing a sort of exposé, from what I could gather. She called it *Money and Magick – Greed and Sin in a Small Town*. There was some other stuff in there about land grants and deeds. She pointed to a lot of shady goings on in the church and here in Table Rock, actually.'

'Can you be more specific?'

I shook my head. 'I don't remember very well. I was reading quickly. And, as I explained, I hadn't read through everything.'

'Nancy was a writer,' Highsmith said. 'She's written a couple of earlier nonfiction books that were attacks on industry and politicians. Nothing big or too splashy. Her publisher is very small.'

'That's what I heard.'

'Oh?'

'Brad Smith told me pretty much the same thing.'

'I see. Her publisher told me she never sold more than a couple thousand copies of anything.' The detective stretched his arms and yawned. 'Frankly, I don't know how she managed to pay her bills.'

I remembered what had been insinuated at the church. 'Suryavayu told us that Nancy was being paid by the church to write about them.'

Highsmith's face darkened. 'Who is Suryavayu?'

'He calls himself the Head Master and High Priest of the Sacred Church of Witchkraft. Brad and I went to see him this afternoon.'

'Do I want to know why you did that?'

'We were curious, that's all. Like I told you, I mentioned what Nancy was working on to Brad and Brad thought we should go have a look around.'

'That could have been dangerous.'

'The church is open to the public.' Though there had turned out to be at least the insinuation of danger.

'This high priest told you that he was paying Nancy Alverson to write something for them?'

'He showed us the cancelled checks.'

'I'll look into it.' The detective grabbed his pad and made some notes.

A horrendous grinding sound started up further back in the office.

'Ignore that,' Highsmith said, nonchalantly.

'I don't think I can,' I said, bringing my hands to my ears.

'It's the construction crew doing some work on the new cells. It will stop in a minute.'

We waited for the noise to die down. Sure enough, a minute later, the racket dimmed then ceased altogether.

'Wow,' I explained.

'You get used to it. The crews try to do most of the work in the evening now that we've moved in. Hopefully, all the last-minute stuff will be done soon. I'll be glad when it is.'

I looked around the spiffy new office. 'How do you like your new location?'

'I love it. We're right in the heart of town. I get to walk to lunch and have my pick of a dozen restaurants.'

'And your girlfriend within easy walking distance?'

The detective colored ever so slightly. 'We were talking about Nancy Alverson.'

To continue to tease him would have been so easy, but I decided to give him a break and returned to our subject. 'Do you think Nancy may have made some enemies along the way? Digging up dirt that somebody didn't want dug up?'

Highsmith smiled grimly. 'I think she made at least one enemy.'

'If that's all, I'd like to get going.' I picked my purse up and set it in my lap, pushing the laptop closer to his desk. I hoped I'd be getting it back soon. 'I've got a cat to feed.'

'Look, Maggie . . .' The detective came to his feet. He laid his hand gently over mine and gazed into my eyes.

'Yes?' My heart thumped.

'VV, Veronica, really could use a friend right now.'

My thumping heart came to a dead stop.

'A friend?'

'Yes. Can't you talk to her? As a friend?'

'Are you kidding? VV likes me about as much as I like getting bitten by a rattlesnake!' I crossed my arms over my chest. 'And I dare say, the feeling is mutual.'

'Come on, Maggie. You don't mean it.' Highsmith smiled, dimples and all. 'Believe it or not, Veronica doesn't have any real girlfriends. I mean, she has social friends, but nobody she is really close with. Nobody she can open up to.'

Oh, I could believe it all right.

'She's got you.'

'I'm not a woman.'

No, he sure wasn't.

Still, a part of me melted. But just a tiny part. And not a critical one. 'Not a chance. She—' My mouth froze at the same time that my arms unfroze and fell limp at my sides.

If I said yes and, if – big if – VV agreed to talk to me, I could do what Brad had been unable to do thus far. I could question her more deeply about Nancy Alverson's murder.

I could hear what she had to say to explain herself regarding what Joho told me about her argument with Nancy at Hopping Mad the day Nancy was murdered. I should say yes. 'She—'

My jaw froze up once more. I felt conflicted. VV and I could barely stand to be in the same room together. How on earth could I be expected to go to her as a friend? What was Highsmith thinking? It was absurd. And VV Vargas would never buy it. Not for one minute.

Detective Highsmith stood leaning over me, his arm resting on the back of my chair. I felt the warmth of his arm on my shoulder. 'She what?'

I trembled. 'She really could use a friend right now, couldn't she?'

Detective Highsmith gave my shoulder a tender squeeze. 'Thanks, Maggie. I owe you.' He helped me to my feet. I seemed to have lost all my leg bones somewhere and was wobbling like a jar of cactus jelly. 'In the meantime, I suggest you stay away from Jakob Waltz.'

'Why?' I said, feeling my balance slowly returning.

'He has a criminal record.'

'Jakob?' I gasped. 'I don't believe it.'

'Nothing too serious. He and some friends stole a car when he was sixteen. A couple of arrests for trafficking marijuana a few years ago.'

'I see.' I slowly buttoned my coat. 'People can change.'

'Yeah,' Highsmith said, 'but not always for the better.'

FOURTEEN

When I got home, I found Brad Smith seated on the front stoop with an open copy of the *Table Rock Reader* in his hands. He looked up as I pedaled to a stop at his feet. His jacket was zipped to his chin. 'It's about time you got home.'

'What are you doing here?' I slid off my bike. 'I thought you were out chasing a missing hot-air balloon?'

'Very funny, Maggie.' Brad folded up his newspaper and stood. The cat was watching him from the sill of the front window.

'I wanted to get a look at that note you said Nancy sent you.'

Brad dusted himself off as I unlocked the door and pushed the bike inside. Carole Two hopped down from her perch with a resounding *plunk*, which reminded me that we were both in need of a diet.

'Help yourself.' I rolled the bike through the kitchen and out to the patio. I removed my purse from the basket and hung it on the coat rack. C2 followed me along. While Brad looked on, I rewarded her with some kibble smothered with a helping of canned salmon.

'And I brought you an old copy of the paper with my story on Herman in it. I thought you might like to read it.' He waved the folded paper in the air.

'Thanks. I'll read it later. Highsmith told me something interesting,' I said.

'What's that?'

'Nancy's laptop has been wiped clean.'

Brad whistled. 'That is interesting. That makes finding the flash drive all the more important.'

'Assuming the killer hasn't destroyed it already.' I knew that anything I told the police was on that flash drive would only be considered hearsay and inadmissible as evidence. Finding the flash drive, if it still existed, could prove crucial.

'Yeah. Where is the note?' Brad tossed his newspaper on the kitchen table.

'Right there on the sofa.'

I returned to the living room as Brad picked up the envelope and thrust his hand inside. 'Interesting,' he said after giving Nancy's note a read. 'And cryptic.'

'Tell me about it.' I had brought us each a margarita.

Brad set the envelope on the table beside the couch and took a glass from my outstretched hand. He sat on the arm of the couch. 'I sure wish I knew what it all meant. The flash drive, the note to you . . .'

'I don't know. But it must be related to her murder.' I ran my tongue along the edge of my glass before taking a sip. I had coated the rim with sugar. 'Have you managed to find Veronica Vargas yet?'

'No. As a matter of fact, I went by her condo right before stopping here. There was no answer.' He sighed and took a gulp. 'I've left several telephone messages for her through her office, too.'

'Sounds like she doesn't want to talk to you.' I knew VV lived in a fancy co-op downtown. She occupied one of the two penthouse units. It was a security building with an electronic lock at the entrance.

'One way or another,' he said firmly, 'she's going to talk.'

Brad was right. But I knew where to find her and it was me she would be talking to.

'I did learn that Nancy Alverson had a boyfriend,' Brad continued. 'I managed to track him down.'

'Jakob?'

'Yeah. Jakob Waltz. Do you know him?'

'Sort of.' I explained how he had done some art-related work for me at the café. 'In exchange, I let him hang his paintings in the café.'

Brad was nodding. 'I've seen them. He's pretty good. Not that I'm an art expert or anything.'

'Me neither, but I agree with you. He comes in the café now and again.' I hoisted my near-empty glass. 'Can I get you a refill?'

'Sure. Thanks.' Brad followed me to the galley kitchen where I put together two more drinks. I handed his glass back to him and we sat down at the kitchen table.

'As a matter of fact, Jakob came into the café the night of the murder.'

'You don't say?'

'He was looking for Nancy.'

'Interesting. Did he say why? Did he and Nancy have a date?'

'No, he told me he wanted to surprise her.'

'Maybe *surprise her* is exactly what he did,' suggested Brad.

My hand went involuntarily to my neck.

Brad stirred the margarita with his finger. 'Jakob told me he last saw Nancy a couple of days ago. According to him, they had lunch. He didn't mention anything about the day of the murder.

'Jakob said he was home working. He even showed me the painting he said he'd been finishing.' Brad frowned. 'Why would he lie?'

'Not everybody likes talking to reporters,' I chided. Carole Two mrowled. She had made herself at home atop one of the empty kitchen chairs.

'According to Detective Highsmith, Jakob had plenty of reasons to reveal as little as possible,' I said.

'Care to elaborate?'

'I'm sure you'll find out sooner or later. The detective said that Jakob has a criminal record.'

'Murder?'

'No, nothing like that. He and some friends stole a car when they were kids. Plus, he was apparently, at one time, a marijuana dealer.'

Brad whistled brightly. 'Very interesting. I'll look into that. Thanks, Maggie. Jakob certainly wouldn't want the newspaper to print anything about his troubled past.'

Brad went into reporter mode, pulling a pen and pad from the inside pocket of his jacket.

I laid my hand over his, stopping his pen. 'You aren't going to put that in the paper, are you?'

'No. It's history but it isn't news. I won't print it unless he turns out to be Nancy's killer.'

'Good.' If he had murdered Nancy, his criminal past would be the least of his worries. If he hadn't murdered her, there was no sense drudging up his less-than-stellar past.

'What time was it when Jakob went by your café that night, Maggie?'

'A little before closing. And Jakob stopped by here at the apartment last night.'

'Oh?'

'Yes. He dropped off that painting for the café.' I pointed to the brown paper-wrapped canvas on the floor near the front door.

'While he was here, I asked him if he had found Nancy that night. He said he hadn't. He seemed upset. He said that maybe if he had found her, she might still be alive.'

'Or,' Brad said, raising his brow meaningfully, 'he did find her, and that's why she's dead.'

'You really think he did it?' It was a chilling thought, especially since I had been alone with Jakob in my apartment. I thought of what Detective Highsmith had told me about the young artist.

Brad slapped his notebook down on the table. 'He's a strong suspect. Do you have a better one?'

'No. But I must say, I didn't like the high priest and priestess very much. I didn't like the way that van followed us.'

'It might have been a coincidence – the van, that is. That was the only road heading into Table Rock from that direction.'

'I suppose. I can't picture either of them with their wild hair, dressed in their outlandish purple and green robes and cloaks, sneaking in and out of Nancy's apartment to murder her.'

'Are you forgetting?' Brad smiled. 'It was Halloween. Those two would have fitted right in.'

'You're right.'

'Then there are those other people I told you about. The same ones we saw entering the high priest's HQ at the Sacred Church of Witchkraft.'

'The two guys and the lady?'

'Like I said, they were in the café the day Nancy was killed and she didn't seem happy about it.'

'I wish I knew who they were,' Brad said, thoughtfully. 'Had you ever seen them before?'

'Not that I can remember. They may not be local.' I realized I hadn't mentioned them to Detective Highsmith. I wondered if he was aware of them.

'You know, no offense,' Brad began while tapping out a beat with his pen against his pad, 'I had been wondering why Nancy chose to send that flash drive to you instead of Jakob. He was her boyfriend, after all.'

'She certainly knew Jakob better than she knew me.'

'That's my point. Maybe she knew him *too* well.'

Then it dawned on me. 'You mean she might have known about his criminal past?'

Brad nodded.

There was a loud knock on the door, followed by another. Carole Two shot off for the bedroom.

For a moment, I wondered if it could be Jakob Waltz returning. Then I remembered that Mark Highsmith had said he would be stopping by. I pushed back my chair and rose. 'That will be Detective Highsmith.' The pounding started up again. 'I had better let him in.'

Brad wrapped his hand around my wrist. 'What's he doing here?'

'He's come to get that.' I pointed to the envelope on the table beside my couch. The note Nancy had scrawled stuck to the outside. 'He said it could be evidence. He's got my laptop, too. He said they want to check it for fingerprints.'

'Ms Miller! Are you in there?' Highsmith hollered through the door.

'Coming!' I scurried to the door, fluffing my hair as I went. I yanked the door open. 'Hello, Detective Highsmith. You came.' I glanced back inside. Brad was moving around.

'Yeah. Where are the envelope and note? I'm sort of in a hurry.'

I stepped aside. 'Come on in, I'll get them for you.'

Highsmith preceded me.

I spotted Carole Two peeking from behind the bedroom door. 'You two—'

I was about to say 'know each other' but the kitchen table was empty. Brad's chair was vacant. Only the newspaper remained. 'Hello?' I called.

'Who are you talking to?' Detective Highsmith was looking at me funny.

I chewed my lip. Where the devil had Brad gone? Bathroom? No, the door was ajar . . . unless he was hiding behind the door or in the shower. But why would he do that?

'Nobody,' I answered. 'I mean, the cat.' I wiggled my fingers at C2. 'You remember Carole Two, don't you, Detective?'

Detective Highsmith's funny look got even funnier and his brow furrowed deep enough to plant corn. His eyes took in the room. 'Ah. Is that it there?'

Even as he pointed, he crossed the short distance to the end table. He picked up the envelope. His lips moved as he read Nancy's note. Next, he pushed open the envelope and took a look inside. He slid the note back into the envelope and stared at the address and post-mark on the outside. 'Anything else?'

'What do you mean?'

'I mean, is this it?' He waved the envelope. 'Nancy didn't leave you anything else, did she?'

'No, that's it.'

Detective Highsmith moved to the kitchen table. He looked at the two margarita glasses. 'Am I interrupting something?' He did a turn around the room. 'Have you got company?'

The truth was I didn't know if I had company or not.

I walked to the front door without addressing his comment. 'Thanks for stopping by, Detective. If you learn anything, I hope you'll let me know.'

Detective Highsmith didn't respond.

I opened the door. 'Will I be getting my laptop back soon?'

'A day or two at most.' Highsmith's eyes were still moving around the apartment as if looking for hidden menaces. Finally, he opened the door and stopped, one foot in, one foot out. 'I mentioned to VV that you would be dropping by tomorrow afternoon. Does that work for you?'

I muffled a sigh. Despite my misgivings, I was determined to go through with it. 'Her office or the penthouse?'

'Neither.'

'I heard your girlfriend has been hard to find lately. Where is she hiding?'

Highsmith bristled. 'Who told you she was hiding?'

'Brad Smith.'

'He's wrong.' Highsmith was quick to reply. 'VV hasn't been in the mood to talk to reporters. She's been laying low at Casa Mirasol.'

'Her father's house?'

'Yeah. I'll get you the address.'

'That won't be necessary.' Practically everybody in Table Rock knew where Casa Mirasol was.

We agreed a time for me to go pay a social call on VV, then the detective drove off.

When I got back inside my apartment, I searched the bathroom and the bedroom. Brad was gone. I went to the kitchen to prepare dinner. That was when I noticed the sliding glass door to the patio was ajar.

That explained how Brad had disappeared, but not why.

FIFTEEN

Kelly called in sick and mom was teaching a morning yoga class at Sol Serena, so it was only me and Aubrey running things at the café in the morning.

Fortunately for us, if not my bank balance, business was slow.

With only two hours left before closing, I was filling a large cola order when the soda dispenser started making a strange whirring sound. Cola sputtered from the spout then stopped, the cup less than half full. I pulled the cup back from the valve lever then pressed it against the machine again. The machine sputtered and whirred some more. Another ounce or two of caramel-colored liquid spat out – mostly onto my arm.

Then the soda machine stopped completely.

I peered into the cup. A little more foam but still hardly more than half a cup of soda. I turned to my customer at the counter. 'Sorry, ma'am. The machine seems to be on the fritz.' I snapped a lid over the drink. 'My treat.'

She nodded a thanks, took the cola and went out the door. Straight across the street to Karma Koffee.

I banged my fist against the soda dispenser. 'On the fritz, again. That's the second time in as many months.'

'I'll call Mr Hooper.'

'Good idea.' Mr Hooper ran Hooper Commercial Equipment Repair. 'His card is in back.'

'I know.' Aubrey sighed.

She should. His magnetic card was affixed to the refrigerator in back and we had had too many occasions to call him.

'Uh, Maggie?'

I turned to see Aubrey looking at me. 'Something more on your mind? Spit it out.'

'It's about this.' She rubbed her hand against the metallic water reservoir of the espresso maker.

'What about it?' The machine now sat on the counter beside the soda dispenser. We had completed its once-over. It looked beautiful sitting there, taking on a golden hue as the rays of sun bounced off its shiny surface. Kelly had been right when she'd claimed it looked something like a steampunk spaceship. I could imagine it blasting off into the big blue Arizona sky.

As good as it looked, the espresso maker would look even better once our coffee cup shipment got delivered and I could start seeing a return on my investment.

'I truly, truly wish you'd get rid of it.'

'Get rid of it? Let's not start this again, Aubrey.' I tucked my hands under my armpits. 'You don't really believe that thing is cursed?'

She lowered her eyes.

'Do you?'

'Well . . .' She set her hand atop the malfunctioning soda dispenser. 'How do you explain this?'

'You think the espresso machine is responsible?'

Aubrey blushed but didn't deny it.

I walked over with a smile on my face. 'It's just a coffee maker. A fancy one, I grant you. But that's all.' I tapped it. 'Nothing magical or malevolent or cursed about it.'

Aubrey pulled a face. 'I wouldn't be so sure . . .'

'Fine.' I could see the poor girl wasn't going to let go of whatever was gnawing at her. 'Tell me, why do you think it's cursed?'

She shrugged with an accompanying blush. 'It just is, that's all. Ask Lee. Ask Terry and Chris. Ask Mr and Mrs Gregory.'

I pulled my brows together. Those were all names of Karma Koffee employees, plus the owners.

Aubrey continued speaking. 'Ask practically anybody at Karma Koffee, for that matter.'

'What do you mean? What does Karma Koffee have to do with *my* espresso machine?'

Aubrey's eyes widened with surprise. 'Because your espresso machine used to be Karma Koffee's espresso machine,' she explained. 'Didn't you know? I thought you knew?'

I shook my head side to side. A coldness grew in the pit of my stomach.

'They only got rid of it because of the curse.'

I looked at the floor, waiting for a gaping black hole to open up and swallow me. Maybe one of those vortexes the New Agers were always talking about.

Nothing happened.

I was stuck right where I was.

'Are you trying to tell me I bought Rob and Trish Gregory's old espresso machine?'

Aubrey nodded.

'Rob and Trish's *cursed* espresso machine?'

She nodded once more, looking uncomfortable. 'I thought you knew,' she repeated at a whisper.

'Are you serious?' I slapped my face with my icy fingers. 'I had no idea! I would never—'

'Excuse me.' A voice called from the counter. 'Is that thing working? Can we get some espresso?'

Aubrey and I spun around together.

I tried to contain my surprise. It was the woman and the two men, one of whom had been seen arguing with Nancy and all of whom Brad and I had seen at the Sacred Church of Witchkraft.

I smiled. 'Good afternoon, folks. I'm sorry, but the espresso machine is not quite ready yet. Rather, it is, but we're waiting on our shipment of glassware.'

I grabbed the ordering pad, ignoring Aubrey's snort of derision – or was it fear? 'We should be getting them in anytime now.' I tapped my pencil against the counter. 'What can I get you?'

The three of them conferred, settling on three orders of pumpkin spice beignets, two coffees and a soda. 'I'm sorry,' I explained, 'the soda machine is temporarily on the fritz. How about some tea or lemonade, ma'am?'

'Do you have green tea?' she asked sternly. Dyed brown hair draped around her heart-shaped face. Her lipgloss was pale pink. Her eyes were blue and a couple of shades lighter than her fancy wool business dress. The men wore dark suits and sunglasses.

'As a matter of fact, we do.' My sister had insisted on it. We got more requests for it than I would have imagined.

The taller man pulled out his wallet to pay for all of them. Clearly, he was the man in charge. I took his twenty and handed him some change. I'd been hoping he'd pay with a credit card so I could learn his name.

Desperate to know who they were, I tried striking up some conversation as I fried up their order. 'Nice weather we're having, isn't it?' I called. 'I suppose this is normal for this time of year.'

I looked at them expectantly.

'I suppose,' the tall, older man answered.

'I'll get a table, Alan,' the woman said. Taking her tea from
Aubrey, she moved to the table in the corner at the window where
Nancy had been sitting the day she was murdered.

The shorter of the two men, narrow-shouldered, with curly, black,
longish sideburns that came to a point near his jawbone, glanced at
me then went with her, carrying two coffees.

I tried again. 'I haven't been here that long. I'm still getting used
to what the seasons are like.' When no response was forthcoming,
I took a more direct aim. 'Are you folks from around here?'

'No.'

'Oh?' I scooped nine beignets from the fryer and set them on
the drip tray for a minute. 'In town visiting – that's nice. Business
or pleasure?' I picked up the shaker and sent a cascade of powdered
sugar over the hot donuts.

'If you do it right, business is always pleasure,' the tall stranger
replied. He ran his tongue along his upper lip as if he'd enjoyed
the taste of what he had said.

I plated their beignets and placed them on a tray. 'You know,
even though you're visiting, we have a weekly giveaway. All you
have to do is drop your business card in the jar to enter.'

'Huh?' Aubrey whispered.

'No, thanks.' His hands reached for the tray.

'Are you sure? Free coffee and beignets, a twenty-dollar value.
Good anytime up to a year.'

I saw hesitation – or maybe annoyance with me – on his face.

'Fine.' He set his attaché case on the floor. Long, manicured
fingers reached into the wallet in his back pocket. He extricated a
business card, white with gold lettering.

I took the card from his outstretched fingers and looked at it
quickly: Alan Steven Klopton, President, ASK Financial Services,
Las Vegas, NV. There was a website address, an 800 number, email
address and another telephone number with a 702 area code.

'Great. Aubrey, drop this in the jar, would you, dear?'

'Uh . . . OK.' She took the card from me. I hoped he didn't notice
the way she was looking around wondering what to do with it.

'What about your friends? Wouldn't they like to enter?'

'I don't think so.' Mr Klopton slipped his wallet back in his
pocket.

He reached for the tray. I held on to it by the lip at the other
end. 'Come on,' I said. 'It will increase your odds.'

I could tell by the look on Alan Klopton's face that he was growing weary of me. He walked stiffly to the table, where they handed him their business cards with amused looks on their faces.

Klopton passed me the additional business cards.

I glanced at the names on the cards before giving them to Aubrey, too. Gary Busby and Stephanie Headley, both with ASK Financial Services. Gary was a VP. Stephanie was a comptroller, whatever the devil that was.

My dead ex-husband, Brian, would probably know, seeing how he used to work in banking. Not that I was about to call him for the answer.

Aubrey had been resourceful. She had gone to the supply room, found an empty glass chocolate sauce jar and carried it out front. She dropped the two cards in with Klopton's and gave it a shake, looking at me the entire time.

'Your jar looks rather empty,' Ms Headley remarked with a touch of suspicion.

'It's the beginning of the contest week.' I grinned. 'So far, your odds of winning are high.'

He joined his associates at the table. While they ate and drank, the three of them studied some papers that Klopton had pulled from his attaché case.

I grabbed a clean, damp towel. 'I'll bus the tables.'

Aubrey grabbed the corner of the towel and held on. 'I'll do that, Maggie. It's my job.'

'That's OK.' I tugged the towel free. 'I feel like it.'

I strolled out from behind the counter and worked my way toward their table. My only other customers were a pair of college-aged kids, a young man and woman, soaking up the sun and looking at their cellphones while they dawdled over their coffee and beignets.

I was working my way closer to my target when the café telephone rang and Audrey answered. 'It's for you, Maggie!'

'Who is it?' I called. Only a couple of feet from the threesome and their papers, I could make out a bunch of columns and figures but none of it made sense.

'It's Mark Highsmith and he wants to talk to you.' Aubrey waved for me to come. 'He says it's urgent.'

'Detective Mark Highsmith? Maybe he has some information about that lovely young woman who was strangled in her apartment across the street,' I said, loud and clear.

I watched Klopton and the others out of the corner of my eye. They had stopped whispering and were eying me intently. I seemed to have struck a nerve.

A frown line appeared between Aubrey's eyes. 'Maybe. Are you coming or what?' One ear was pressed to the phone. 'He sounds angry.'

I retreated and took the phone from Aubrey. 'Yes, what is it, Detective?' My eyes were glued to Klopton and his cronies.

'Ms Miller, what are you doing there?'

'Working,' I said, confused. 'What would you expect? Tell me,' I turned and whispered into the phone, before he could interrupt with another dumb question, 'what do you know about Alan Klopton and ASK Financial Services?'

'I don't know anything about him or it.' He sounded vexed. 'What I know about you is that you promised to go spend a little time with VV.'

'And I will. You have my word.'

'Your word was that you would be there at two o'clock. It is two-thirty now.'

'Oh.' I glanced at the clock. 'So it is.'

'I told VV that you would be there in ten minutes. Don't make me look bad.'

'I'm leaving now.' I handed the telephone back to Aubrey. Klopton and his companions had disappeared. 'Can you handle everything alone until closing, Aubrey?'

'I guess. Where are you going?'

'I promised a certain somebody that I'd spend some time with my BFF.'

Audrey arched her brow. 'Who might that be?'

'Veronica Vargas, of course.'

Audrey chuckled. 'Oh, 'course.'

I grabbed my coat from the back and rolled my bike to the front of the store. 'Thanks, dear!'

'Wait!' Aubrey called from behind the counter. 'What do you want me to do with this?' She held up the jar that held the business cards.

'Can you make up a little sign and tape it to the jar? We may as well make it a real contest.'

'Sure.' She set the jar next to the smaller tip jar at the register.

I leaned my bike against the wall. I went to the jar, grabbed Alan

Klopton's business card and slipped it into the pocket of my coat.
'See you tomorrow!'

SIXTEEN

C asa Mirasol was an elegant estate in the toniest neighborhood in town. It was located within steps of the Table Rock Hotel and Convention Center, the town's popular upscale resort.

Most of the Spanish-influence adobe homes in the enclave were barely visible to the naked eye, except for sculpted, earth-toned rooflines and their upper stories where they had them, unless their driveway gates were open, because these sprawling homes were built in the courtyard style with walls running all around the properties.

The people who lived in these homes had money and lots of it. They also placed a high value on their privacy.

Casa Mirasol was no exception. The house sat against the edge of the hills and had million-dollar red rock views.

I coasted to a stop outside the massive, intricately carved wooden gates at the driveway to Casa Mirasol. Each gate contained a carved, two foot in diameter sunflower.

Straddling my bike, I pressed the intercom.

'Yes?' came the tinny voice.

'Maggie Miller. I'm here to see Ms Vargas.'

'One moment.'

A minute later the gates lurched, then opened wide. I walked my bike inside. The courtyard was huge and filled with a variety of plants. I recognized prickly lettuce, golden rod, scarlet creeper and black foot daisies along with enormous cacti and other succulents. A couple of gurgling fountains added nature's music to the surroundings. Stone benches provided seating.

The big gates eased shut behind me and I was isolated from the world. But not nature. I'd never seen anything like it.

But I could get used to it.

I'd have to sell a lot of beignets, though . . .

The top half of the door to the main house was stained glass, the bottom some sort of exotic wood. I left my Schwinn at the side of the long drive and walked up the flagstone path to the entrance.

A rotund man in a creamy guayabera opened the door on my approach. 'Ms Vargas will be with you in a moment.'

He instructed me to wait in the foyer and disappeared down a long hall with a Saltillo tile floor.

The interior of the house was all stucco walls and Southwestern décor. I strolled to the entrance of the dining room. It was big enough to hold a troop of Girl Scouts. Two identical sculpted bronze chandeliers hung from the tall ceiling.

A telephone rang someplace far off and I heard a muffled voice answer it. There was still no sign of VV. I wouldn't have been surprised if the man who'd let me in returned to tell me she was unavailable or unable to see me.

I wouldn't have cared if he had.

I heard low voices on the other side of the house and wandered toward them, admiring artwork that looked like it had been collected from exotic locales the world over.

Peering obliquely through a pair of highly-polished double doors with glass inserts, I saw Mayor Vargas seated at a plush brown leather sofa at an angle to a massive fireplace of river rock and flagstone. He was smoking a thick cigar. I moved closer under the protection of a pale lavender vase at the corner that contained tall dried cattails.

Gary Busby and Stephanie Headley occupied a smaller leather sofa and Alan Klopton was seated in a leather chair with a wooden frame. Klopton was doing most of the talking. The mayor nodded, adding an occasional word. I did not notice any animosity among them. It all seemed rather cozy and friendly. I couldn't hear a sound.

What was their conversation all about?

What did Mayor Vargas, Nancy Alverson's murder and the Sacred Church of Witchkraft have in common? Where did ASK Financial Services fit in?

I felt a tug on the back of my coat.

'What are you doing?'

Veronica Vargas glared at me.

'Hi,' I stammered. 'There you are.'

'What are you doing snooping on my father?'

'Snooping? No.' I extricated myself from behind the plant. 'I was admiring the pot. I wanted to get a look at it from the other side.' I glanced at the window. 'Is that your father in there?'

'Come on,' VV said with a world-weary sigh, as if entertaining me in her familial home was a heavy burden.

Dressed in gray velour pants and a white cashmere sweater with slip-on shoes, VV was far more casually dressed than I was used to seeing her. Her hair fell luxuriously around her face. Though that face did look a bit drawn and tired. Even VV's fancy makeup couldn't cover the worry lines.

I followed her out the front door. Was she getting rid of me so soon?

'I'm staying in the *casita*,' she explained as we stepped along a flagstone path beside the house. The path led to a small adobe bungalow near the swimming pool.

Like the main house, the door to the *casita* contained a beautiful stained-glass insert. The interior of the guest house was every bit as fancy and immaculate as the main house, too. A hint of flowery perfume hung in the air. The room's décor continued the distinct Southwestern flair.

A painting over the stone fireplace showed a woman in a black dress with white lace trim. The mature woman had dark hair piled high on her head and looked a lot like VV.

'My great-grandmother,' VV said, catching my gaze. 'Granddaddy built the *casita* for her.'

'Your grandfather built Casa Mirasol?'

'Yes. It's been renovated and modernized over the years but the bones are the same.'

And lovely bones they were. The *casita*'s open kitchen was nearly as large as my whole apartment and appointed with chef-grade appliances.

'Does the name *mirasol* have any particular significance?'

'*Mirasol* means sunflower in Spanish. The sunflower is native to Mexico, which is where my family has its roots.'

'Do you still have family there?'

'Of course, but Table Rock has been our home since the eighteen hundreds.'

'Wow. I'm still working on year one.'

'Have a seat.' VV crossed to the bar and poured herself a drink. 'Would you care for a Bloody Mary?'

'OK, sure.' I wasn't particularly thirsty, but a girl should never have to drink alone. I accepted the drink and took a sip. 'This is the best Bloody Mary I've ever had.' I stirred the thick, dark red liquid with my celery stalk.

'The trick is to let the ingredients marinate for twenty-four hours or more.'

VV slipped off her shoes, picked up her drink and carried it to a butter-colored leather sofa that looked out over the pool patio. 'Have a seat.' She set her drink on a low glass table, curling her legs under herself as she sat.

I claimed a pillow-backed rocking chair near the sofa. Remembering that I was there to provide solace, as Highsmith requested, I asked, 'How are you holding up, Veronica?'

'Fine.'

VV didn't sound fine.

'Good.' I stared at the floor for a moment. 'Mark was concerned you might be depressed.'

'I don't get depressed.'

'Right. Still,' I shifted in my seat, 'you must be tired of all the questions, the police, the reporters . . .'

'Reporters are toads.'

'Right,' I said again. 'Then you aren't worried about—'

'I don't get worried,' interrupted VV.

'Of course not. Why would you?' I felt sweat building up under my armpits. We were both finding this awkward. I set my Bloody Mary on the tile-topped iron table beside the rocker. 'I'm sure we can both agree that this has been a mistake. I should probably go.'

'Go?' VV appeared surprised. 'Yes, I suppose you're right. Mark gets some crazy ideas sometimes.'

'Tell me about it,' I quipped. Getting me to come comfort VV and act like her bestie had been his craziest yet.

'He's a good detective.'

'The best.' I picked up my purse.

'You know, I believe he actually thinks I might be guilty.'

'You don't say.' I moved to the door.

I heard her chuckle softly behind my back. 'He thinks I'm keeping secrets.'

My hand went to the doorknob and I froze. 'Secrets?' I turned around. 'Are you? Keeping secrets, I mean?' Was Veronica Vargas about to spill her guts?

The corner of VV's lip turned down. She extended her legs and stared up at the beamed cathedral ceiling. 'I wish I had never gone to Nancy Alverson's apartment that night . . .'

I hurried silently back to my chair and sat. I picked up my

unfinished Bloody Mary. 'Tell me about it. Why did you really go see Nancy on Halloween night?'

VV's prior claim that she had been jealous that Mark Highsmith and Nancy might have been having an affair had always seemed absurd and false to me.

VV swiveled her head my way and wiggled her toes. 'I was helping her with her research.'

'Research? You mean the book she was writing?'

'That's right.' VV sat up. 'You know about that?'

'Yes, I heard about it. Nancy used to come into the café.' I wasn't about to tell her that at one time I'd had a copy of that work-in-progress. I'd let VV think that Nancy had told me herself. Since Nancy had sent me the flash drive, she had, in a sense, done just that. 'What did she want from you?'

'Oh, the usual, background about the town and its history. As you know, the Vargas family goes way back. She wanted to pick my brain for ideas and stories.'

'Did she talk to anybody else in your family?'

'She might have talked to Daniel. You'd have to ask him. She originally tried to talk to Daddy but he was too busy to talk to her. That's how Nancy and I originally met.'

'Did you read her manuscript? Do you know what sort of book she was writing?'

'A history of the region, I suppose. I never read it, although she promised me a copy when it was published.'

'So, on Halloween night, you went to see her because she wanted to interview you some more?'

VV finished her drink and crossed to the pitcher at the bar. 'Care for a refill?' She broke off a couple stalks of fresh celery.

I did and said so. She brought the pitcher to me and refilled my glass. 'Thanks. You were saying?'

She slid a fresh celery stalk into my glass.

After filling her own glass, VV crossed to a wide picture window overlooking the pool and gazed outward. She pulled out the celery stalk and took a small bite before speaking. 'Nancy had been . . . interviewing me earlier. When Mark got the call while we were at Hopping Mad and had to leave, I thought I would run over to Nancy's apartment and continue our conversation there.'

'So Nancy was not expecting you?'

'No.'

'When you got there, did you see anybody else?'

VV turned, a wan smile on her face. 'You sound just like Mark now. He questioned me a lot. Too much. I told him I might never forgive him.' Her smile turned coquettish. 'I will, though. Just don't tell him I said so,' she added with a wink. 'To answer your question, the only person I saw was you.'

'You didn't see Jakob Waltz?'

VV's pert little nose wrinkled up. 'Who?'

'He and Nancy were seeing each other.'

'Oh, yes.' VV resumed her seat at the sofa. 'Nancy mentioned him a time or two. No, I've never met him. I got the impression that it was not serious.'

I took a generous drink before asking my next question. 'What were you and Nancy arguing about at lunch the day she was murdered?'

VV's eyelashes fluttered quickly. 'Arguing? What makes you think we were arguing?'

'Hopping Mad is a busy place. There were witnesses.'

'We were having a lively discussion,' replied VV. 'Anybody who implies anything else is flat-out wrong. And,' she said, leveling her gaze on me, 'liable to be sued.'

I had a feeling my visit was coming to an end, and an ugly one at that. Therefore, I had nothing to lose in asking my next question. 'Who are those people in the house talking to Mayor Vargas?'

'What people?' VV had decided to stonewall.

'Alan Klopton, Gary Busby and Stephanie Headley.' I stared right back at her in defiance. 'ASK Financial Services. Who are they? What do they want?'

'You'd have to ask Daddy that question. They are probably here on town business.'

'Town business or personal business?'

'What is that supposed to mean, Ms Miller?'

'What do they have to do with Nancy Alverson's murder?'

'I think we have indulged Mark enough.' She banged her empty glass on the table and jumped to her feet. 'You had better go.'

'What were those people doing at the Sacred Church of Witchkraft?'

VV grabbed my purse and pushed it into my hands.

'What does the church have to do with the town of Table Rock and your father, the mayor?'

'Goodbye, Ms Miller.' She gave me a nudge out the door.

As I headed indignantly to my bicycle, having been so ignomini- ously ejected from the *casita*, I noticed that the mayor was still in conference with Klopton and his associates.

But I had no clue what was going on.

SEVENTEEN

'I'm telling you, Laura, Veronica Vargas is hiding something. I just don't know what it is.'

I had filled her in on my visit to VV and the puzzling events of the past few days, from Nancy Alverson's last morning in the café to my ill-advised visit with the mayor's daughter.

I needed somebody to talk – and vent – to. Laura's Lightly Used was on my way home from Casa Mirasol. I needed a friend, a real friend.

Luckily, Laura Duval was at her store. Laura was about my size, with inquisitive blue eyes and ash-blonde hair. Her nature was as friendly and unassuming as was her dress. I liked her a lot.

'Maybe it's the fact that she strangled Nancy Alverson,' Laura suggested.

Today she wore a flowing blue print skirt and baby blue turtleneck and ankle boots. Her hair was styled in a fashionable A-line bob but I had a feeling she'd had the cut long before it had become popular.

'Maybe,' I conceded. Having VV locked up for murder would certainly get the woman out of my hair, but I couldn't come up with a plausible explanation for what would have provoked her to strangle Nancy Alverson.

A customer wandered by and we held our tongues until she was gone. We were seated in a couple of bamboo-framed chairs in the far right corner of the thrift shop. The chairs were for sale, like everything else in sight. If we sat still long enough, we'd be for sale too.

'Did you ask VV about the tea?' Laura asked. I had told Laura what Detective Highsmith had told me about Nancy's tea being drugged.

'No. Shoot, I forgot.'

'It would be illuminating to know how the sleeping medication got in the tea.' Laura removed her earrings – delicate silver pentacles. She set them in her lap and rubbed her earlobes. 'Assuming she didn't put it there herself, which, I agree, seems unlikely.'

'The tea was in a Karma Koffee takeout cup. I'm guessing that Nancy had a guest, probably the same guest that killed her. They must have drugged the tea at some point when she wasn't looking.'

'Still,' Laura jiggled the earrings in her hand, 'it had to be a friend, someone she trusted.'

'Exactly. The question is who? Anybody could have gone up to her apartment from the street without passing anyone else on the way up,' I said. 'The only time there's much traffic on the stairs is before and after classes at the yoga studio on the second floor.'

Laura put her earrings back in her lobes. 'These things always make me itch. They are supposed to be silver but I think they're plated. It's the nickel I'm allergic to.'

'They are nice. Don't tell me you're a witch too? You aren't a member of the Sacred Church of Witchkraft, are you, Laura?'

'No.' Laura laughed. 'Why do you say that?'

'The earrings. They're pentacles.' I explained how several of the robed members wore similar, although not identical, objects around their necks.

Laura removed her left earring and held it between her fingers. 'I don't know about witches. The pentacle represents the four elements of nature. This point,' she indicated the lower left point, 'represents the earth. The upper left point is air. Fire is the lower right point and water is the upper right.'

'And the fifth point?'

'The divine spirit.' Laura looked embarrassed. 'Silly, I guess.' She replaced the earring and shook her hair. 'Was this Nancy person into witches?'

'There was something about witches in her manuscript but it mostly seemed to concern church business more than witchcraft itself.' I pressed my palms into my forehead. 'I wish I had made a copy of that book so I could read the rest of it.'

'It still seems quite odd that she sent it to you. You were almost a complete stranger.'

'Brad said the same thing. I think that's exactly the reason why she mailed the flash drive to me. I was the last person on earth anybody would expect her to send it to.'

'That makes sense.'

'What I can't understand is why was Nancy killed?'

'From everything you've been telling me, it sounds like somebody didn't like what she was writing.'

'Yes, but, I mean, why now?'

Laura could only shrug. 'Do the police have any suspects besides Veronica?'

'If they do, they aren't sharing them with me. I'm hoping Brad will be able to come up with something on those ASK Financial people. There was a lot of business stuff in that manuscript. Nancy talked about fraud and all sorts of financial shenanigans. I think she was trying to build a case for something. I just may never know what without knowing how her book was going to end.' I yawned. The day was taking its toll on me. 'I'll talk to Brad. Hopefully, he's learned something.'

Laura grinned. 'What's going on with you and Brad?'

'Nothing,' I said, crossing my legs. 'We're sharing information.'

'Sharing any saliva yet?' Laura made kissing movements with her lips.

'Stop that,' I insisted. 'You're disgusting. Besides, it's not what you think.'

'He's cute,' teased Laura.

'He looks like my ex-husband,' I said sharply.

'Interesting,' Laura said, tapping her index finger against her cheek. 'It sounds like Brad is exactly your type.'

'Do you think we could get back to the subject of Nancy Alverson for a minute?' I'd had enough talk about my love life, or lack thereof. 'If I want to be on the receiving end of a hard time, I'll talk dating with Donna and Mom.'

'Sorry.' Laura's giggle said otherwise.

I gave her a look that brought the giggle to a halt. 'I learned from the police that Jakob Waltz, Nancy's boyfriend, has a criminal record. He lives here in Table Rock.'

'Jakob Waltz?' Laura rubbed her forehead. 'I think I know him. An artist, right?'

'That's right.'

Laura nodded. 'He's bought painting materials and a couple of secondhand easels from me. You say he has a criminal record?'

I explained about Jakob's past. 'And he was definitely in the area around the time Nancy was murdered.'

'So it could be that Nancy's murder has nothing to do with what she was working on. It might have been a lover's quarrel.'

'I must admit, after Nancy's murder he did seem more concerned than distraught.'

Laura nodded. 'Think about it. Strangulation. That does sound like an act of passion, doesn't it?'

'You're right. I may have been looking at this all wrong. I'm going to have to see what more I can find out about Nancy's relationship with Jakob, and pin down what he did and where he went after leaving the café that night.'

'Surely the police would have asked him those same questions?'

'Jakob says he was home. I'm not sure if the police have verified that or not. I have no idea how seriously they may be treating him as a suspect.' I worried my lip. 'Detective Highsmith did warn me to keep my distance from Jakob.'

Laura's brow went up. 'I'd listen to that advice if I were you, Maggie. Jakob may or may not be a murderer, but he does have a criminal record. I still can't get over Highsmith asking you of all people to go and try to console Veronica.'

'You and me both. It's funny, though. For a few minutes there, I thought we might really bond. After that, I thought she might stomp on me like a bug.'

'Veronica Vargas seems quite inscrutable. You said she argued with Nancy?'

'So?'

'Maybe she got angry enough at her to want to stomp on her like a bug, too.'

'I don't know why I bother talking to you,' I joked. 'You give me more questions than answers.'

'That's what friends are for – somebody to bounce ideas off.'

'Somebody to sell evil espresso makers to?'

'What?'

'That espresso maker you sold me.'

'The La Floriano?' Laura said with surprise.

'That's the one.'

'What about it?'

'Like I said, it's evil. More precisely, it's cursed.'

Laura cast a dubious eye at me. 'Cursed, Maggie? How many Bloody Marys did you have this afternoon?'

'Not enough, and that's beside the point. If you don't believe me that the machine is cursed, just ask Aubrey. She's the one who told me.'

'She must have been pulling your leg.'

'Nope, she believes it. One hundred percent. And, while I'd never admit it to her, I'm starting to believe it myself. I mean, my life has not been exactly running like a well-oiled machine since you sold me that evil thing.'

'In the first place, the La Floriano is a wonderful antique espresso maker. I gave you that machine at barely above cost, as I remember.'

'Sure, probably because you wanted to get the cursed thing out of your store.'

'Very funny.'

'Did you know that Rob and Trish Gregory previously owned that espresso maker?'

'They were the ones who sold it to me. Of course, they did seem very eager to sell it. They sold it to me cheap, too.'

I could tell Laura was razzing me now.

She wiggled her fingers in the air. 'Probably because of the malevolent spirit that inhabits it. That's it, Maggie! Your espresso machine has been possessed!' She leaned toward me, elbows on her knees. 'Would you like me to arrange an exorcism for you?'

'OK, maybe it's not possessed.' I pointed a finger at her. 'You, on the other hand, might be.'

We both laughed.

'Seriously, Maggie. If there's anything at all wrong with the espresso machine or you are simply unhappy with it, I'd be happy to buy it back.'

'No, I couldn't ask you to do that.' I sulked. There was no good way out. I was stuck with the cursed machine. I could throw it in the Grand Canyon but I was pretty sure there were laws against such things.

'OK, if that's what you want. Remember, the offer of the exorcism still stands.'

One of Laura's assistants, Robin Pahe, a twentysomething Navajo woman with liquid brown eyes, interrupted. 'Excuse me, Laura. A customer is asking if you can do better on the price of that Frigidaire chest freezer.'

Laura rose with an accompanying sigh. 'Let me go see which one you mean. Tell them I'll be right there.'

Robin nodded and left.

Turning to me, Laura said, 'Sorry, Maggie. Enough girl talk. Duty calls.'

'No problem. I have to go feed the cat and get ready for my yoga class.' I stood and gathered my coat and purse.

'You're taking a yoga class? That sounds fun. Maybe I'll join you.'

'Great. It's the beginners' class at Yoga By Rob.'

'OK, now I know I'm hearing things.' Laura tugged at her ears. 'First you tell me that your espresso machine is cursed, next you tell you are taking a yoga class, and then you tell me that Rob Gregory is the teacher?' Her voice rose in pitch.

She knew how much Rob and Trish irritated me.

'His yoga studio and his store are directly below Nancy Alverson's apartment.'

Understanding came to Laura's face. 'Oh, you're going to snoop. That I get. Maybe I'll pass for now.'

Laura rearranged the pillows on our chairs. 'Let me know if you learn anything interesting.'

I promised I would.

Back at the apartment, I fed Carole Two and gave her a rubdown with some weird glove my sister had given me when the cat came to live with me. The red glove was peppered with soft silicone tips that were supposed to massage the scalp and remove loose hair.

Carole Two liked it.

I loved it. Yes, there were times that I massaged my head, shoulders and lower back with the glove. In fact, I was thinking of buying a second one so I could use them in tandem.

Thinking about Donna and Andy reminded me of the promise that I had made to my nephew, Connor. I wasn't looking forward to that conversation any more now than I had been at the time he had asked me. It wouldn't be fair to put it off much longer.

But one more day couldn't hurt, and I didn't have time that night.

I nuked my dinner, a delicious frozen chicken pot pie that contained more grams of fat than protein – trust me, always an essential statistic if you wanted flavor over nutrition, which I, as a rule, did.

I ate quickly and held myself to one glass of wine. After all, I had a bicycle to ride in the dark and a yoga class to attend. Most of all, I wanted to keep my wits about me and see if I could learn anything new about Nancy Alverson's murder.

My hope was to get a chance to take a look in the apartment. With luck, that might just happen.

Unfortunately, I hadn't had time to go shopping for yoga clothes. I threw open the closet and looked at my meager selection. Rob would not be happy if I showed up in my Maggie's Beignet Café outfit.

I riffled through the hangers and opened and closed drawers. Nothing seemed right. I finally settled on a simple short-sleeved black T-shirt with an embroidered white poodle with a pink bow between her ears in the center, and my best pair of sweatpants – dark blue with only one tiny hole in the butt from when I'd accidently sat on a fork I had left behind on the sofa.

I studied my image in the bathroom mirror. Not terrible. And, if I tugged down the T-shirt, the hole in the butt didn't show at all.

Satisfied, I grabbed a headband for good measure. Having watched Mom do her full-body contortions, I knew I was in for some mind and body-bending exercises and wanted to be prepared.

I even put on my best pair of cotton socks, blue-and-white striped with red chili peppers. They had been a Valentine's Day present from my dead ex-husband. The socks were in perfect condition because I had never worn them.

Now was the time.

I threw a fleece jacket on, told Carole Two to hold down the fort and pedaled to Karma Koffee.

EIGHTEEN

It was five minutes till seven. Rob said his class started promptly at seven. I unlocked the front door of Maggie's Beignet Café. There was no point leaving the bike exposed on the street with my shop just across the way. I rolled the Schwinn inside the café and parked it in the dining room. I grabbed my little purse from the basket and clutched it in one hand while I locked up behind me.

I ran across the street with one eye on my watch. Two minutes to seven. I was going to make it. Everything was going to be OK.

I shot a quick peep through the window of Karma Koffee, curious to see how busy the place might be at that time of night. Call it professional curiosity.

I glimpsed a familiar shape inside and slammed to a stop, sideswiping a pedestrian. 'Sorry, sorry,' I muttered.

I pressed my face to the picture window as my victim moved on with an easy look back in my direction. 'Herman?' I said out loud.

Herman the Swede stood at the counter. Lee was on the other side, handing Herman a white paper sack.

I pretended to read the newspaper in the rack attached to the sidewalk at the curb. Herman exited Karma Koffee and turned in the opposite direction.

I was about to follow him when he glanced over his shoulder and noticed me.

'Maggie Miller.' He stopped and turned. He was dressed as I had last seen him. My guess was you didn't need much variation in your wardrobe when you were treasure hunting in the mountains and the desert. The only addition to his wardrobe tonight was a bulky military-style camo jacket.

'Hi, Herman. This is a surprise.'

He crumpled the Karma Koffee bag under his left arm and quickly closed the distance between us. 'I was looking for you, Maggie Miller.'

'You were looking for me? Why?'

Herman glanced furtively around. His eyes were barely visible under his hat. 'Your beignet store was closed.'

'We aren't open at night. In fact, I'm on my way to a class.' I groaned inwardly. I was definitely going to be late now.

Herman touched the sleeve of my coat near the wrist. 'But we need to talk.' His head swiveled from side to side. His right hand, I couldn't help noticing, was gripping the handle of that deadly-looking knife he wore on his belt. 'Seriously.'

'I'm sorry.' I took a step backward. 'I really don't have time.'

A patrol car cruised slowly toward us. Herman spotted it at the same time as I did.

'Later,' he said. He turned on his heel, moved the bag to his right hand and marched with a noticeable hitch in his step down the street.

I pulled open the door and raced inside Karma Koffee. Lee was alone at the counter. 'What did Herman want?'

'Who?'

'That guy who was just in here.'

Lee grinned. 'Yeah, Table Rock gets its share of characters, doesn't it, Maggie?' He lazily wiped the counter with a white towel. 'As a matter of fact, he was asking about you.'

A chill went up my spine. 'About me?' I squeaked.

'Yeah. He said he stopped at your café and it was closed. He saw we were open, so he came in here. He bought a muffin and a coffee. I keep telling you that you ought to open in the evenings. You're losing business.'

'Believe me, it's in the works. I'm planning to expand the menu.'

'So Aubrey tells me. Good for you.'

I noticed the time on Lee's watch and gasped. 'I'm late! I'd better get upstairs.'

Lee's brow went up. 'You taking a class with Rob?'

'Yes. Wish me luck.'

'Good luck. How about a Heaven's Building Block before you go? They're fresh.'

'I really shouldn't,' I said, at the same time digging my wallet out of my purse in search of cash. 'I swear, Lee, I think you invented these muffins just for me.' The Heaven's Building Block had been his creation.

Lee wrapped up my muffin in waxed paper and dropped it gently in a bag. 'The biggest of the bunch,' he said with a smile, handing me the bag.

'Thanks.' I rushed to the exit, ran six steps, yanked open the street-level door leading upstairs to the studio and raced to the second floor. Yoga By Rob was stenciled on the solid oak door.

I threw open the door and was hit by a wall of fragrant sandal-wood. I had entered a small alcove with an open doorway leading to a larger space. The alcove contained a simple trestle table and a couple of shelves. There was a narrow door to the left.

Rob stood at the far end of the larger room. A group of men and women, mostly women in clothing that left little to the imagination, faced him.

Rob took one look at me, panting as I slammed the studio door closed behind me, and glared.

I felt like melting into the fancy rug with its abstract mountain and cloud design.

I unzipped my jacket and threw it on the small white sofa in the corner next to somebody's backpack. I took a deep breath and ran my fingers through my hair.

I was about to step out and join my new classmates, but found that Rob was blocking the entrance. 'Hi, Rob!'

'You are late, Ms Miller. Instruction began ten minutes ago.'

'Yes. Sorry about that. I had a little trouble.' I tried to edge past him but he wasn't budging. For the life of me, I didn't want to rub against him. Rob was wearing a silvery-gray sleeveless shirt with a pair of calf-length silver yoga pants. The pants were skintight.

One passing glance at his lower body was enough to scar me for life, and I made a promise to myself to avoid any below-the-waist sights thereafter.

'With you, Ms Miller, everything is always more than a little trouble.'

'Right, sorry,' I said again, determined to stay on his good side, at least for as long as it took to get some answers.

'You are not entering my studio like that.' He held up a hand while looking down his nose at me. 'And take off your shoes.'

'Oh, I didn't know.' I kicked off my shoes, suddenly self-conscious of my silly socks. I cursed my dead ex-husband and his cheap and crass idea of an anniversary gift.

Rob made *tsk-tsk* sounds. 'You are completely inappropriate. Your clothing is inharmonious, Ms Miller.'

'It is?' I tugged at the poodle on my shirt. What was so inharmonious about a curly-haired poodle? 'I didn't have time to shop.'

'It is. Yoga is about the spirit as much as it is about the body.' Rob stepped past me and went to the shelves behind the table. The long shelves contained shirts, pants, slippers, mats and more, grouped by size and sex. The guy was running a yoga lover's mini-boutique.

Rob faced the shelves. 'You'll need some clothes. And a yoga mat.' He pulled down a pale green shirt and matching pants. 'What size are you – large?'

'Medium,' I said sharply. 'At best.' I sucked in my gut.

Rob looked at me dubiously. He replaced the clothing, dug through the stack and handed me two pieces in my requested size. 'You can change in there.' He pointed to the door on the left. 'Join us when you have finished changing.'

He aimed his thumb at the wall. 'You'll need a mat, too. You can pay me after class.'

'Thanks. I'll only be a minute.' I took the clothing and opened the door to find myself in a small bathroom. I couldn't find any price tags on the items and hoped I wasn't going to be in for sticker shock. Between the cost of the class, the clothing and the mat, this was not going to be a cheap night. Too bad I wasn't a private detective – I probably could have deducted all this stuff.

Maybe even the muffin.

I struggled into the tight-fitting yoga pants, banging my elbows against the walls of the small space. The elastic waistband dug into my stomach. The material pressed to breaking point against my thighs. I should exchange them for a large but I wasn't going to give Rob the satisfaction.

I sucked in my gut again and exited the bathroom.

I selected a yoga mat from the offerings and tiptoed into the studio, remaining far in the back, careful not to create any further disruption.

A row of windows faced Laredo. Maggie's Beignet Café was visible in the glow of the streetlights.

Rob was in the middle of some sort of one-armed, one-legged, no-brained stretch. Who in their right mind would risk planting their face in the floor doing a thing like that?

A sudden gagging sensation was all I needed to remind myself once again not to look below waist level.

I rolled out my mat. I had selected a pretty blue one. It was reversible, plain blue on one side and the Tree of Life on the other. Mom would love it and I would give it to her after class – because I was never, ever coming back.

The woman next to me smiled as I lowered myself tentatively to the floor.

Up front, Rob had descended into some head down, butt up, one leg off the ground maneuver that I could never hope to replicate. Lulling instrumental New Age music played from speakers in the upper corners of the space. If he would just turn off the lights, I could have taken a nap.

Rob's personal yoga mat looked like a Southwestern magic carpet with its fringed edging and Native American motif in shades of white, grape, orange and mauve. I half-expected him and the mat to lift off the ground and zoom lazily over the class side to side while he offered comments and suggestions.

Forty-eight agonizing minutes later – yes, I was counting every bloody minute and would have counted the seconds too, if my watch had had a second hand – we were done.

Class had gone on nonstop. There had been no chance to sneak away for a second look at Nancy's apartment. Not that I had figured out a way to get inside, even if I had had the chance.

And I was finished – physically, that is.

The woman next to me told me how great I had done. 'First time?' she asked with a big white smile.

'Last time,' I quipped, wiping the sweat that poured from my face with a paper towel from the bathroom.

She laughed, rolled up her yoga mat and said, 'See you next week.'

I smiled in reply. There was never going to be a next week if I could help it.

I hobbled out to the alcove where Rob was chatting with a few of the lingering students – most of whom I noticed were of the adoring female persuasion judging by the looks in their eyes.

I wondered if any of them had ever persuaded Rob to join them on their yoga mats.

There was no sign of Rob's wife, Trish.

As the last students were leaving, I pulled my sweatpants over my yoga pants and my T-shirt over my new shirt. I stuck my shoes on my feet and pulled on my jacket. I picked up my purse and the Karma Koffee bag containing my muffin.

I saw Rob smirking at me. I should have hidden the lousy bag from his sight.

Rob handed me a bill and I handed him my credit card. For what he had charged me, class should have included roundtrip air tickets to Las Vegas with dinner and a show.

Rob ran my card through the small electronic scanner on the corner of the desk. 'What did you think of the class?' he asked.

'It was something,' I said. Something I would never forget and hoped never to repeat. 'What sadist invented yoga?'

Rob handed me back my card and pulled the receipt from the machine as it spat out. 'Yoga goes back at least five thousand years, Ms Miller. It was developed by the Indu–Sarasvati civilization in Northern India. It is a sacred tradition and art.'

He glanced at the appointment book on the desk, then closed it. 'You need to keep your mind open.'

'Sorry,' I replied, feeling as though I'd been chastened. 'I'm trying.' I dropped the yoga receipt in my purse. 'Did you ever talk yoga with Nancy? Did she ever attend your classes?'

Rob frowned at me. 'As a matter of fact, we did talk about it once or twice. She never came to class, though. She was always busy working.'

'Right, busy working on that book she was writing.'

'I suppose.'

'Do you know what she was writing about?' I asked innocently.

'Not really. It wasn't something she liked to talk about.' Rob turned his back on me, straightening the merchandise on the shelves.

'Did she have any enemies that you know of? Anybody that would want to harm her?'

Rob spun around, hands on his hips. 'Alverson was my tenant, Ms Miller. I was not her confidante or her psychologist. Why all the questions?'

'Just curious. You know.'

'No, I do not know,' Rob replied sternly. 'As for who killed her, it was probably that boyfriend of hers.'

'Jakob Waltz?'

'That's the one.'

'Why do you think he might have killed her?'

'It's late, Ms Miller. Time to leave.'

I hovered as he re-entered the main studio, turned off the music and dimmed the studio lights. 'See you next week?'

'I hope so.' That wasn't technically a lie because I did not say *where* he would possibly see me.

He moved to the door and raised a brow. 'Well?'

'Do you mind if I use the restroom before I go?' I asked in desperation.

Rob looked at me oddly. 'What's wrong with the bathroom at the apartment? You haven't clogged up the toilet again, have you?'

I grimaced. Once, maybe twice, I had poured dirty cat litter down the toilet and clogged the pipes. The Gregorys had had to call out a plumber to snake them out. Couldn't he let that go? 'I'm kind of in a hurry.'

'You have a facility at your café.'

'I forgot my key,' I answered with an apologetic shrug.

'Fine. But I am in a hurry.'

'You go ahead. I'll lock up as soon as I'm done.'

Rob gave it some thought and then agreed. Mostly, I believe he simply wanted to get away from me.

Whatever.

I listened as Rob thumped down the stairs and locked the door behind him. I grabbed my muffin bag and crossed the studio floor in my shoes. If Rob had seen me, no doubt he would have screamed bloody murder.

What he didn't see wasn't going to hurt him.

There was a door at the far end. If I was right, it matched the general location of the door I had seen in Nancy's apartment.

The door locked from the inside. I unlocked it and opened it slowly. I found myself on a small, dimly lit landing.

Down had to lead to Karma Koffee. Up had to lead to Nancy's apartment.

And it did.

NINETEEN

What was the significance of this second stairway? Did Nancy's killer know about it? If so, what part did it play, if any, in her murder?

The existence of the stairway meant that whoever had killed Nancy could have used these stairs, not the stairs VV and I had used the night of the murder.

The killer could have come from Karma Koffee, but that was unlikely. More likely was that the killer had gone through the yoga studio just as I had.

Unless that killer was Rob Gregory!

He was the only one, along with Trish, who would have keys to Karma Koffee, the yoga studio and Nancy Alverson's apartment. Could he and Nancy have been having a secret affair? It was clear from the position of the body that Nancy had known her killer. She'd certainly known Rob.

I heard a noise above and willed myself upward, one deliberate step at a time.

My heart quickened as I reached the top of the stairs. The door to Nancy's apartment hung open. I tiptoed up the last few steps and paused on the landing. My heart was racing. I took slow, shallow breaths. There was a light on inside and I heard somebody moving around.

'Hello?' I whispered.

There was no reply.

Across the apartment, I could see a slant of light coming from the door at the opposite end. The door stood ajar. Whoever had been in the empty apartment had probably gone out that way.

Against my better judgment, I stepped inside and moved into the living room. There was no one in sight. A light was on in the kitchen.

There was no one there.

The bathroom door hung open. It was empty too.

That left only the bedroom.

I bit down on my lower lip and held my purse and muffin bag in my overhead fist, ready to clobber anybody that might be lurking.

I stepped inside the bedroom. The curtains were pulled tight and the space was all shadows. The floor creaked as I put my weight on the boards.

I felt my arm tensing, ready to strike. I saw a blur and screamed. It came from behind the bedroom door. I tried to run but steely fingers clamped down on my left shoulder. I screamed again, dropping my purse and muffin bag, all thoughts of using them as a weapon gone.

I kicked savagely at the dark shape with my right foot and connected with something hard. My assailant cursed and let go of me.

The bedside light blinked on. I winced, partly from the sudden strong light, but mostly from the pain in my shoulder.

'Ms Miller?'

'Rob?' I grunted.

Rob Gregory winced and rubbed his tibia. 'What are you doing here?' He was still wearing his sleeveless shirt but had thankfully thrown a pair of charcoal sweatpants over his yoga tights.

'Me? What are you doing here?'

'Being attacked by a berserk intruder, apparently.' Rob scowled and paced back and forth between the desk and the bed in an effort to ease the pain. He stopped and turned on me. 'I thought you were gone?'

'I was. I mean, I am. That is, I heard footsteps and, since I knew the apartment was empty, I figured I should come see.' It was scary sometimes how easy the little lies came to me.

I rubbed my tingling shoulder. 'I thought you were gone. What are you doing up here?' Two open suitcases, a backpack and a tote bag sat on the bed. One was full, the other half so.

'Gathering Alverson's things.'

'Then what were you hiding for?'

'I thought you were a burglar. After what happened here, I wasn't taking any chances.'

'Are the police OK with you moving Nancy's things?'

'Of course.' Rob huffed indignantly. 'Her brother is coming for them tomorrow.'

'Brother?' I picked up my purse and pastry bag off the floor.

'That's right. The police gave him permission to collect her personal belongings. Which is fine by me, because I'd like to get this place rented again.'

He put his hands on his hips and examined the room. 'I don't suppose you know anybody who is looking for a nice one-bedroom at the moment? It is fully furnished.'

For a place where a young woman had just recently been murdered? I didn't think so. 'I'll ask around,' I said, trying to be diplomatic. I was pretty positive that I didn't know anyone with a ghoulish enough disposition to want to rent that apartment – especially if the Gregorys didn't change the furniture.

Who wants to sit in a dead woman's chair?

'I don't suppose I could get a look at her things?' My eyes were on the two suitcases and the backpack.

'No.' Rob slammed the last case shut. 'I don't suppose you could.' He picked up the case and carried it to the front door.

I followed. 'I heard from the police that Nancy's tea was drugged.'

Rob looked at me. 'I heard that too. What's your point?'

'The tea is a mystery, don't you think? And it was in one of your cups.'

'It's not a mystery to me. I gave her that tea myself.'

'You did?' I took a step back. Was he a mad killer?

Rob seemed to read my mind. 'I *brought* her the tea, Miller. I didn't murder her, and I didn't spike it. I was on my way up; she was on her way down for some tea. I offered to bring it to her. I did.'

'Do the police know that?'

'Of course,' he answered with a sigh. He returned to the bedroom for the second suitcase and planted it next to the other beside the door. 'Detective Highsmith thinks Nancy let someone into the apartment – a friend – and that person put something in her tea.'

Rob opened the door and gave me a nudge. 'Goodbye, Miller.'

'But I want to know—'

I could have finished my sentence but doors rarely answer. Accepting my defeat, I went downstairs gingerly. My muscles were beginning to tighten and complain.

I had a feeling I was going to regret my inaugural yoga class for a very long time. I retrieved my bike and pedaled stiffly home.

I unlocked the door, expecting to be greeted by Carole Two. She was nowhere in sight. 'Probably snoozing,' I whispered. I turned on the light and still she didn't appear.

I kicked off my shoes and dropped my purse and muffin on the table. My stomach grumbled. I couldn't wait to demolish that muffin. After the night I had had, I deserved a Heaven's Building Block. I deserved a dozen of them.

I rolled the Schwinn to the sliding glass door at the edge of the kitchen to put the bike on the patio for the night as I generally did.

I pulled back the curtain . . . and screamed!

'Maggie Miller,' the muffled voice in the darkness said. 'It's me.' Herman patted his chest. 'Herman. Only me, Herman.' He threw his arms in the air to show he was harmless.

All I saw, though, was a big, scary, crazy man with a long-bladed knife.

'What do you want?' I hollered. Glancing over my shoulder, at my purse on the kitchen table, I wondered if I could reach it and the cellphone inside before Herman smashed through the glass and strangled me.

Now I knew why there was no sign of the cat. She had probably sensed his presence on the patio and been scared witless. No doubt I would find her huddled far under the bed, cringing in fear. I felt like joining her.

'We need to talk, Maggie Miller.'

I barely heard him over the thumping of my heart. 'About what, Herman?' Did the crazy man think I knew where his City of Gold was? Did he think I was after his treasure? I clutched my throat. Was my neck about to meet the knife?

'About Nancy.'

My hand fell to my side. That was the last answer I'd expected to hear from Herman. 'Nancy Alverson?'

He bobbed his head eagerly up and down.

I narrowed my eyes at him. 'What about Nancy?'

His eyes glistened like jewels. 'She was murdered.'

'Yes, I know.' Definitely a case of heatstroke. Instead of fearing the poor man, I was beginning to wonder if I should call a doctor for him.

'She gave you something.'

I gasped.

He smiled and removed his hat. 'Can I come in?' He nodded at the door. 'We need to talk.'

My hand went to the handle. Did I dare let this crazy man in the house?

Before my hand could make up its mind, the doorbell rang, startling us both. 'One minute,' I said, raising my finger. I hurried to the door. 'Who's there?' I called through the thick wood.

'Open up, Maggie. It's me.'

I unlatched the door and turned the knob. 'Brad. First you disappear and then you reappear.' I stepped aside. 'Come on in.'

'I'm not intruding, am I?'

'No. As a matter of fact, a friend of yours is here too. We were about to have what I think is going to be a very interesting chat.'

Brad wiped his feet at the door – cowboy boots, I noticed – and stepped inside. He unbuttoned the top two buttons of his jacket and glanced toward the living-room furniture. 'What friend is that?'

'Herman the Swede.' I started toward the kitchen. 'He's over here on the—'

The patio was empty.

Another man had disappeared from my home.

Was that supposed to be some sort of sign?

'He was right there . . .' I pointed my arm toward the sliding glass door.

Brad pushed his brows together. 'Who?'

'I told you. Herman. He was standing right there on the patio.' I pushed my face against the glass and looked outside. The patio was deserted. 'I don't understand. He said he wanted to talk to me.'

I turned back around. Brad was peering out the window now too. 'Are you sure it was Herman?'

'Of course I'm sure.' Once you've met Herman the Swede you don't soon forget him.

'What was he doing on your patio? And at this hour?'

I blew out a breath. 'That's what I'd like to know.'

'What did he want to talk to you about?' Brad went to the kitchen and pulled open the refrigerator. 'Mind if I grab a beer?'

'Only if you grab me one, too.'

He opened a can and handed it to me.

'He said he wanted to talk about the Nancy Alverson murder.'

Brad paused with an open can of beer suspended inches from his lips. He lowered the can slowly and whistled. His eyes went to the dark, empty patio. 'You don't say.'

'I do say. The question is what did Herman want to say?' I raised my brow in question at Brad.

'I wonder why he disappeared.' Brad unlocked the slider and stepped onto the patio.

'You probably scared him off.'

Brad frowned. 'Right.' He opened the gate and peered into the yard. 'I wonder how he got here?'

I joined him. 'Good question.' I couldn't begin to imagine how long it would have taken him to hike in from the area where Brad had said his camp was located.

'Hitchhiked, maybe?' Brad unfastened the rest of the buttons on his jacket.

I pictured Herman the Swede standing at the side of the highway after dark, armed with his thumb out. 'I wouldn't pick him up. Would you?'

'No.'

We went back inside and settled side by side on the sofa, the empty middle cushion between us. At least it was for a minute or two, until C2 showed up. She mrowled something incomprehensible to either of us, curled into a big furry ball on the cushion and went back to sleep.

Lucky girl.

'Why did you disappear without a word like that when Detective Highsmith came over yesterday night?'

'I wanted to follow him. I was hoping he would lead me to VV. I went out the sliding door and hopped into my car.'

'Where did he go? Did he lead you to VV?'

'No.' Brad stroked the cat's side. 'He went to Karma Koffee, ate a pastry, then he went home.' He eyed me suspiciously. 'What are you smirking about?'

I batted my eyelashes oh-so-innocently. 'Was I smirking?'

'Spill it, Maggie.'

I set my can down on the side table. 'As it happens, I had a chat with VV this afternoon.'

Brad straightened. 'You did? Where? How?'

I held up my hand. 'Whoa, reporter boy. Enough of the questions. Let me explain.' I told him how Highsmith had asked me to stop by and talk to her.

Brad was rolling his eyes. 'Did that guy really think VV would appreciate having *your* shoulder to cry on?'

'Hey, it worked.' I wanted to be offended but it was impossible. Brad was right. 'At least for a little while.'

'Where is she hiding out?'

I could see from the look on Brad's face that he was like a shark that had scented blood in the water. 'Casa Mirasol.'

'Her father's house.' Brad snapped his fingers. 'That figures.'

'Yes, so if you are thinking of storming the gates, I'd think again.'

'Storming the gates of the mayor's house would not be good for my career. Do you think you can get me an appointment with her?'

'I don't think she'd even agree to talk to me again, let alone you.'

'Rats.' Brad finished his beer and set the empty can on the floor. 'On the plus side, I found out about those guys.' He moved the can around on the hardwood with his toe.

'What guys?'

'Those guys we saw at the church.'

'Oh. ASK Financial Services.'

'You already know?'

'They were in the café this morning. I got their business cards. How did you find out who they are?'

'I was down at city hall making my usual daily rounds. I saw them go into the records room. The clerk there is a buddy of mine. He told me who they were but wouldn't budge when I asked what they were looking for.'

'Too bad.'

'Yeah. I looked them up on the internet. They're from Vegas.' I didn't bother to tell Brad that I knew that too. There was only so much disappointment a man could take.

Brad continued, 'I dug around and found out that the three of them are staying at the Table Rock Hotel and Convention Center. Klopton is staying in bungalow four. The other two are in separate rooms.'

In addition to the main buildings, there were a half-dozen garden bungalows for guests.

'That's not far from the mayor's house,' I noted.

'Hey, that's right.' Brad pulled his cellphone from his front pocket and showed me the ASK Financial Services website. It was slick, same as them. 'I haven't interviewed them yet, but I will.'

'On what pretext?'

'I'll think of something,' he said with a confident shrug.

I yawned. C2 peeked at me then lowered her lids.

Brad stood and picked his empty beer can. 'I'll let you get some rest. I know you have to be up early.' He went to the kitchen. 'You have a recycle bin?'

'Under the sink.'

Brad opened the lower cabinet and dropped the can inside. He moved to the sliding glass door. He checked the lock and closed the curtains. 'I don't think Herman will be back tonight.'

'No, I don't suppose he will.' I dropped my own empty can in the bin. 'I can't stop wondering what he wanted to talk to me about regarding Nancy's murder . . .'

'We'll find out tomorrow.' Brad buttoned his coat.

'We will?'

'Sure. You said you want to know what he was doing here, right?'

I nodded.

'I'll pick you up tomorrow at the café. What time works for you?'

As much as I was burning to know what was on Herman's mind, I knew I couldn't blow off work. I didn't know yet whether Kelly would be off sick another day and couldn't leave Aubrey and Mom shorthanded. 'We close at three.'

'Three it is.'

I sat down at the kitchen table with a second beer. Too tired to even think about microwaving, let alone cooking on the stovetop, I opted for a muffin dinner. I nibbled on my Heaven's Building Block while reading the old copy of the *Table Rock Reader* that Brad had left for me the other night.

Brad had done a bang-up job on the story. Then again, he'd had great material to work with. Herman the Swede was certainly one colorful character.

I couldn't wait to hear what he had to say tomorrow. At the very least, it was sure to prove interesting.

TWENTY

Audrey and I were working the counter the next day around noon when Donna and Andy strode in hand in hand. Mom was on her lunch break.

'Two more adorable lovebirds, I've never seen,' I quipped, setting the fryer tub back in place and wiping my hands on my apron.

During a break in the action, I had decided to change out the oil in the fryer because I noticed it had been getting rather smoky. Always a sign that it was time for some fresh cottonseed oil.

'Hey, Sis.'

'Connor said you wanted to see us?' Andy said.

'He did?' I scratched the top of my head. 'Why would he—' Oops. The kid had seen through my delaying tactics and outmaneuvered me. 'Oh, right. Have a seat.' I poured fresh oil in the tub and turned the heat to 370 degrees.

I brought a couple of hot green teas to the table. 'Here you go.' I offered them each a cup. They both refused the sugar. It wasn't organic.

'What's wrong with you?' Donna asked.

'What do you mean?' I replied.

'You were wincing.'

'I was?'

'With every step,' agreed Andy. 'You look like you're in pain.'

'I took a yoga class last night.' I pressed my knuckles into my lumbar region. 'I am a little sore.' Truth be told, I'd had to roll out of bed onto the floor. From there, I'd crawled on my hands and knees, every muscle burning with exquisite pain, to the shower, where I had laid on the tile floor for nearly twenty minutes letting the water pummel me back to life.

'You took a yoga class?' Andy sounded incredulous.

'Don't act so surprised. I'm always open to new experiences.'

'Like pain?' Donna smirked.

I drilled her with my eyes.

Andy changed the subject. He slapped his hands on the table. 'So why are we here? What's up with Maggie Miller, entrepreneur? Need to borrow some money?'

'This isn't about me.' A more solvent person might have been offended.

'It isn't?' Donna looked puzzled.

'No.' Knowing my tendency to avoid sticky situations, I jumped right in. 'Here's the thing.' I grabbed a chair, turned it backwards and sat. 'Connor has a girlfriend.'

'What?' They said in unison.

'Well, maybe not a girlfriend, but he—'

'What are you talking about, Maggie?' demanded Donna, her hand wrapping around her cup.

She and Andy looked adorable in jeans and flannel shirts. His shirt was green and black, hers blue and brown. Both wore them untucked.

'Yeah, Maggie. What gives? Are you saying that Connor came to you and told you he has a girlfriend?' Andy pulled his ponytail over his shoulder, his eyes locked on mine.

'Connor came to the café the other day. He told me that he met this girl at a dance.'

'The Halloween dance at the school?' Donna interrupted.

'Yes. I guess so. Anyway,' I played with my fingers, 'he wants to ask her out. You know, on a date?' I looked from Andy to Donna.

Donna pouted. 'We already know that, Maggie.'

'Yeah.' Andy smiled. 'Connor already asked us. He's inviting the girl to dinner, right, Donna?' He turned to his wife. 'What was the girl's name?'

'That's right,' my sister agreed. 'I think Connor said her name is Madison.'

Andy nodded.

I shook my head. 'No, that's just it.' I clamped my hand over my sister's, preparing her for the truth. We all know that sometimes that can hurt. '*You* invited Madison to dinner. At your house. Connor wants to take her to the movies.'

Donna pulled her brow together. 'The movies?'

'Just the two of them?' Andy added.

'Just the two of them.' I grinned. 'It's perfectly normal. Connor is fourteen. Movies, soda, popcorn. It's all part of growing up.'

Andy and Donna shared a troubled look.

Donna tugged at her engagement ring. 'I suppose . . .'

Andy grabbed her other hand. 'If you think it will be all right, honey.'

'That's what he really wants?' Donna asked, turning to me.

'That's what he really wants,' I said. 'Don't worry. If the date works out, you can invite her over for dinner another time. But keep the meal simple – none of those far-out dishes like that tofu brains and turnip casserole of yours,' I suggested. 'We don't want Madison's parents accusing you of child abuse.'

Donna managed a smile.

'There is one other thing.'

'What's that?' asked Andy. He leaned back and took a sip of his tea.

'Connor wants to go to public school.'

'What?' They went off in unison again.

'You're joking?' Donna accused.

'Connor told you that?' Andy set his cup down. I could tell he was really upset because he was playing with his hemp bracelet.

After a moment of silence, Donna spoke. 'If that's what he really wants. I suppose that will be OK. I'll miss him, of course. But we want him to be happy, don't we, Andy?'

Donna and I looked toward Andy.

Suddenly, the tears were flying, but they weren't Donna's. Andy leaned forward, sobbing. Donna jumped up and threw her arms around him.

'Oh, Andy. Don't cry.' She thumped him on the back. 'It's OK. It's going to be OK. Connor's growing up.'

Andy mashed his fists into his eyes. 'I know.' He sniffed. 'It's just so hard.'

'Come on,' Donna said. 'Let's get you home. The boys are there. We can have a nice family discussion. OK?'

Andy scooted back his chair and stood. 'OK,' he sniffed again.

Donna nodded a goodbye and led Andy out the door.

'Smooth, Maggie. Truly, truly smooth,' chided Aubrey.

I removed the towel hooked under my apron string and hurled it at her. It flew over the counter and landed atop the waffle maker, where it began to sizzle.

I had been expecting a few tears, just not Andy's.

Brad showed up at the curb outside the café at three on the dot.

'Everything OK?' he asked as I eased myself into the car.

'Yes. Why do you ask?'

'You looked like you were, I don't know, walking funny.'

'I'm a little stiff today, that's all. Maybe it's my mattress. I probably need a new one.'

I was not mentioning yoga class again and going through a second razzing of the day.

As we drove out toward the Sacred Church of Witchkraft, I told Brad about some of the other things I had learned concerning the mystery of Nancy Alverson's death.

'Rob was the person who delivered the tea to Nancy that night. And it was spiked with two hundred milligrams of diphen, diphen . . . something.'

'Diphenhydramine?' Brad slowed at a deep rut.

'That's right.'

'Somebody sure wanted to incapacitate her.'

'Making it easier to strangle her.'

'Yeah.' Brad ran his tongue over his lips. 'Do the police suspect Rob Gregory?'

'I'm not sure,' I replied, rising in my seat to soften the impact as we took another severe bump. 'But I do. He has a lot of students, female students in that yoga studio of his. I wouldn't be surprised if he had a groupie or two.'

'And you think Nancy might have been one of those groupies?'

'Maybe, and maybe she threatened to tell his wife about them.'

I played the scenario through in my mind and came up with an alternative. 'It could also be that he came onto Nancy and she rebuffed him. Rob has a big ego. I don't think he would take that very well.'

Brad chuckled. 'You really don't like the guy, do you?'

'He charged me nearly two hundred dollars for a yoga outfit and a rubber mat,' I said in my own defense. 'Besides, he took Nancy the tea and he was acting very suspiciously.'

'It would be pretty stupid of him to drug the tea and admit that he'd delivered it.'

'Stupid or clever like a fox?'

'Meaning that he would have to be crazy to make himself look suspicious and might have thrown suspicion on himself knowing that that would only make him look innocent?'

'I'm not sure what you said, but yes.' Trying to follow that sentence had given me a headache. But I understood what he'd been trying to say. 'Exactly.'

'I'll do a little digging,' Brad offered. 'See what I can find out. Maybe I can talk to some of these students of his. Did you get any names?'

'No, but it shouldn't be hard to find out. There's a list on his desk of all the class times and students enrolled in each.'

'Perfect.' Brad slowed once more and pulled onto the same track where we'd first come across Herman, who had appeared to pop up out of nowhere.

'I'm still wondering why Herman decided to come see you, Maggie. He barely knows you. Why didn't he choose to come see me instead if he wanted to talk about Nancy Alverson's murder?'

Brad sounded a trifle hurt that Herman had chosen me over him. 'I am a reporter and he knows me.'

'He told me last night that Nancy gave me something.'

'What do you mean?'

'I mean he didn't *ask* me, he *told* me.'

Brad turned off the main road. 'That is weird. I can't wait to hear what Herman has to say. I hope he's near his camp. If he's off prospecting somewhere, we may never find him.'

It would be even worse if Herman didn't want to be found. Looking at the rugged landscape, I knew that a man could hide practically forever out here if he chose to.

Before long, Brad pulled over to the side. I felt and heard the underside of his sedan scrape the uneven ground. 'This is as close as we can get in the car. Too bad I don't have a four-wheel-drive truck.'

We climbed out. The sun was high in the sky and the weather was warm. November in this part of Arizona wasn't bad at all. I held my hand up to my forehead, wishing I had brought a hat.

Brad started walking. 'It's this way, I think.'

I stumbled after him, glad that I had worn sneakers to work. 'You didn't tell me this was going to involve a hike,' I complained, dodging past a cactus twice my height with stickers three times the length of my longest finger.

'You knew what it was going to be like out here.' Sure, he was wearing sturdy brown high hiking boots, thick jeans and a long-sleeved chambray shirt. I had on my café clothes, thin khaki slacks and a polo shirt.

We walked for a solid twenty minutes over the rough terrain, past boulders large and small. I only fell twice, skinning my knees the first time because Brad had failed to catch me. The second time, he had been prepared and caught me before I hit the ground.

I hoped we didn't run into any ticked-off javelinas or hungry coyotes.

I recognized the hills that Brad had described the other day as the ones where Herman had pitched his camp. 'Please tell me we are getting close,' I complained.

'It's just around this rock formation,' Brad panted.

We were both tired and thirsty. Neither of us had thought to bring a water bottle.

As we rounded the house-sized reddish brown boulder, I saw a low beige tent a hundred yards off.

I stopped. My eyes widened. 'That's Nancy's truck.' I pointed, though it was completely unnecessary. There was no other vehicle present.

'Are you sure?'

'Positive.' I began walking toward the ancient Land Rover. It was definitely Nancy's. 'What the devil is it doing here?'

'I don't know.'

We came within thirty feet of it and Brad stopped.

He cupped his hands around his mouth. 'Herman! Herman, are you here? It's me, Brad Smith. I've got Maggie Miller with me!'

There was no movement from the low tent.

I walked over to the Land Rover and peered inside. Brad followed me. 'It's empty,' I said. 'But it's definitely hers. I recognize it down to the Route 66 bumper sticker.'

'Let's go check out the tent.' Brad started walking. 'Maybe he's sleeping.'

'Or waiting to slit our throats,' I replied. I clung to Brad's side as we made our approach. We saw a few scattered footprints and animal tracks. I was hoping they were deer prints and not coyote. Deer I could cope with.

Deer are cute.

We stopped again a dozen yards from Herman's camp. Besides the tent, there was a small ring of stones with a cold campfire in its center. A half-dozen five-gallon plastic jugs sat outside the tent on the right.

There was no sign of Herman the Swede. I checked the hills for any sign of him. Nothing.

Not a sound came from anywhere around.

'Herman?' It was my turn to call. 'It's me, Maggie.' I stepped slowly toward the tent. The flap hung loose and partially open. A couple steps from the tent sat a lone, olive-green, canvas-backed folding chair. 'You wanted to see me?'

Brad moved toward a small cairn on the left, near which sat several tools including a shovel, a pickax and a sledgehammer.

I hovered over the circle of stones. The fire had long gone out. All that remained were a few unburned twigs, a scorched stump the thickness of my wrist and . . . something. I reached into the ashes. It was the charred remains of some sort of report. I held the document lightly in my fingers, gingerly turning it right side up for fear it would disintegrate.

What was it?

I skimmed the pages. It was a financial report, a Security and Exchange Commission financial report, to be precise. And the subject of the report was ASK Financial Services.

I shivered. What had Herman been doing with a financial report on a company out of Las Vegas? What interest would he have had in a financial services company?

Was he looking for a company to manage his riches? Had he found his treasure?

I laid the scorched document gently on the ground and approached the tent once more.

'Herman?' I wrapped my fingers around the edge of the tent flap and bent to peer inside.

Sunlight spilled into the musty space. The tent was cluttered with everything the modern treasure hunter could need except a toilet and a shower. The interior smelled of sweat. I saw a big chest cooler, a selection of freeze-dried foods and other foodstuffs, including a paper sack from Mother Earth/Father Sun.

There was a solar-powered lantern atop a small folding table. An empty leather sheath and a handful of change sat beside it.

The table also contained an assortment of books and maps, most related to history, geography and minerology, and a compass. Beside the low table was a cot with an unzipped sleeping bag rolled over it. The cot was empty. There was no sign of Herman.

I exited the tent. Brad looked over, his hands wrapped around the pickax, probably dreaming of life as a gold prospector. 'Anything?'

I shook my head. 'Nothing.' I let go of the flap.

'I'll take a look up this way.' Brad pointed up a path that looked regularly travelled.

'OK. I'll look around here some more. Maybe Herman will come back.'

'Good idea.' Brad waved and trudged between some scrub brush.

I strolled past the cold fire, stopped and looked again at the Land Rover. It all made no sense. A quick glance at the hill overhead still revealed no lurking killer coyotes or crazy Swedes.

I kicked one of the big plastic containers with my toe, listened to it slosh and unscrewed the cap. I took a sniff. 'Water,' I said aloud. 'That makes sense.'

I cupped my hands and tilted my head toward the looming hill behind the tent. 'Herman?'

All I got in reply was the echo of my call.

I ambled around the corner of the tent to see what else I might find that could give us a clue as to where Herman had gone to for the day. Why couldn't he have left behind a day planner stating something like: *Gone to X marks the spot. Follow the red arrow to the one-armed cactus, then turn left and walk twenty paces to the rock that looks like Snoopy.*

It would have made things so much easier.

A scream caught in my throat as I rounded the backside of the tent.

Herman was stretched out on the ground, dressed much like I had seen him the night before. He stared up at the sun without complaint.

Because his throat had been cut.

TWENTY-ONE

'**B**rad!' I stumbled backward, tripping over myself. 'Brad!' I turned and ran as fast as I could, running in the direction he had disappeared. 'Brad!'

Brad's head appeared on the horizon and then the rest of him. Seeing my agitation, he raced forward. 'Maggie! What's wrong?'

I stopped, planted my hands on my knees, and gasped for breath. 'It's – it's Herman. B-back there!'

'OK.' Brad wrapped his arm over my back to support me. 'Let's go see him.' He gave me a gentle squeeze. 'You OK? I want to find out what this is all about.'

'N-no!' I yanked at his arm. 'Call the police!'

'What?' Brad pulled me upright and cupped his hands around my face. 'What is it? Breathe, Maggie.'

I nodded and complied. Breathing was exactly what I needed to do. I took several lurching breaths with Brad watching me like a hawk. 'OK.' I nodded. Finally able to speak. 'Herman is behind his tent. He's dead.'

The frown line between Brad's eyes deepened. 'Dead? Are you sure?'

'I'm sure. His throat has been cut.' And I had seen the empty sheath on a table in his tent. Had someone used his own knife to murder him?

Brad lowered his hands to my shoulders. 'Are you OK?'

'Yeah, I guess.'

We walked quickly back to the tent.

Brad stopped in front. 'Why don't you wait here? I'll go check.'

'Not a problem,' I replied. I had no intention of revisiting the scene.

Brad pulled his phone from his pocket and handed it to me. 'Call the police, Maggie.'

I nodded. Brad was only gone a minute. When he returned, his face was white and he looked about as good as I felt. I had a hunch he had never seen such a gruesome scene before either.

'The police are on their way,' I said, handing him back his cellphone.

'Thanks.'

'I gave them the best directions I could. I hope they don't have trouble finding this place.'

'They should be able to follow our tracks,' Brad assured me. 'If they don't show up soon, we can go back up the road a ways and wait for them.'

'Good idea.'

Brad looked at his phone. 'I'll be right back.'

'Where are you going?' I cried.

He held up the camera. 'I want to get some pictures.'

'Pictures? At a time like this?'

Brad shrugged an apology. 'I'm a news reporter. This is a story. I'll be right back.'

I moved further from the tent, wanting to put as much distance between myself and Herman's corpse as I could. As I walked, I noticed a mottled impression in the ground with footsteps all around. The impression was rectangular and maybe five foot wide and eight foot long. Three faint lines, equally spaced, ran the length of it.

I studied the impression, wondering what on earth it could be.

Brad came up from behind, startling me.

'What are you looking at?'

'This.' I pointed to the ground.

Brad bent for a closer look. 'What is it?'

'You tell me.'

Brad straightened and took a couple of photos of the impression.

'Maybe it was from some alien spacecraft,' I joked, despite the somberness of the occasion. Table Rockers were big on aliens. For all I knew, Brad was a believer.

Brad lowered his phone and tilted his head. 'You know,' he stooped and ran his hand along the edge of the ground, 'I think you're right.'

I raised my brow. 'You do?'

'Yeah.' He waved his hand at me. 'I don't mean I think this is an alien spacecraft.' He straightened once more and rubbed his hands to remove the dirt from his fingers. 'I think this was an earthly spacecraft.'

I angled my eyes at him. 'An earthly spacecraft?'

Brad pointed at the ground. 'Yeah. Those are human footprints, not alien.'

I looked at the few impressions that were visible. The ground here was patchy, sometimes soft, sometimes hard. There were definitely some other footprints and they weren't all mine.

Brad smiled. 'I think this was made by a hot-air balloon. More precisely, by a hot-air balloon basket.'

We heard the sound of sirens in the distance.

'A hot-air balloon?' I looked at the area in question. I'd never been in a hot-air balloon and it wasn't high on my bucket list – why anybody would want to leave the ground with nothing but a balloon full of hot air between themselves and death was beyond me – but I could see how that could have been made by a balloon's basket.

'Didn't you recently do a story about a missing hot-air balloon?'

'Yeah,' Brad said, his voice tight. 'I think we might just have found it.'

'Or at least where it's been.'

'Come on,' said Brad. 'The cops are here.'

Detective Highsmith arrived first, followed by two Table Rock squad cars and an ambulance.

Detective Mark Highsmith unfolded himself from his unmarked blue sedan and approached us stiffly. 'Mr Smith, Ms Miller,' he said grimly. 'Where's this body?'

'Over here,' I said. 'Behind the tent. There's something else I think you should see, though.'

'Let's see the body first,' Highsmith replied.

The three of us approached the tent.

'You two wait here,' Highsmith ordered.

Officers Singh and Collins accompanied the detective while Officer Kurkov remained with us.

Detective Highsmith reappeared alone a minute or two later, his face set. 'There's no ID on the body. Do either of you two know who he is?'

'His name is Herman,' Brad offered. 'I did a story on him for the paper. He's a prospector.'

'What's his last name?'

'He didn't want to tell me and I didn't push him on it.'

Highsmith's mouth tightened into a line. 'The medical examiner is on her way.' He turned to the EMTs and told them to stand by. Then he turned his attention to me and Brad. 'Let's talk.'

'Detective, there is something we think you should see first,' I said.

'Maggie's right,' said Brad.

'What's that?'

'We'll have to show you. It's over there.'

Highsmith groaned but complied, following at my side as we headed toward the odd depression in the ground.

When we reached the spot, some thirty yards from the campsite, I pointed at the mottled earth. 'There.'

Highsmith worked his jaw side to side. 'What is it?'

'We think it's the indentation from a hot-air balloon, Detective,' answered Brad.

The detective's brow went up. 'A hot-air balloon?'

'A hot-air balloon basket, to be precise,' I added.

'And you are showing me this in the middle of a crime scene investigation, why?' His gaze went from one to the other of us.

'You tell us,' Brad said.

Highsmith huffed a bit. 'Fine. Consider it off limits.' He waved his arm. 'Consider this entire area off limits. Follow me.' He walked us to Brad's car. 'What were you two doing out here, anyway?'

'We came to see Herman,' Brad replied.

'Was he expecting you?'

'No.' I took this one. 'He came by my apartment last night wanting to talk. Then Brad came and scared him off. So we thought we would come see him today. I don't close the shop until three and—'

Detective Highsmith held up his hand. 'Stop.' He turned to Brad. 'Why did you scare Herman off? Did you two have an argument?'

Brad shook his head. 'Give me a break.'

'It was nothing like that,' I interjected. 'When I got home from yoga class last night—'

Both men looked at me in surprise. I chose to ignore them. 'When I got home from yoga class, Herman was waiting on my patio. He said he wanted to talk. Then Brad showed up at the front door and I think Herman got scared, not knowing who it was, I guess.'

'And that's the only time you saw him?'

'As a matter of fact, I ran into him earlier on the street last night.'

'Where exactly was this?' Highsmith asked.

'On Laredo. Near my café.'

'When?'

'Right before my class. I signed up for a class with Rob Gregory at his upstairs studio. Herman had been in Karma Koffee. Lee, the man that works there, told me Herman had been asking for me. Then he saw me on the street.'

'Why didn't he just talk to you then rather than wait for you on your patio?'

I pushed my brows together, trying to remember. 'I think he wanted to. Then he saw a police car and I think it spooked him.'

Highsmith leaned up against Brad's car and pulled out his notebook. Brad and I watched in silence as he wrote. Finally, he looked up and started up with the questions once more. 'What time did you get home last night?'

I shrugged. 'Tennish?' I looked at Brad for help.

'Yeah.' He ran a hand across his scalp. 'Something like that. Listen, Detective, it happened just like Maggie says.'

'I'm sure it did.' Highsmith looked back at the crime scene, now crawling with official personnel. 'Do you know what this Herman fellow wanted to talk to you about, Ms Miller?'

'Yes.' I folded my arms over my chest. 'He wanted to talk to me about Nancy Alverson's murder.'

The way the detective's brow shot up, I knew I had gotten his attention. 'Why would he want to talk to you about Nancy Alverson's murder?'

'I honestly don't know.' And probably never would.

Detective Highsmith turned to Brad. 'What was your relationship to the victim, Mr Smith? Did you know this Herman fellow?'

Brad frowned. 'Like I explained, I wrote a human interest piece on him for the *Table Rock Reader*.' His voice rose in annoyance. 'Doesn't anybody read the paper?'

'Sorry,' the detective said, not at all ruffled. 'I guess I missed that. A human interest piece, you say?'

Brad nodded. 'Herman was a treasure hunter. He was looking for one of the lost cities of gold.'

'Another one of those, eh?' Highsmith jotted something down in his notebook. 'In this interview of yours, Mr Smith, did Herman ever mention Nancy Alverson?'

'Not once.'

'That's her Land Rover, by the way.' I nodded in the direction of the dusty SUV.

'I know. I ID'd the license plate,' he replied. 'Did either of you drive it here?'

'No, we came together.' Brad stuffed his hands in his back pockets.

'In that car?' Highsmith pointed to Brad's vehicle.

'That's right.'

'Did either of you see someone in the vicinity riding a small motorbike?'

'No,' I answered. 'Why?'

'There are some tracks around. It could mean nothing.'

I hadn't noticed.

'A dirt biker, maybe?' suggested Brad. We did get a lot of them buzzing around the hills.

'Nope. The tire treads are wrong. I think we are done for now.' Detective Highsmith clicked his pen open and closed.

'There is one more thing I think you should be aware of, Detective,' I said.

'What's that?'

'I found a burnt document in the ashes of the fire.' I pointed at the campfire ring. 'It's some sort of SEC financial statement concerning ASK Financial Services. You can see it there on top that rock.'

Brad's brow went up.

'You shouldn't have touched it, Ms Miller. This is a crime scene.'

'I didn't know that at the time, Detective.'

His mouth went flat. 'Right. What's ASK Financial Services got to do with this?'

I lowered my chin. 'Why don't you ask VV that question, Detective?'

Highsmith's face darkened. 'I have to get back but I am going to want to talk to both of you again, get your official statements, OK?'

We both nodded readily.

'Fine. You can both go. And Ms Miller, I was going to bring your laptop back to you today. It's on the front seat of my car. Help yourself.'

'Thanks,' I said. 'No fingerprints?'

'Just yours.'

I was afraid of that. 'What about the tea?' I asked as Highsmith distanced himself from us.

He paused and turned. 'What tea?'

'The tea that Nancy drank. Were there any fingerprints on that cup?'

'Only hers and Rob's.'

I raised my brow ever so slightly. 'Is he a suspect?'

Highsmith pointed toward the tent with the pen clutched in his right hand. 'I'm walking over there. If, when I get to the tent and turn around, you two are still here . . .' He paused for effect. 'I'm holding the two of you on suspicion of murder.'

He turned his back on us without waiting for an answer.

'Is he kidding?' griped Brad, balling up his hands. 'Who does that guy think he is?'

'A man with handcuffs,' I said. 'Come on, let's go!' I hurried around to the passenger side of Brad's Honda and hopped in.

Brad jumped in and started the engine.

'Wait!' I threw open my door.

'What is it?'

I didn't stop to reply. There was no time to waste because Highsmith, curse his long legs, had nearly reached the tent.

I threw open the door of Highsmith's car and grabbed my laptop. I clutched it to my chest and ran as fast as I could. I practically threw myself inside Brad's car.

As I balanced the laptop on the dashboard and Brad put the little car in gear, I saw Detective Highsmith staring at us from the edge of the tent.

We had made it by the skin of our teeth. It was a good thing too, because I didn't look good in handcuffs – they made my wrists look big.

TWENTY-TWO

B rad dropped me off at my apartment. I had walked to work that morning knowing he was picking me up.

'Do you want to come in? I could order a pizza.'

'No, thanks. I'll take a raincheck. I need to get back to my desk.'

I couldn't help grinning. 'Don't tell me, you've got a story to write.' Herman's murder wouldn't be big news – after all, he was just some crazy treasure hunter in the eyes of the world – but it was news.

He nodded. 'Before one of the big papers beats me to it.'

I exited the car and hovered at the curb with my hand on the window. 'Any thoughts on who might have slashed his throat?'

'No.' Brad's wrists hung over the steering wheel. 'It wasn't the same MO as Nancy's murder.'

'My money is on Alan Klopton, Gary Busby and Stephanie Headley.'

'You think all three of them did it?'

'All three, one, two out of three. Take your pick. Personally, I say start at the top: Alan Klopton, president and potential killer.'

I grabbed my laptop off the floor of the car. 'Why else would there be a copy of an SEC financial report on ASK Financial Services at a treasure seeker's campsite?'

I didn't really think he was looking to hire ASK as his financial consultants. And it seemed like every time something bad happened, somebody from ASK was around.

'If it was important, wouldn't the killer have taken it?' Brad countered.

'I suppose you're right.' I was getting tired of questions with no answers.

Brad took off, promising to check in with me tomorrow. I dragged myself inside, showered and changed into a pair of comfy jeans and an old ASU sweatshirt.

I fed C2 and had a large pizza delivered to myself. I didn't plan to eat the entire pie. I'd save the cold leftovers for breakfast.

When the pizza arrived, I carried the box to the coffee table in front of the sofa next to my margarita glass and pulled out a warm, gooey slice – fresh mushroom, onion and garlic. Garlic, one of the perks of being single.

While I ate, I powered up my laptop and did a little internet snooping.

Two hours of fishing, four slices of pizza and a margarita and a half later, I closed the laptop in frustration.

Not a single bite. Not even a nibble.

I'd found nothing interesting on ASK Financial Services. Whatever they were about, they hid it well.

It was late. I squeezed the pizza box into the fridge and went to check that I had locked the front door. Two murders in a matter of days had me seriously spooked.

I picked up Jakob Waltz's wrapped painting. I'd been meaning to take it to the café and fill the hole in the wall. I yawned and unwrapped the package, curious to see what he had for me this time.

It was a colorful landscape that captured the beauty of the surrounding red rock countryside. I set it carefully on a kitchen chair and turned off the lights.

I headed to the bedroom, then paused. Something tickled at the back of my brain. I returned to the kitchen, turned on the light and gazed at the painting for a long moment.

There was something oddly familiar about it. I scanned the sky, the trees and the rocks. That was it. My finger rubbed gently against one particular rock.

I had seen that rock the day Brad and I had driven out to the Sacred Church of Witchkraft. I remembered it because it had reminded me of a cactus itself. I had mentioned to Brad how it looked like someone had actually carved a giant cactus out of the mountainside.

Jakob had painted that scene. That meant he had been near the Sacred Church of Witchkraft.

Wait. My heart skipped a beat. I studied the painting, the angle of the strokes, the brushwork. I was no expert but at first glance it seemed to me that maybe, just maybe, Jakob had also painted those canvases I had seen in the church's headquarters when Brad and I had met with the headmaster and headmistress.

Was Jakob one of them?

Was he their hired killer?

I laid the frame gently on the kitchen table and stared at it. Was I staring at the work of a vicious murderer?

I sat at the table. Nancy and Jakob knew each other. Nancy and the three suits from ASK knew each other. Suryavayu claimed that the church had hired Nancy to do some sort of write-up about the church for them. It looked like Jakob was affiliated with them as well.

I gasped, remembering now the recently sold painting of Jakob's that I had so admired. He told me that he had hired a hot-air balloon so he could see and sketch out the scene he was trying to capture and then paint it.

I slipped my cellphone out from my purse and looked at the time. It was late but I took a chance and dialed Brad's number. If I was wrong about Jakob, I didn't want to damage his reputation with false accusations. He'd been in trouble with the police more than once already. He didn't need any more bad publicity.

On the other hand, if I was right, and Jakob was the killer, I wasn't about to face him alone.

The phone rang and rang. Finally, I heard somebody on the other line pick up.

'Hello, Brad?'

'Hi, Maggie. What's up?'

'Do you remember that new painting that Jakob Waltz brought to my apartment?'

'The one for consignment in the café, sure. What about it?' I could hear Brad typing in the background.

'I opened it.'

'Is it any good?'

I took a breath. 'More than good. I think it could be a key to Nancy Alverson's murder.'

'How's that?'

'I think Jakob might have killed her.'

The sound of typing ceased.

'What?'

'Do you remember that rock we saw that I said looked like a giant cactus?'

'Yeah. So?'

'There's a rock just like it in this painting.'

'Are you sure?' Brad sounded dubious.

'I'm looking right at it, Brad. I think Jakob killed Nancy.'

'A lover's quarrel?'

'I don't know,' I replied. 'Maybe. I remember that there were several paintings in the office of the high priest and high priestess at the church. I think Jakob painted those too. I don't know how I missed it before, but the style is similar to say the least. He could be working for the Sacred Church of Witchkraft. And if Nancy was writing some exposé about them—'

'I don't know, Maggie . . .'

'There's only one way to find out. Talk to him. Now.'

'Now?' Brad's voice rose. 'I've got a story to write.'

'Think about it,' I teased. 'If Jakob is the killer, this could be an even better story.'

Brad grunted. That meant I was right and he knew it. 'Fine. Give me a few minutes to wrap things up and I'll come get you.'

'I've got my bike. Tell me where he lives and I'll meet you outside.' I could use the fresh air and the exercise.

Brad looked up Jakob's home address and I wrote it down on a scrap of paper.

I bundled up and left through the patio. Jakob's modest home was a mile or two from my apartment. The streets of Table Rock were laid out mostly in a grid fashion, so I had no trouble finding the place.

There were several lights on inside the modest house. I rolled to a stop beside the thick trunk of a wide-canopied oak. Straddling my Schwinn, I watched from the relative safety of the shadows.

The curtains were drawn. I could see Jakob moving about inside. A minute later, he stepped out carrying a suitcase. He popped the rear hatch of an old-model SUV in the gravel driveway. He threw the suitcase in the back then returned indoors.

Was he leaving?

I glanced at my watch to see the time. Where was Brad? If he didn't show up soon, Jakob could get away.

I bit the inside of my cheek in frustration. I stared at my watch. The minute hand went around two more times and that was all I could take.

I was going to have to go in alone, knowing that Brad would be right behind me.

Or so I hoped . . .

I rolled onto the sidewalk and lowered the kickstand. With trepidation, I started up the sidewalk. Jakob's house was a cream-colored cottage with a shingled roof and a narrow, covered front porch.

I mounted the steps and knocked.

I heard light sounds from inside and a TV playing in the background.

The front door opened and Jakob stood there. 'Ms Miller, what are you doing here?' He wore paint-spattered jeans and a dark blue, long-sleeved turtleneck shirt. Leather moccasins covered his feet.

'Brad and I wanted to talk to you.'

'Brad?' Jakob's brows pushed together and he looked past me.

'Brad Smith, the reporter from the newspaper. The one who interviewed you. Brad's meeting me here. He'll be along in a minute.'

I wanted Jakob to know that upfront and I wanted to make that very clear.

'What do you guys want to talk to me about?' Jakob thrust his hands in his front pockets. A strong smell of paint mixed with smoke wafted past him.

'Nancy.'

Jakob's mouth tightened into a thin line.

'Can I come in?'

After a moment's hesitation, Jakob stepped aside. 'If you want.' He motioned me inside.

The door opened up into a cramped living space with a low ceiling. A black woodstove sat in the right corner. A white fan hung in the middle of the room. Beige carpet, worn and dirty, ran from wall to wall.

A futon loveseat was pushed up against the wall. Jakob walked to the TV on the coffee table facing the futon and turned it off. The table held a remote control, several empty beer bottles and an ashtray. A pair of stuffed green duffle bags leaned into the corner. The frame of an easel protruded from the opening of one of them.

'Going somewhere?' I asked.

'Huh?'

I pointed to the bags.

'I thought I'd get out of town for a couple of days. Take a break. Get away from . . . everything.' Jakob fell onto the chocolate-colored futon mattress and indicated that I should sit in the solitary dining chair in the front window.

I sat. The walls were covered with original art. All Jakob's work, by the looks of them. He was good. Against the wall stood several overstocked bookcases with books of all sizes piled in every possible space. Most were art books, design and history.

Beyond the living room was an Arizona room, a small glassed-in patio on which I could see several easels.

To the left there was a hall that I pictured leading to a couple of bedrooms and a bath. I could see the tiny galley kitchen to the right. A black backpack leaned in the doorway between the kitchen and the living room.

Jakob leaned forward, his elbows pressed against his legs. 'What's this about Nancy? What did you want exactly?'

I glanced out the window, hoping for a sign of Brad. There was none. The street was quiet. 'I took a look at that painting that you brought me the other night for the café.'

'Is there something wrong with it? Don't you like it, Ms Miller?' He began to rise. 'I can pick out something else, if you like.'

'No.' I waved for him to sit. 'It's nothing like that. The fact is I thought I recognized it.'

Jakob's brow furrowed deeply. 'Recognized it how?'

'There was a rock in the background, one that looked like a cactus.' I watched Jakob's eyes as I spoke for telltale signs. 'I saw a rock formation like that. It was near the Sacred Church of Witchkraft.'

Jakob's hands clenched.

I glanced once again out the window for Brad. What was keeping him? 'Do you know it?'

Jakob jumped to his feet and I gasped. He paced from the futon to the Arizona room and back again. 'Yes. I know it. So?'

'Do you know Alan Klopton?'

'Who?' Jakob looked at me from the other side of the coffee table.

'Alan Klopton, Gary Busby and Stephanie Headley. They are with ASK Financial Services.'

'I've never heard of them.'

I couldn't tell if he was lying or not. He clearly looked troubled. 'They work for the church. At least, I think they do. What about you, Jakob? That rock formation is on or near the church. Do you work for them, too?'

'I don't know what you're talking about. I don't work for anybody.'

'I saw some of your work there,' I pressed. 'In the high priest's office at the church. Your work is unique.' I hoped my hunch was right. 'I recognized several of your paintings.'

Jakob stared at his hands for a minute before speaking. 'OK, so I did some paintings for the church on commission. I admit it. It's no crime.'

He stood and began pacing once more. 'The pay was good. As you may have noticed, I'm not exactly rolling in dough, Ms Miller.'

'Was Nancy working for the church too?'

'What?' Jakob shook his head. 'No. I mean, I don't think so. Why would she?'

'From the way Nancy talked, she didn't like those people at all.'

'Did you know Nancy was being paid by them?'

'No.' He seemed genuinely surprised.

'Do you know a prospector named Herman?'

'No.' Jakob went to the kitchen and grabbed a bottle of beer. He popped the cap with an opener screwed to the wall.

He raised the bottle to his lips and chugged half of it down his throat. 'What's with all the questions, Ms Miller?' Anger had built up inside him. 'Huh? Do you think I killed Nancy? Is that what this is all about?'

I glanced nervously out the window, wishing that Brad would pull into the driveway. And the minute he did, I was going to kill him.

'Of course not,' I said to calm him. 'After all, the police questioned you. You have an alibi, right?' I stood and inched my way closer to the front door. 'Where was it you said you were the night Nancy was strangled?'

I knew that Jakob had told Brad that he had been home that night. But Jakob had also been in the vicinity of Nancy's apartment near the time of her murder. He'd certainly had the opportunity to commit murder.

Like he did now. That was an uneasy thought.

Jakob's bottle was clenched in his fingers as he stepped toward me. 'This is crazy.'

His arm darted toward me. I leapt backward, hitting the bookcase.

'You want a beer?'

I gulped. 'N-no.' I picked up several books that had fallen to the floor and laid them haphazardly on the nearest shelf.

'Look, you want the truth, I'll tell you the truth.'

I held my tongue, giving him free rein.

'I was young. I got in a little trouble.'

'Trouble?'

'Small stuff. A few fights. A couple of buddies and me borrowed a car. I sold some weed to friends.'

'I understand,' I said with as reassuring a smile as I could muster. I dearly hoped this wasn't one of those famous confessions by the killer just moments before he kills his last victim and makes his getaway. 'We're all young once, right?'

'I *was* young. I know I did wrong, Ms Miller. People can change.' He jutted his chin.

'Of course.'

'It's not what you think. I didn't murder Nancy.' Tears formed at the corners of Jakob's eyes. 'I loved her.'

'Did she love you?'

He shrugged a shoulder. 'Not really, I guess.'

'Did that make you mad?'

Jakob scowled. 'Not enough to kill her, if that's what you are suggesting?'

I raised my hands. 'No, not at all.'

'Nancy didn't really like a whole lot of people, let alone love them. She was pretty much a loner as far as I could see.' Jakob took a sip from his bottle. 'She made it clear to me that she wanted to keep things casual. I don't mind admitting I wanted more.'

Jakob rested the bottle on the bookcase near my shoulder. 'You're probably wondering if Nancy knew about my past.'

'Did she?'

'Yep.' Jakob sounded pleased. 'I told her early on. She said we all have a past and that it is only our future that matters.'

'Wise words,' I commented.

'Look.' His hand shot out to the bookcase and he retrieved a book. He thrust it into my fingers.

'Nancy's book?'

'Yeah. It's one of her earlier books.'

It was titled *Solar Sham*. I flipped the pages. 'This is the book you told me about.'

'Yeah.' He turned the page to the foreword. 'I haven't had a chance to read it yet. She inscribed it to me. See?'

I saw. The inscription on the title page read: *To Jakob, May your future be bright. Nancy*

'That's sweet.' I closed the book.

'Being an artist is hard, you know?'

'I'll bet. Being a small business owner isn't exactly easy, either,' I replied, in an effort to gain some camaraderie with him.

'Look, the police already know, so you may as well know too.' He leaned back on his heels. 'I don't want you to think badly of me but I'd rather you think badly of me than think I'm a murderer. I like to consider us friends, Ms Miller.'

'Me too, Jakob.' Assuming you aren't a murderer.

'After I left your place the night Nancy was killed, I drove into Sedona.'

'You weren't here, at home?'

Jakob shook his head. 'I was in Sedona. Picking up some weed.' He lowered his chin. 'The police know all about it. They talked to my . . . friend.

'I told that reporter guy that I was home that night because I didn't want him printing anything about that or, well, any of my past. I'm trying to make a go of things here.'

'I understand completely.' I hesitated before asking my next question. 'I have to ask you one other thing, Jakob.'

'What's that?'

'That painting of yours that sold recently at the café.'

'What about it?'

'I remember you telling me that you had gone up in a hot-air balloon so that you could capture the view from above.'

'Yeah, so?'

'Do you know how to fly a hot-air balloon?'

'Fly one?' Jakob pinched his brows together. 'No. I paid some guy to take me up and run the thing while I sketched. You want his number?'

I clutched the book in my fingers. 'That won't be necessary.'

'You believe me, don't you, Ms Miller?'

'You know what, Jakob? I do.' I patted him on the arm. 'Do you mind if I borrow this?'

Jakob glanced at the book. 'I guess not.'

'Don't worry, I'll take good care of it and bring it back as soon as I'm finished with it.' I laid my hand on the doorknob. 'I'd better be going.'

'Sure thing. You know, I'm glad you stopped by.' Jakob rubbed the back of his neck. 'I feel better getting everything out in the open like this.'

I pulled open the door. 'Good night, Jakob.'

Jakob followed me on to the porch. 'Say, what happened to your friend?'

'That's what I'd like to know.' I stepped off the porch and raised the book overhead. 'Thanks again for the book!'

TWENTY-THREE

B rad came by the café the next day carrying a dozen roses wrapped in green paper. 'These are for you, Maggie.' He extended his right hand over the front counter.

'Thanks.' I took them. I gave them a sniff. Delicious. 'Are these for my grave?'

'Huh?'

I glowered at him. 'I could have been killed last night.'

'Oh, that.'

'*Oh, that*, is right.' I grabbed an empty water pitcher and filled it from the tap. I removed the paper from the bouquet and arranged the roses inside the water pitcher. 'What happened to you last night?'

'A call came in from my editor. There was a wreck on the highway. A semi and a tour bus collided.'

I gasped. 'Was anybody hurt?'

'A few scrapes and bruises. The bus driver has a broken ankle.'

'That's a relief.'

'I had to cover the story, Maggie. I had no choice.' Brad looked contrite. 'Forgive me?'

'Fine,' I said with a well-rehearsed pout.

'Great.' He was all smiles again. 'Did you really go to Jakob's house alone?'

'I did.' I poured Brad a coffee and handed it to him. Glancing at the jar we had set up for our giveaway, I was happy to see it was filling up nicely with business cards.

'Was Jakob there? Did you talk to him?' Brad took a sip of his coffee.

'He was and I did.' I was going to play hard to get. Lucky for him I wasn't killed last night. Lucky for me, too.

'Come on, Maggie.' Brad drummed his fingers on the counter. 'Fill me in.'

'Fine,' I said, trying to sound as put upon as I possibly could. 'Let's sit.'

Kelly and Aubrey were busy with customers – well, that and listening in on my conversation with Brad, so moving to a table seemed like the thing to do.

I untied my apron and went around the counter, joining Brad at a spot near the door.

I told Brad that I didn't think Jakob was our killer. Brad told me that he was meeting Alan Klopton from ASK Financial Services after lunch on the pretense of doing a company profile.

'Then I'm supposed to go to the station and sign my statement concerning yesterday.' Brad cracked his knuckles. 'Hopefully, I'll get some new info on Herman's murder.'

'I'm supposed to go down later, too.' I pushed back a hair that had been tickling my nose. 'I can't wait to hear what Mr Klopton says. I'm surprised he's willing to even give you the time of day.'

'Klopton didn't seem too eager to talk to me but when I mentioned I was friends with the mayor, he came around.'

'You said you were friends with the mayor?' I raised my brow. 'You lied?'

'Journalistic license,' replied Brad, avoiding eye contact.

'Ask Mr Klopton about Arimexico Ventures.'

'What's that?'

'A failed solar energy company. Nancy Alverson wrote a book about it. There was a lot of fraud, according to her, involving people in high places.'

'You mean politicians?'

'Politicians and business persons.'

'How do you know all this?'

'It was in one of her books.' I explained Jakob had shown me the book and let me borrow it. 'I was up all night reading it. To be honest, she wasn't a great writer and there's a lot more innuendo than there are facts.'

There was more in Nancy's book about VV, or rather, about her father, our dear mayor. I wasn't going to mention that yet to Brad, though. I'd need to talk to her about it first.

I rubbed my eyes, swollen and itchy from lack of sleep. 'But if even half of what Nancy purports to be true is true, there was a whole lot of bad going on.'

Brad had news of his own. 'I managed to get a look at that class schedule of Rob Gregory's that you told me about. 'Guess who was a walk-in the night of Nancy's murder?'

'Who?'

'Stephanie Headley.'

I leaned back against my chair. Was ASK's comptroller also a strangler?

Brad left but he called later to say that Alan Klopton had been a no-show. 'Do you believe it?' complained Brad. 'I wasted an hour at High Steaks waiting for the guy and he never appeared.' High Steaks was a popular steakhouse on Main Street at the square.

'Did you try the hotel?' I leaned against the counter, massaging my back. My muscles were slowly returning to their normal state. As long as I avoided yoga and any other form of exercise other than riding my bike, I figured I'd be OK.

'I called his bungalow. There was no answer. His associates didn't answer their room phones either.'

I yanked my ear from the receiver as Brad cursed because I noticed smoke coming from the waffle maker on the counter.

'Hey, Kelly!' I cupped my hand over the receiver while Brad continued his tirade against corporate America, and whispered, 'The waffle maker!'

I waved at the machine. Smoke billowed from between the plates. The cord was sizzling, making funny noises and wriggling like a headless rattlesnake. The insulation wrapped around the cord appeared to be melting before my very eyes.

'Yikes!' Kelly threw the contents of a glass of lemonade at it. She then ran to the back and suddenly all the power went out.

I heard the sound of running footsteps. Kelly poked her head over the swinging doors. 'OK, now?'

'What happened to the power?' I said. Brad was still talking. 'I'll call you back.' I hung up the receiver.

'I turned off the circuit breaker.'

'Good call.' I planted my hands on my hips. I had a dining room full of customers looking at me for an explanation. 'It's OK, folks.' I raised my arms. 'No problem. Just a drill.' I pulled the molten plug of the waffle maker from the wall. 'Turn the breaker back on now,' I whispered to Kelly.

In a flash, the café sprang back to life and my customers went about their business.

Aubrey, who had been working in the storeroom, appeared with Kelly. She walked over to the damaged waffle maker.

'Careful,' I warned her as she picked up the end of the waffle maker cord in her fingers.

'Well.' Aubrey sighed. 'The good news is that the soda machine got fixed this morning while you were at the bank, Maggie.'

Aubrey picked up the waffle maker. 'The bad news is that your waffle maker is dead.' She carried it to the trash can and let it go.

It plopped loudly to the bottom of the can.

Aubrey turned meaningfully to the espresso maker. 'Do we have to watch the whole café fall apart before you do something about *that*?'

I bent over and picked the waffle maker out of the trash. 'This can be repaired,' I said, setting it under the counter. 'It probably only needs a new cord.'

'To say the least,' quipped Kelly.

'You know, Maggie,' Aubrey draped her arm over my shoulder, 'I had Lee come look at the espresso maker.'

'What did he say?'

'He thinks you need a spiritual cleansing. Well, not you, that.' Aubrey pointed at the espresso maker slash steampunk spaceship slash demon's spawn.

'You mean like an exorcism?'

'Exactly. Lee offered to do it but he said it probably wouldn't work unless Rob or Trish did it themselves. The machine had belonged to them, after all.'

I freed myself from her grasp. 'I'll keep that in mind. In the meantime, the cups for that machine arrived late yesterday. How about unpacking them and we give it a trial run?'

Aubrey and Kelly shared dubious looks.

'Come on, ladies. It's an espresso machine, not the devil incarnate! Fine,' I said, noting their hesitation. 'I'll do it myself and show you just how wrong you've been and how silly the two of you are being about this whole thing.' I wagged my finger at the two of them.

I stormed to the backroom for the case of porcelain espresso cups. Carrying the box with both hands, I pushed through the swinging doors. 'Here, let's open these and . . . whoops!'

My feet landed in a puddle of lemonade.

The box flew from my hands, bounced off the edge of the counter, and then struck the ground. Hard.

My butt hit the ground hard, too. Right in the puddle of lemonade. On the plus side, my pants soaked up most of the spill so I wouldn't need to worry about mopping.

On the minus side . . . the box of cups had burst open and, at first glance, looking at the carnage scattered around the floor, it appeared that twenty or so of the two-dozen pairs of cups and saucers had broken.

Kelly looked on in wide-eyed horror. 'Are you OK, Maggie?'

Aubrey reached out her hand and hoisted me off the floor.

'I think so.' Nothing was broken. Except maybe my spirit. Besides the dishware, of course. I could feel the cold, wet lemonade seeping into my underwear and wriggled.

'I think I had better go home and get changed,' I whimpered.

'Good idea, Maggie.' Kelly grabbed a broom and dustpan from the backroom and began sweeping.

Aubrey was scooping up big shards of porcelain with a damp cloth.

I grabbed my bicycle and pushed it to the front door. I leaned on the handlebars. 'What is the going rate for this spiritual cleansing?' I inquired.

Aubrey popped her head over the counter. 'Trish charges one hundred dollars, according to Lee.'

'One hundred dollars?' My hands flew from the handlebars as I turned my gaze toward Karma Koffee. The bike, of course, fell to the floor.

On my toes.

I bit my lip to keep from screaming.

Aubrey was practically smirking. 'What time should I tell her to come?'

'Make it after hours,' I said through the pain. 'Unless we need to wait until the moon is propitious and Uranus is in alignment with Jupiter and Mercury is in the House of Oldsmobile or some such mumbo-jumbo.'

'After hours, it is.' Aubrey disappeared behind the counter.

I could hear her and Kelly whispering and giggling as I limped out the door. Being a business owner wasn't the dignified position I had imagined it to be.

As I had told Brad, Detective Highsmith had called me earlier at the store requesting that I come down to the police station to give my formal statement.

I pedaled over and was ushered to his cubicle, where we carefully went over the events and my movements of the day before.

'Do you have any idea who killed Herman?'

'No.' Highsmith wasn't giving anything away.

'What about a time of death?'

'The initial report places it as sometime between midnight and four a.m.'

'What about the weapon?'

'We found a knife matching the description you gave me of the one Herman owned. There was evidence of blood and tissue on the blade but no prints on the haft. We discovered it about twenty yards from the body.'

'Did you question VV about ASK Financial?'

Highsmith slapped the folder against the table. 'Yes. I asked her, Maggie. She said they were in talks with her father, *the mayor.*'

'What sort of talks?'

'That's none of your business. It isn't even any of *my* business.' His tone was angry.

'I don't mean to tell you your business—'

'You could have fooled me,' Highsmith interrupted.

'I just wanted to say that you might want to talk to those people from ASK Financial Services, that's all.'

'We've already interviewed them. And since I know you are going to ask, they all have alibis. For Nancy *and* Herman Alverson's murders.'

'Are you sure, I mean—' I jerked. 'Wait. Did you say Herman *Alverson*?'

'That's right, Maggie. You may as well know. It's going to come out anyway.' Detective Highsmith pulled a cherry licorice stick from a ripped open bag and chomped off the end. He held the bag out to me but I declined. 'Herman was Nancy's brother.'

I sucked in a breath. 'First her and then him? Why? What does it mean?' Now that he mentioned it, I could see the resemblance. The shapes of their faces, the set of their eyes.

'Believe me,' Detective Highsmith said, rising from his chair and motioning for me to do the same. He yanked off another few inches of licorice with his teeth. 'I intend to find out.'

Highsmith escorted me to the door up front and hit a buzzer releasing the lock. 'Thanks for coming in.'

'Wait. What about those marks near Herman's campsite? Were they made by a hot-air balloon basket?'

'Yes,' Detective Highsmith reluctantly admitted. 'It appears so.'

'Did you know that a hot-air balloon was stolen from one of the tour operators a few days ago?' I stopped beside a bench near the entrance.

'I am very aware of that. I've read the police report,' Detective Highsmith answered, his voice flat.

'Do you think it's connected to Herman Alverson's murder?' I couldn't get over the fact that Herman and Nancy had been related. 'They must be connected, right?'

'No comment.'

'What about Nancy's Land Rover? Do you have any idea how it ended up at Herman's campsite?'

'That I can tell you.' Highsmith swallowed the last bit of his licorice. 'Apparently, he drove it there himself. His prints were all over it.'

'But the keys.'

'They were Nancy's. Jakob Waltz recognized them. She must have let him borrow them. We'd been looking for the Land Rover. I intended to impound it for the duration. Herman must have driven off with it before we could send a tow truck out.'

'But how did he get to and from town without it? You saw how far it was to his camp.'

'My guess is that he hitched.'

'Is that really likely?'

'You'd be surprised.'

'I am. At a lot of things.' A text came in on my cellphone. I pulled the phone from my purse and tapped the screen. It was a message from Aubrey. I read it quickly. 'Very funny,' I mumbled.

'What?'

I turned the phone's screen so he could see for himself.

'Operation Espresso Exorcism is a go. Nine p.m.' He frowned. 'What does that mean?'

'It means Aubrey thinks she's a comedian and that my espresso maker is possessed.' I put the phone back in my purse without further explanation.

'Right. Well, thanks for coming in—'

'What about that financial report I found burnt in the fire?' I blurted quickly.

'You ask a lot of questions, Maggie.'

'I wouldn't have to, if you would be more forthcoming in your information.' I batted my eyelashes.

He rolled his eyes in reply. It was like a finely practiced tango. 'According to that priest named . . .' Highsmith paused and extracted his notebook from his inner coat pocket, 'Suryavayu, representatives of ASK Financial Services had been to see them. Apparently, they dropped off several information documents, including that SEC report.'

'How did it end up being used as kindling in Herman's campfire?'

'I can't answer that. I can tell you that this high priest guy claims that the church had a break-in last night. Several items were taken.'

'Meaning that Herman might have stolen it?'

'It is a distinct possibility. His campsite is technically on their land.'

'You're right. I hadn't thought of that. Did they know he was out there? I mean, they must have, right?'

'They did. And the priest says they didn't care. They considered him harmless.'

Maybe. I wondered what they would have thought if he had discovered the lost City of Gold on their property. Would they slit his throat so they could keep the gold for themselves?

'Did anybody from the church report this break-in?' I asked.

'Yes. A representative reported it this morning. Officer Collins handled the call herself. The door to the office was broken. No prints. Not much to go on. The report didn't mention the financial document, however. Only some ritual instruments and religious objects. When I went back out to speak with Suryavayu, he said he hadn't mentioned it because he didn't think it was important.

He claims he noticed his desk had been searched but wasn't concerned because he knew it contained nothing of value.'

Maybe the high priest of the Sacred Church of Witchkraft didn't think it was important, but I did.

The corner of Detective Highsmith's mouth turned down. 'I can't say I agree with that. Everything is important in a murder investigation.'

Highsmith shoved his notebook back in his pocket. 'Suryavavu claims he didn't realize that particular document was missing until I showed him the charred one. He searched his desk with me standing there watching him and discovered his copy was gone.'

'This whole thing stinks.' I tried to put the puzzle together in my head but there were too many pieces. 'The church paid Nancy six thousand dollars. I saw the canceled checks,' I reminded him.

'She never cashed them and we didn't find the checks or any significant amounts of cash in her personal belongings.'

I squeezed my brows together. 'What does that mean?'

'I don't know. Yet.' Detective Highsmith glanced over his shoulder. 'Let's walk.'

He took my arm and escorted me out of the town hall and down to the sidewalk. We came to a stop beside the bicycle rack. A cold wind was coming from the north. I stamped the ground and shoved my hands in my pockets for warmth.

'Be careful, Maggie.' He looked up and down the sidewalk as if to be certain we were out of earshot of passers-by.

'Do you think I could be in danger?'

'There is a killer on the loose and somehow, like it or not, you are involved.'

'Is there anyone in particular that you think I should be careful of?'

To tell you the truth,' he confessed, 'at this point, there isn't anybody in Table Rock that I don't suspect might be involved in the murders of the Alversons.'

He trudged up the steps and left me there to wonder whether that *anybody* included Mayor Vargas and his daughter, VV.

TWENTY-FOUR

By the time I got home, fed the cat and myself and changed from my work clothes to a pair of stretch jeans and a pink flannel shirt, it was dark outside.

It would be cutting it close but, if I hurried, I could have a word with Veronica Vargas before the espresso exorcism planned for nine p.m. at the café.

I pedaled to Casa Mirasol. The driveway gates were open so I rode right in and parked beside a gurgling fountain. I grabbed my purse from the basket of my bicycle and marched to the *casita*.

I banged my hand on the door.

Veronica answered. She was wearing an elegant gold cocktail dress, black pearls and black heels. Her dark hair was done up in a loose French braid.

'Ms Miller? What are you doing here?' Her lips glittered with gold. An ice cube-filled cocktail glass jiggled in her fingers. A slice of lemon lay buried under the stack of cubes.

'I wanted to talk to you about this.' I unzipped my purse and yanked out Nancy's book.

'A book?' VV looked down her nose at me.

'Not just any book.' I turned the spine toward her. '*Solar Sham* by Nancy Alverson.'

VV looked past me toward the house. 'Come inside.'

'Thanks,' I quipped. 'I thought you'd never ask.'

A strong fire burned in the stone fireplace.

Veronica crossed to the bar. 'Have a seat.' She silently prepared drinks, pouring from a crystal cocktail shaker. 'I don't have much time. Mark is coming by to pick me up for dinner. Daddy is hosting a small party at a restaurant downtown.'

'Oh? Will Alan Klopton and his associates be joining you?' I sat in the chair with the book on my lap, watching the flames dance.

VV's mouth flattened. 'I hope you don't mind mojitos.' She handed me a tall glass.

'Thank you.' Sugar, mint, lime and rum. What was there to mind?

VV settled herself on the leather sofa and crossed her legs, exposing acres of thigh. Not that I was judging. If I had legs like that, I'd be wearing dresses that short, too.

'I suppose you've read it,' she said calmly.

'Not all of it,' I said. 'But enough.' I set the book on the table between us. 'Enough to know that your father is an investor with ASK Financial Services.'

A flash of anger shot from VV's eyes. She slammed her glass on the table. 'Was an investor, Maggie. *Was.*'

'Nancy had a lot to say about ASK in that book. It wasn't until I read that bit in chapter seven where she lists what she calls co-conspirators that I put it all together. Mirasol Enterprises. That's one of your father's businesses, isn't it?'

'You know it is.'

I did. Everybody in town knew that the mayor owned several business, including Mirasol Enterprises, which, in turn, operated several local businesses. 'Nancy claims that Mayor Vargas helped to cheat investors of millions of dollars in the Arimexico project.'

'Innuendo! Nancy was a hack. Slinging mud wherever she went!' VV snarled.

I was taken aback by her reaction. Had she been mad enough to kill Nancy in an effort to prevent her publishing her next book? 'Are you saying it isn't true?'

'I'm saying it's true that Daddy was an early investor in the project, Ms Miller. When he discovered what was going on, he got out.'

VV stood and crossed to the fireplace, pushing her hands toward the flames. 'He warned others to do the same.' She swiveled her neck.

'You lied to me.' I folded my arms and cradled my drink in my hand. 'You were covering up for your father. That's why you were talking to Nancy. That's why you were seen arguing with her at Hopping Mad.' I leaned in. 'That's why you went to Nancy's apartment that night, isn't it? Was it to confront her or was it to beg her not to print her new book?' I asked.

VV fingered her pearls as I said, 'I didn't get a chance to read the entire draft of the book she was writing because it was stolen but I read enough to know it involved financial shenanigans and corruption.' I moved in for the kill. 'Is that why you strangled her? You were afraid she would destroy your father and your family's reputation?'

'You are being ridiculous,' yelled VV, eyes flaring. She crossed to the table and picked up the book. 'This is garbage. Nancy Alverson was a third-rate writer and couldn't see the truth if it was staring her in the face.'

VV hurled the book into the fire. Flames shot up and ash flew around the room.

I was going to owe Jakob a new copy of the book.

'Just like you, Ms Miller.' VV suddenly slumped to the floor, resting her arm on the sofa.

I watched in fascination as she tipped her mojito to her lips and sipped. 'Yes, I argued with her. Yes, I begged her not to publish that pack of lies and innuendo.' VV locked her eyes on me. 'But I did not murder her, Ms Miller. Nancy was dead when I got there. I was running to get help. As for Alan Klopton, Daddy despises him. The pompous fool came here hoping to get Daddy to invest in yet another of his schemes. Can you believe that miserable worm actually threatened to go public about Daddy's prior investment in Arimexico? Oh, it would be slander and lies. But the damage would be done. Daddy's reputation would be ruined.'

VV climbed to her feet. She grabbed the fireplace poker and stirred the flames. We watched the book melt away. 'But Vargas' are not murderers, Ms Miller. Daddy wasn't about to give in, nor was he about to invest in another scheme of Klopton's.'

'What sort of a scheme?'

VV shrugged. 'I don't know the particulars. All I do know is that ASK Financial Services is pooling investors to buy up a chunk of outlying town property. Their intention is to build a large resort.'

'A resort?'

'I've seen the artist's renderings. It's ambitious, with a spa, thirty-six-hole golf course and timeshare units.'

To my surprise, tears were pooling up in VV's eyes.

VV slid a makeup mirror from a gold-sequined purse at the bar. Seeing her reflection, she groaned and began dabbing at her eyes with a tissue.

'Do you know if Alan Klopton is still in town?' I asked. Maybe they had left town. Klopton hadn't kept his lunch meeting with Brad.

'I have no idea,' sniffed VV.

The ASK Financial Services name and Alan Klopton's, in particular, had come up quite a bit in *Solar Sham*. I glanced at my watch.

It was nearly nine p.m. but I wanted to strike while the iron was hot.

I said goodnight and climbed on my Schwinn. The Table Rock Hotel and Convention Center was less than a block away. I could have walked but I didn't want to have to come back for the bike. Besides, if the gates were closed when I returned, my bike would be spending the night.

The exclusive bungalows were toward the back edge of the enclosed garden grounds of the hotel. I parked my bike near a side entrance and strolled into the garden. Fairy lights glittered from the trees. I heard the sound of laughter coming from an outdoor bar and restaurant midway between the main building and the bungalows.

Brad had mentioned that Alan Klopton was staying in bungalow four. As I neared, I spotted Gary Busby and Stephanie Headley standing at the bar with drinks in their hands.

When they saw me watching them, they set their drinks on the bar and disappeared in the direction of the main hotel.

I turned my attention to the bungalow. The door stood open. A small amount of light spilled out.

Reaching the covered porch, I strained my ear at the entrance but heard nothing from within. 'Mr Klopton, are you here?'

With no reply, I entered. A narrow hall opened into a large living area. There was a bedroom to my right. The open kitchen was to my left. A lamp beside the sofa facing the fireplace glowed.

'Mr Klopton?' I peeked in the bedroom. Nothing and no one stirred. The door to the private patio was open. I stepped to the door. The enclosed patio ran the length of the bungalow. It contained outdoor furniture and a cold stone fire pit.

But no Klopton.

Re-entering the bungalow on the living-room side, I gasped. Alan Klopton lay sprawled on the floor between the sofa and the glass table. 'Mr Klopton!'

He was wearing dress slacks and a white shirt. A blue silk tie spilled over his shoulder. I fell to his side and felt for a pulse.

As I did, I heard the sound of steps.

'Hello?'

'Help me!' I called, Klopton's warm, floppy wrist in my hand.

'Ms Miller? Is that you?' Lee hurried to the sofa. He grasped the edge of the cushion. His mouth fell open. 'What's going on?'

'It's Mr Klopton. I think he's passed out or something.' I placed the back of my hand on his forehead. 'We need to call an ambulance.'

'Of course,' agreed Lee. His hand went to his pocket. He wore an unzipped tan jacket over an indigo chambray shirt and brown trousers.

'What are you doing here?'

'I had an appointment with Mr Klopton. I heard he was looking for investors and his associates convinced me to invest,' Lee replied rather sheepishly. 'We were just talking at the bar.' He rummaged through his pockets. 'Now, where is that phone of mine?' He frowned. 'I must have left it behind. I don't suppose you have your phone, do you, Maggie?'

I stared at him.

'Maggie?'

'Or, rather, I stared at the silver pentacle dangling from his neck as he leaned over the sofa. The exact match of those I had seen on other members of the Sacred Church of Witchkraft.

'It was you, wasn't it?' I whispered. My hands fell to my sides. My knees were pressed to the hard tiled floor.

'What are you talking about?' Then Lee's eyes noticed where my eyes were looking. He glanced down and leered. 'Oh, I see.' He fingered the medallion. 'Tsk-tsk. This is a shame.'

I bolted for the patio door.

TWENTY-FIVE

I ran from the living room to the patio. Lee snarled and came after me. I heard his steps behind me. I ducked in through the bedroom hoping to circle around and out the front way.

Instead of chasing me, however, Lee had anticipated my move and was coming straight for me from the living room.

I cried out and dodged back onto the patio. I threw my fingers over the lip of a moon-faced fountain built into the rough adobe wall and began pulling myself up and over.

Hands grabbed at my legs. I screamed and kicked repeatedly until he let go and I was able to hoist myself onto the top of the wall.

Breathless, I looked all around. I could see the lights of Casa Mirasol. The driveway gates were still open. All I had to do was get to the estate and the Vargas' could call the cops. Emilio Vargas was the mayor, for crying out loud. The police would be there in a flash!

I tumbled to the ground and landed hard on a prickly pear cactus. I screamed in agony. My rear end felt like it was on fire. My eyes filled with tears. There was no time to stand around and try to remove the thousand spikes sticking in my butt.

Lee cursed and leapt up the wall. I ran as fast as I could, wishing I hadn't left my phone in my purse, my purse in the basket of my bike and the bike at the edge of the garden in the opposite direction I needed to go!

I did the hundred-yard dash to Casa Mirasol's driveway and it felt like a hundred million. Through the picture window, I saw VV standing by the fire in the *casita* and raced over.

I grabbed the door handle and flew inside.

'Miller!' VV dropped her cocktail glass. The glass hit the rug, spilling its contents. 'What the devil are you doing?' She picked up her glass and took a step toward me. 'You can't barge in here like this!'

'It's not what the devil I'm doing,' I said, struggling to lock the door. 'It's the devil that's after me! How do you lock this thing?' I yelled.

VV rolled her eyes. 'Calm down.' She took another step my way. 'You're turning the lock the wrong—'

Lee slammed into the door and yanked it from my hands. He leapt into the room with a mad look on his face and a big kitchen knife with the Karma Koffee name laser-engraved on its long, sharp blade in his right hand.

It looked like my nemeses, the Gregorys, were going to be the death of me for real this time.

I screamed. VV screamed too. She drew back her arm and threw her glass, smashing Lee in the face. He howled and stumbled backwards, his hands flying to his nose.

'Don't just stand there!' I grabbed VV, who seemed frozen in place. 'Move!' I grabbed her and pulled her toward the bedroom.

'What are you doing, Miller?' VV shouted.

I yanked open the door and pushed her inside, then jumped in after her. Hopefully, there would be a telephone in the bedroom or a window we could escape through to the main house.

Only it wasn't a bedroom.

It was a closet.

It was dark. VV's chin was against my nose. Her bra against my chest felt like it was diamond studded. Heavy clothing pressed against us. Coat hangers dug into my spine.

'Nice going, Miller,' VV hissed. I smelled the alcohol on her breath. 'Now that nut has us trapped.'

Lee jiggled the handle. 'Come on out, you two! Let's not make this anymore unpleasant than it needs to be.' He jiggled some more.

'What a sicko,' VV whispered.

I blew her hair out of my face. My hands had a death grip on the closet doorknob. 'I don't suppose there's another way out of this thing?'

I couldn't see VV's face but I could imagine what it looked like.

'Forget I asked.'

We both yelped as Lee slammed his shoulder against the door. He cursed and banged his fists at us.

'Who are you?' VV screamed through the door. I felt her breath in my face. 'Who is he?'

'Lee . . . something.' I didn't know his last name. Great, I was going to be killed by a guy whose last name I didn't even know. 'He killed Nancy.' I pressed my mouth to the door. 'Herman, too! Right, Lee? You killed them both, didn't you?'

He was kicking the door now, crazy with frustration and murderous intent.

'Stop provoking him, Miller,' hissed VV.

'Why?' I yelled. 'He's killed two people – what's two more? Right, Lee? Tell me,' I hollered. I wanted him mad, filled with blind rage. Maybe he'd do something stupid. Maybe even something as stupid as I had done by trapping myself and VV in a closet with no way out.

'Why did you do it?' I taunted. 'To protect your precious church? I'll bet that was it! Am I right?'

Suddenly the door splintered and the sharp end of the fireplace poker pressed against my cheek.

I squeezed against VV before he could spear me. I liked shish kebab as much as anybody, but not when it included the head of Maggie Miller.

I'd had enough. Lee had viciously murdered two people and had nearly skewered me. 'I am not going down without a fight,' I vowed to VV.

She planted her sharp claws in my shoulder. 'What are you going to do?'

'Follow my lead,' I whispered in her ear. 'When this door opens, run like hell. Got it?'

'Are you sure this is a good i—'

I cut her off. 'One.' I squeezed my hands on the doorknob. 'Two,' I whispered. 'Three!' I twisted the knob and threw the door open as fast and hard as I possibly could.

Lee was hit by the door and fell flat on his back.

'Run, VV! Run!'

No need to ask her a third time. The woman stuck her arms out and practically ran me over in an effort to get to the door. In the NFL, I was pretty sure that would have been an illegal hit.

No matter. I was right behind her. VV turned left out the door and I followed. This was her family's property, not mine. Surely, she knew what she was doing.

We heard the slam of Lee's steps coming closer as we skirted past a patio set.

I paused long enough to grab an aluminum chair. I turned and heaved it at Lee. It clipped his leg and he yelped. I sprinted forward. Unfortunately, VV had stopped to see what I was doing.

I slammed into VV and we both tumbled into the swimming pool. My head went under and I came up hacking and gasping for air. I started dog paddling.

'Swim to the other side!' I coughed. The water was frigid. Didn't they heat this thing?

Lee crouched, knife in hand, looking like he was trying to make up his mind whether to jump in after us or intercept us on the other side.

From behind Lee, a dark blur shot from the courtyard onto the pool patio. It was Detective Highsmith. He snatched the upside-down chair I had thrown and swung it sharply across Lee's back.

Lee never made a sound.

Well, until he hit the water face down, that is.

Splash!

'About time!' I spat, my mouth foul with chlorinated water.

Detective Highsmith sauntered over. He was looking rather nice in what was probably his best suit and tie. Dress shoes, too, I noticed – easy to do, seeing as his feet were almost level with my eyes.

Highsmith leaned down. 'I'd join you, ladies,' he quipped, but I forgot to bring my bathing suit.'

I was going to give him a piece of my mind, but the minute I opened my mouth it filled with pool water again – so I coughed instead.

'Mark, get me out of here!' commanded VV. Her fists pounded the surface of the water.

'OK.' Mark chuckled as he knelt at the edge of the pool and extended his hand. 'I guess I'd better fish him out, too,' he added with a glance at Lee as he floundered helplessly in the deep end.

'Help!' blubbered Lee. 'Can't swim! Can't swim!'

Personally, I didn't much care if he sank.

TWENTY-SIX

The following day I stayed home, ate pizza and played with the cat. I mean, come on, I'd almost been sliced to death by a crazed killer!

I deserved a day off.

The day after that I was back at work at the café. OK, so I rolled in around noon. I got there. That's the important thing.

Aubrey and Kelly chided me for having missed the big espresso-maker exorcism. Mom, Donna, Andy and the kids had attended. Even Laura Duval had come to see the machine get cured of whatever devil's spawn had possessed it.

Mostly, I think they had come hoping to have some good-natured fun at my expense. Of course, the joke had been on them because at the same time the espresso machine was being rid of its demons, I was busy getting almost stabbed to death by Lee Lawsen – that was his last name, Lawsen, good to know. I was stabbed in the butt by a prickly pear cactus, stabbed in the chest by Veronica Vargas' boobies, and I'd swallowed gallons of chlorinated, ice-cold pool water.

All in the name of justice, so maybe it was worth it.

Oh, and by the way, because Rob and Trish had performed the exorcism as a duo – not that I had asked them to – the session had cost me one-fifty. I was thinking of taking it out of next month's rent.

'It was a bit uncomfortable having the Gregorys here,' Aubrey confessed when I finally came in for work. She had left them to work for me. 'When they were doing the exorcism, I asked them why they didn't do this for themselves.'

'What was their answer?'

'Trish said they tried it but "it didn't work but who knows maybe this time,"' replied Kelly.

I didn't like the sound of that.

Nonetheless, I plugged in the machine for its inaugural brew. 'Get ready, ladies.' I rubbed my hands together. 'This is going to be great.'

I was in a fantastic mood. A customer had come in with a rolled-up copy of the *Table Rock Reader* under her arm and had asked me to sign it. Me! Maggie Miller!

Brad had interviewed me for the paper and I was something of a minor celebrity. At least, I would be for the next day or two. Hopefully, it would lead to a few new customers, the same way this fancy espresso maker was bound to do.

I explained in my interview how Lee had been a member of the Sacred Church of Witchkraft. Aubrey had told me Lee was a devote churchgoer. I just hadn't realized that the church he was devoted to involved witchcraft. And that he was a senior member of the church.

Lee had learned about Nancy's latest interest in witchcraft from Nancy herself and told her proudly that he was a member of the church. On the pretense of striking up a friendship, she had tricked Lee, convincing him that she was simply interested in learning more about the church as part of the background of her book.

What she was really doing was using him to gain access to the church and gather inside information to be used against them in her book.

Lee had recently caught on to her true intentions. Growing suspicious, he had waited until Nancy was out of the apartment, snuck upstairs and read her work-in-progress. He knew then that he could not let her publish that book. Doing so would publicly humiliate the church and ruin its reputation.

Lee had been desperate to protect the church at any cost, including murder. Nancy had returned to the apartment before he could destroy her work. Besides, he knew that destroying the document would never be enough. If he didn't stop Nancy dead in her tracks, she would only doggedly restart.

Nancy had first learned about the existence of the church from Herman, who had been squatting on church property for several months and had learned a thing or two about them. She had already heard rumors of ASK Financial Services attempting to buy up land in the region.

Sensing a big story, Nancy had become intrigued and came to Table Rock to see for herself.

Sadly, that story ended in her death and that of her brother.

Not realizing that Lee was now plotting her death, Nancy had told Lee how she had mailed a copy of the book-in-progress to me for safekeeping. Brad and I conjectured that Nancy had mailed the flash drive to me rather than her brother, Herman, at his camp because he didn't exactly have a mailbox or a safe place to store anything. Of course, poor Herman ended up dead, anyway.

One way or the other, Lee had been determined to get the flash drive back. Working across the street, it had been relatively easy for him to sneak into the café while all of us were busy out front, and that was exactly what he had done.

Just as it had been easy for Lee to drug Nancy's tea prior to strangling her. He'd claimed he didn't want her to put up a fight.

It was true that Rob had taken Nancy the tea. What he had forgotten to mention was that he had asked Lee to prepare that cup. Seizing the opportunity, Lee had slipped on a pair of food service gloves, doctored the tea and handed it off to Rob for delivery.

Voila, no fingerprints!

After giving the sleeping medication time to do its job, Lee went upstairs to finish Nancy off. He found VV's scarf – the one she had left behind – and took it as a sign. He used it to strangle Nancy as she sat unresponsive at her desk.

I got the shivers every time I thought about it.

Herman had been poking around himself trying to discover who Nancy's killer was and what had happened to her manuscript. That was why I had seen him in Karma Koffee the night of my ill-fated beginners' yoga class.

Herman had been questioning Lee, who had already been nervous about Herman because Nancy had told him previously that he was her brother. Having killed once, Lee apparently figured a second time couldn't hurt.

With cold-blooded planning, he had convinced Herman that the two of them should talk. Herman had agreed and Lee rode his scooter out to Herman's camp with a bottle of tequila under his jacket, waited until Herman was good and drunk, and then slit his throat.

Lee had intended to haul Herman's body off to some remote area of the mountains. He figured nobody would notice or care if the crazy treasure hunter disappeared. Herman would be one more footnote in Arizona's long and colorful history.

But something spooked him. Lee said he saw a bright light coming from the sky, so he'd dragged the body behind the tent, intending to come back later to finish his grisly task before anyone discovered the body.

Detective Highsmith figured that what Lee saw was the stolen hot-air balloon making a temporary landing. The missing balloon – somewhat the worse for wear – had been found nearly one hundred miles from town. There was no clue yet as to who had stolen it or why. 'Probably a drunken joyrider,' Highsmith had conjectured.

Lee had also confessed to staging the break-in of Suryavayu's office, making off with the ASK document and planting it in Herman's campfire, hoping to further implicate ASK in the murders and remove suspicion from his church.

The church officially denied knowing anything at all about Lee's plans or actions. There was no way for the police to prove otherwise.

From behind the counter at Karma Koffee, Lee had seen Nancy arguing with Alan Klopton in the street. Hoping to point the finger of suspicion at Klopton, Lee had waited for his chance. He sneaked into Klopton's bungalow, hoping to plant Nancy's flash drive there after having removed all references to the church. The contents of the drive had been ruined when Lee got knocked in the swimming pool.

Lee had planned to phone the police anonymously afterwards to tell them where they could find the missing flash drive. But Klopton caught Lee in his room. The two fought and Klopton lost. He was a greedy, unscrupulous little man, but not a very strong one.

Lee was on his way out the door when he saw me coming. He hid in the bedroom, then hoped to trick me into believing he had entered after me.

Luckily, Alan Klopton lived. He, Gary Busby and Stephanie Headley weren't looking too good but it did not appear that they would be facing any charges as long as they left Table Rock and never came back. That last part had been Mayor Vargas' condition.

VV's daddy, the mayor, of course, had done nothing wrong and had been every bit as honorable as VV had claimed. ASK Financial Services was trying to buy up a lot of property, including the big piece of land the Sacred Church of Witchkraft sat on.

According to the high priest, the church was not budging. He still insisted that the church had given Nancy six thousand dollars but no one knows what happened to the money – if there ever was any. Personally, I think the priest wrote out the checks then ripped them up just to confuse the situation.

Job done.

As for Nancy's latest book, that project had died with her.

The espresso maker hissed pleasantly. I added some ground coffee to the top thingy. I gripped the handle and crossed my fingers, hoping to remember the steps Laura had taught me. 'Get ready, girls.'

Veronica Vargas strode into the café like she owned the place. 'Ms Miller!' She sashayed to the counter, dressed in a navy-blue silk set and black heels, balancing a five-hundred-dollar leather purse on her left shoulder.

'What is it, Veronica?'

She planted her perfectly manicured hands on the counter. 'I hear you have espresso?'

I pinched my brows together. 'That's right.'

VV set her purse on the counter, opened said purse, pulled out a wallet that looked like it was fashioned from ostrich or alligator or some other poor, hapless, possibly endangered creature, and slapped a gold-plated credit card on the counter.

'I'll take a double shot, one teaspoon of raw sugar, a dash of cinnamon and a hint, just a hint,' VV squeezed her thumb and forefinger so close they nearly touched, 'of allspice.'

I frowned. I had a *hint* I'd like to give her.

Aubrey interposed. 'One *café verde norté.*'

Huh? Did Aubrey just make that name up?

'That will be six dollars,' Aubrey said, cheerfully accepting VV's card.

Six dollars? I held my breath, waiting for VV to scream in outrage and stomp on Aubrey like a bug.

But she didn't. VV pushed the card toward Aubrey at the register. 'To go.'

Six bucks for a cup of coffee with a fancy name? There was no way I could turn that down.

I was doomed.

I turned past Aubrey and muttered as I crossed to the copper and brass espresso maker slash steampunk spaceship slash devil's spawn behind us. 'You were right, this machine is cursed.'

I quickly grabbed a hot cup from the bowels of the machine, burning my fingers on its hellishly hot metal interior.

The infernal instrument had conjured up Veronica Vargas and drawn the vixen into my once-pleasant little café.

What would people think?

What would become of me?

What would become of Maggie's Beignet Café once customers learned that VV Vargas was frequenting the place?

'Cursed, I tell you!' I muttered at the espresso machine as I brewed. 'Cursed!'